DON'T BELIEVE A WORD

Recent Titles by Patricia MacDonald

THE UNFORGIVEN
STRANGER IN THE HOUSE
LITTLE SISTER
NO WAY HOME
MOTHER'S DAY
SECRET ADMIRER
LOST INNOCENTS
NOT GUILTY
SUSPICIOUS ORIGIN
THE GIRL NEXT DOOR
MARRIED TO A STRANGER
STOLEN IN THE NIGHT
FROM CRADLE TO GRAVE *
CAST INTO DOUBT *
MISSING CHILD *
SISTERS *
I SEE YOU *
DON'T BELIEVE A WORD *

* available from Severn House

DON'T BELIEVE A WORD

WORD

Patricia MacDonald

Severn House Large Print
London & New York

This first large print edition published 2016
in Great Britain and the USA by
SEVERN HOUSE PUBLISHERS LTD of
19 Cedar Road, Sutton, Surrey, England, SM2 5DA.
First world regular print edition published 2013 by
Severn House Publishers Ltd.

British Library Cataloguing in Publication Data
A CIP catalogue record for this title is available from the British Library.

ISBN-13: 9780727894908

Typeset by Palimpsest Book Production Ltd.,
Falkirk, Stirlingshire, Scotland.

To my agent and friend, Meg Ruley, for her charm and cheer, insight and integrity. I can never thank you enough.

Acknowledgements

I am blessed with extraordinary agents and publishers at home and abroad. Special thanks to Peggy Boulos-Smith and her compatriots at JRA in NYC, Edwin Buckhalter and Kate Lyall Grant at Severn House in London, and Catherine LaPautre and Anne Michel in Paris. My deepest gratitude to my publisher at Albin Michel, Francis Esminard, who understood me, even though my French was incomprehensible. And a wistful au revoir to the incomparable Danielle Boesflug.

One

Eden Radley raised her collar and pulled her jacket tightly around herself as she picked her way along the icy sidewalk on the Brooklyn street where she lived. She had a wool scarf wrapped high around her neck, but her nose and cheeks were stinging in the chilly night air. She glanced ahead and saw golden light from inside the Brisbane Tavern spilling out onto the sidewalk. She hurried toward the door, eager to slip into the warmth.

Normally her favorite watering hole was the bar in the Black Cat Restaurant, across from her apartment, but it was Sunday night, the Giants were playing a night game, and Eden had heard that they showed the Giants games on several large TV screens in the Brisbane. At least, if this date was a bust, she could keep an eye on the score. Judging from her past internet dating experience, she didn't expect to be here for very long. Just a drink or two, and then she planned to watch the second half alone, in her apartment, preferably under the covers.

Eden had had over a dozen dates since she joined the online dating service. The guys she met had ranged from weird to merely dull, except for one, a lawyer whom she liked immediately. They had talked for hours, and he seemed positively reluctant to part from her. She went

1

home on a cloud, expecting a text from him any minute to request another date.

Two weeks went by and she didn't hear from him. She finally broke down and texted him, careful to sound casual. 'I thought we had a good time,' she said. 'I was hoping we could do it again some evening.' His reply came back: 'I have a lot on my plate these days. If I have a window, I'll call you.'

A window? Really? she thought. To hell with internet dating. From now on she was going back to hoping against hope that she would meet someone in a normal way. This date with Jake Latham, a chemist working for a drug company, was the last item on her dating service to-do list.

They had agreed to meet at a table in the back of the Brisbane, far from the noisy bar, but it was late in the football season and the Brisbane was packed. A table seemed to be out of the question. Eden scanned the room, trying to spot tonight's prospect from the photos on his profile. Nobody was alone or looking around as if trying to find someone. No Jake Latham. She hesitated by the front door, and then strode up to the bar and hoisted herself on a barstool between two parties of boisterous fans. The bartender, a guy who she reckoned to be in his mid-thirties, his dark hair already shot through with gray, looked at her with raised eyebrows. She asked for a glass of white wine. He wiped off the shining dark wood surface of the bar, poured out a glass of wine and set it in front of her. The delicate wine glass looked lost in the forest of dark green and brown beer bottles which crowded the bar.

'Game night,' he said, almost apologetically.

'I know,' said Eden. 'That's why I'm here.' Ordinarily, she would have felt uncomfortable to be alone, seated on a barstool, but she was a Giants fan, at ease with this group of customers. She looked up at the TV screen and sipped her wine.

''Scuse me,' said a deep voice.

Eden turned to look. The guy was ruddy-faced and looked more like a bobsledder than a chemist. It was not the guy in the profile picture. She smiled at him anyway.

'Mind if I slip in here? I'm with these guys,' he said, pointing to the group next to her.

Eden shook her head. The ruddy-faced guy turned his back on her and high-fived the men to her right. He took no further notice of Eden.

Her face flamed but she continued to watch the game. It's not your fault, she reassured herself. You look good tonight. She examined her reflection between the gleaming bottles on the mirrored back of the mahogany bar. Her long dark hair fell in a shining curve over her shoulders, and her blue-and-raspberry wool scarf was perfect for her pale complexion and rosy cheeks. The bartender, who was facing the mirror, caught her eye and gave her a thumbs up.

Embarrassed, Eden hesitated, and then smiled back. The bartender served the customer next to her. Then he turned to Eden. 'So, you're a fan,' he said.

She shrugged. 'Yeah. Although I'm actually here to meet someone.'

'A fellow fan?' he asked.

3

'We'll see,' she said. 'We've never met.'

'Are you from the neighborhood?' he asked.

Eden nodded. 'But the Black Cat is my local.'

'I like their food,' he said. 'Those Thai spring rolls.'

She smiled. 'I know. Me too.'

He nodded and then answered the summons of the next customer.

Eden looked at the clock and glanced back at the door again. All of a sudden she felt her phone vibrate against her hip. She fished for it in her jacket pocket, expecting it to be from Jake, and quickly noted the name of the sender: Tara Darby, her mother. In spite of herself, Eden's temper flared.

'Hi, Eden. Miss you. Can you talk? Call me.'

Oh sure, Eden thought. And tell you about how I am trying to meet a stranger on an internet date? She knew exactly what her mother would think about that. Tara's life was not about stilted, planned meetings. It was about stars colliding. During Eden's childhood, Tara was a stay-at-home mom who worked on the accounts for her husband, Hugh's, masonry business. When Eden was in high school, Tara took a part-time job in a local bookstore that belonged to their neighbors across the street. Tara was in charge of arranging events. She invited a short story writer from New York City, who had grown up in their village of Robbin's Ferry, to do a reading and signing. Flynn Darby was a handsome Harvard grad, thirteen years her junior. The two of them fell hopelessly in love. Tara threw away everything – Eden, her

4

father and their home together – for her grand passion, her destiny.

All their friends and family claimed to find Tara's behavior unforgivable. But beneath the widespread condemnation, Eden often thought she detected a tiny hint of admiration for a woman who would follow her heart so recklessly. At the age of forty-two, Tara even had a baby with Flynn. After that, her careless rapture fell to earth with a thud. The child, Jeremy, now four, suffered from a rare genetic, usually fatal disorder, and the three of them had moved last year to Ohio to be near the Cleveland Clinic, and the one researcher who was concentrating on Jeremy's terrible condition.

While Eden understood that choice intellectually, and was sorry that her frail half-brother had to endure such suffering, it also meant that she almost never saw her mother. And on the rare occasions when she did, Tara was always too distracted to show much interest in Eden's life.

Eden hesitated and then texted her mother back. 'Can't. Watching the game.' She slipped her phone back into her pocket.

That will piss her off, she thought. Sunday afternoons, when Eden was a girl, she used to sit beside her large, gentle father on the sofa, watching the TV, and he would patiently explain what every player did, and why. At first she only pretended to listen. She really didn't care about the game. It was enough that her father enjoyed it, and wanted her company. But by the time his daughter was nine or ten, Hugh Radley had converted her into a hopeless fan. Sunday

5

afternoons in the season, plus the odd Monday, Thursday and Sunday nights, if the Giants were playing, Eden and Hugh were glued to the NFL on TV.

Tara Radley, a classic beauty with long, wavy black hair, often went out to read on the porch of their charming Victorian house in Westchester County, just to escape the roar of the fans, the excited commentary of the announcers, the war whoops or cries of disgust from her husband and daughter. Sometimes, when it was a four o'clock game, Tara would escape for wine and appetizers to a bar in the trendy downtown area of Robbin's Ferry. She would meet her friend, Charlene Harris, a realtor who was divorced, childless, and free on Sundays. Eden and Hugh would breathe a little easier once Tara was on her way, and they could watch in peace. Tara always came home mildly tipsy, but usually in a better mood than when she left.

'I don't know how you can stand to watch football,' Tara said to Eden once, lifting her penetrating, brown-eyed gaze from her book and frowning, perplexed, at her only child, her daughter. 'It's so . . . violent.'

'It's exciting,' Eden had said defensively.

'Grown men knocking each other over to get at a ball,' Tara sniffed.

'Dad likes it,' Eden protested.

'I know,' said Tara, stifling a sigh. 'I don't understand him either.'

At the time, her mother's words had seemed amusing. Tara was a reader and a dreamer, not a football fan. Everyone to their own taste, Hugh

Radley always said. Now, looking back on it, Eden saw it differently. Tara's complaint had been a narrow fissure in the rock that was their world, their life together, their family. To Eden, her parents seemed content together. But beneath that placid surface, there were numerous cracks, and they were widening into crevices which would wind up breaking Eden's world apart.

The divorce marked the end of so many things in Eden's life. In order to divide their assets, Hugh was forced to take out a second mortgage on their house and money became extremely tight. Six months after her mother left them, Hugh suffered a heart attack and could not work for several months. Instead of attending Yale, where she had been accepted, Eden enrolled as a commuter at Mt St Vincent's in the Bronx, and commuted from home. She had no social life at college. It was all she could juggle to attend her classes, work in the library and rush home to her father. In the ensuing years, he often told her how guilty he felt that she had missed out on so much of college life in order to stay with him, and help him recover.

It doesn't matter, she always replied. What she actually meant was, it wasn't your fault. You weren't the one to blame.

'Hear from your friend?' the bartender shouted amiably above the din.

Eden shook her head. 'He's late.' She looked at the clock again. It was nearly eight-thirty. 'Very late. And he hasn't called.'

'Check your messages again,' he suggested. 'You can't hear anything with the racket in here.'

7

Eden nodded, realizing that this was true, and pulled out her iPhone again. Sure enough, she had missed a call. She tried to listen to the voicemail, but it was a broken, garbled message, indecipherable in the noisy bar.

She was getting ready to text him. To explain that she couldn't hear the message. To ask why he was late. She was starting to key it in, and then she hesitated. Why bother? she thought. If she were honest with herself, she was actually relieved that he hadn't shown up. She had waited a sufficient amount of time, and she was off the hook. Why not just ignore it and go home?

She considered it for a moment, but she had been raised to be more courteous than that. *Can't hear your voicemail*, she texted. *Where are you?*

She waited for a few minutes, and finally he replied. *Traffic at a standstill.*

Eden looked at the message with narrowed eyes. Was this real, or an excuse? That was the problem with dating a complete stranger. How were you supposed to know? *Let's do this another time*, she wrote, and sent it.

'Did you get him?' asked the bartender, holding the bottle of wine tilted over her empty glass.

Eden shook her head and covered the glass with her palm. 'No, I'm going to go,' she said.

'Stay a while. Game's just starting.' He had a sad-eyed smile and was good-looking, sturdy but trim. Probably an actor, or a would-be writer, she thought, bartending to make ends meet, like most of her friends in the neighborhood.

She smiled in reply. 'No, I can't. But thanks.' She stuffed her phone resolutely back in her pocket, and pulled out her credit card, handing it to him.

He glanced at the name on the card and then handed it back to her, shaking his head. 'It's on the house, Eden,' he said.

Eden was taken aback. She wondered if he routinely bought drinks for the girls who were stood up on his shift. Perhaps that was considered good public relations at the Brisbane. 'Oh. Well. Thanks. That's nice of you.'

'Vince Silver,' he said, extending his hand across the bar.

Eden took it and shook it. 'Thanks, Vince.'

'Maybe I'll see you in the Black Cat,' he said.

She smiled and nodded, slipping off the barstool. She could hardly wait to get out of the Brisbane Tavern. She would watch the game from her own comfortable sofa. She pulled on her coat and edged her way through the crowd, as an excited fan quickly slipped in behind her and settled himself on her vacated stool.

The game ran into overtime, and it was past midnight before it was over. Eden's eyelids were heavy by the time the final kick won the game for Detroit. She thought about calling her father to review the game, but that was never any fun when the Giants lost. Besides, she was too tired. She brushed her teeth, turned off the light and got into bed, expecting to be asleep instantly. But the constant exchange of the lead in the game had invaded her head. She tossed and turned for over an hour before sleep overtook her.

The next morning she was groggy on the train

9

to Manhattan, but she felt a bit more awake by the time she had walked from the subway stop to the offices of DeLaurier Publishing. She had worked for the publisher for four years, and she had recently been promoted to the position of Associate Editor, with a small office all her own. Eden greeted the editorial assistants whom she passed in the hallway with a hail of 'Good morning' and 'How was your weekend?'

'Looks like you had a rough one,' observed Gillian Munroe, a roving assistant who worked for Eden as well as two other editors.

Eden shrugged. She was not fooling anyone. 'I wish I could tell you I was doing something exciting. But I couldn't sleep after watching the Giants game.'

Gillian grimaced. 'Football?'

'Absolutely,' said Eden.

'Whatever floats your boat.' Gillian was only twenty-two, and had a peachy complexion which no amount of sleeplessness could dim. Eden thought that twenty-two seemed like a lifetime ago, although in truth she was only twenty-seven herself. But sometimes Gillian made her feel a little bit . . . past her prime.

Don't forget, she reminded herself, Gillian works for you. She'd love to be in your shoes. Eden was pleased with her progress at DeLaurier Publishing. She was on the editorial fast track. The editorial director, Rob Newsome, was already including her in new, high-level projects, encouraging her ambition. All in all, Eden reminded herself, as she poured a cup of coffee and picked up a muffin in the break room, she

10

was doing pretty well. She took her breakfast back to her office and sat down to eat it at her desk. It was a morning ritual she thoroughly enjoyed.

When she went to college, Eden's dream was to get her degree and move to New York City so she could become part of the publishing industry. In this one way, she had been more like her mother, always gravitating to books and literature. Of course, unlike her mother, she reminded herself, she had made her dream come true. She was actually working with authors on the publication of books, not just daydreaming and selling a few copies in a bookstore.

'Hey,' said a friendly voice.

Eden put down her coffee cup and looked up. Sophy McKay, a senior editor, stood in the doorway, tapping on the open door.

'Come on in,' Eden said, indicating a chair.

Sophy came in and slid into the chair in front of Eden's desk. 'So . . . how was your weekend?' she said suggestively.

Eden shook her head. Sophy had met her husband on match.com, and was a tireless proselytizer for the benefits of internet dating. Sometimes Eden wondered if it wasn't a case of misery loving company. 'It was fine,' she said.

'So. Spill. You had a date?'

'I had a date,' Eden said. 'But he didn't show up.'

Sophy frowned. 'I'm sorry.'

Eden shrugged. 'No big deal. I met a nice bartender while I was waiting.'

'A bartender? Eden, you're trying to meet a professional.'

11

'No, I'm not,' said Eden evenly.

'Did you see your dad this weekend?' Sophy asked.

Eden knew that this question was a trap. Sophy made no effort to disguise her opinion that Eden spent too much time worrying about her father. She shook her head. 'My dad went to a *Beef and Beer* for some guy he used to work with. I think he took our neighbor across the street.'

'Ah, chasing after the ladies, is he?'

Eden laughed. 'Hardly,' she said. 'They're old friends.' Gerri Zerbo, who, with her husband, had owned the bookstore where Tara had fatefully gone to work, was recently widowed. Magnus had been ill for several years before his death from lung disease, and they had been forced to close the bookstore. Now, despite having two grown children – a son and a daughter, who were married with children and lived nearby – Gerri found her new, unwanted status to be lonely. Hugh sometimes invited her to events he thought she might enjoy.

'Maybe there's more to it than that,' said Sophy. 'You never know.'

Eden shook her head. 'Trust me.' For as long as she could remember, Gerri and Magnus had been a fixture in their lives. Gerri was more shocked and dismayed than almost anyone when Tara ran off with her short story writer. Part of her felt guilty for having offered Tara the job at the bookstore which led, ultimately, to Hugh and Tara's breakup. 'Your mom and dad had a good marriage,' Gerri often said, shaking her head as she dropped off a plate of cookies, or drove Eden to the train station when her dad was working. 'What was she thinking? I will never understand it.'

'How was your weekend?' Eden asked politely.

Sophy ticked it off on her fingers. 'Holiday dance recital. Dinner at Jim's parents' house 'cause his younger brother is home from India . . .'

As Sophy recounted her busy domestic life, Eden's attention wandered. She glanced at the homepage on her desktop. The usual headlines with photos were on display for a moment, and then they were replaced by the next tragedy. 'Murder/Suicide in Cleveland, Ohio.' Cleveland, Eden thought with a shiver. That's where her mother lived. 'Police in Cleveland, Ohio have reason to believe that a mother killed herself and her severely disabled young son by carbon monoxide poisoning . . .' Eden glanced at the house on the screen, surrounded by snow. She had never been to visit Tara in Ohio. But she had seen photos on Facebook of Tara with her new family, in front of their house. It was a small, relatively new house painted French blue, like the house on the screen. Gooseflesh rose on her arms.

'. . . and I had to bake cupcakes for Jenny's preschool. Eden, are you listening?'

Eden shook her head.

Sophy frowned. 'What's the matter? You look white as a ghost.'

'This headline,' Eden muttered.

'What about it?' Sophy asked.

'It sounds like . . . But it couldn't be.'

Sophy frowned. 'What happened?'

13

Eden shook her head. 'A woman and her son. They're saying it was a murder/suicide.'

'So?' said Sophy.

'My mother lives in Cleveland. The house in the video. It looks just like my mother's house. Their house is that same French blue.'

'Oh, Eden. The colors are always distorted on those videos. Besides, I'm sure you would have heard something . . .'

Eden ignored her, scrolling through the article, as sweat broke out on her forehead and under her arms. Details were scant. They were withholding names until the next of kin could be contacted.

Just then, the phone rang on Eden's desk. She picked it up.

'Eden Radley,' she said.

'This is Melissa in reception. Your father is here to see you.'

Instantly, Eden's hands began to shake. She knew. 'I'll be right out,' she whispered.

She stood up, brushing off the muffin crumbs from her shirt. 'My father is here,' she said to Sophy. Her legs felt stiff as she stood up. It was difficult to move.

Sophy looked worried. 'Do you want me to come with you?'

Eden shook her head. She went down the hall and out the doors to the reception area. Melissa sat alone at a large desk beneath the DeLaurier logo. She inclined her head toward the comfortable furniture grouping in the corner.

A man stood up from his chair. Hugh Radley was a tall man, as wide as those Giant linebackers whom he admired so much. Even though he was balding, and slightly too thick around the middle, Eden always thought her father was handsome. He had even features, keen eyes, and he exuded a quiet authority. He was solid, but not suave, even under the best of circumstances. He rarely came to New York. He found Manhattan baffling. Eden saw the look in his eyes, and her knees felt as if they would buckle beneath her.

'Dad . . .' she whispered.

'I didn't want you to hear this on the phone,' he said.

Eden tried to speak, but she could not form the words. 'What is it . . .' she managed to croak.

Hugh's face was pale and grim. 'I've just had a call from the Cleveland police.'

Eden's heart lurched. She felt her world crumbling into pieces again, the way it had nine years ago, when her mother announced that she was leaving them to remarry. 'What happened?'

Hugh gave a shaky sigh. 'Sweetie, I'm so sorry. It's your mother. And your half-brother, Jeremy. They were found this morning. Dead. In the house.'

'It was online. I saw it was Cleveland, I had a bad feeling . . .'

Hugh shook his head sadly. 'Carbon monoxide poisoning.'

'They called it a murder/suicide.'

'I wish they'd stop saying that,' Hugh said angrily.

Eden was trembling all over. 'She just texted me last night.'

'Your mom? What did she want?' Hugh asked.

'To talk,' Eden whispered. Was it possible that her mother was considering the most terrible deed imaginable and called her for help? Eden shook her head. That simmering anger which she frequently felt toward her mother was like a crutch. A crutch which had now been unceremoniously kicked out of her reach.

'I thought you might want to come home with me,' said Hugh. 'It's such a shock. You can't possibly stay at work. I know I couldn't.'

Eden was thinking about that text. Watching the game, she had said. You can wait, was the subliminal message, until I'm damn good and ready. She had enjoyed defying her request to talk. Now, they would never talk again.

Melissa, the receptionist, came tiptoeing up to them, her face at once concerned and apologetic. 'Can I help? Is there anything . . .?'

'My daughter's things,' said Hugh. 'Her pocketbook and such. They're probably in her office. Could you go and get them for us? I'm taking Eden home. We've had a death in the family.'

'Sure,' said Melissa. 'Oh, Eden, I'm so sorry. I'll be right back.' She hurried past her own desk and pushed open the door to the editorial offices.

Hugh had his arm around Eden, supporting her. She was reminded of the days after his heart attack when he would lean on her in order to walk. It had been quite a while since she needed to lean on him. 'Take it easy,' Hugh said. 'I'll get you home and you can rest.'

Eden shook her head as a tear streaked down

16

her cheek. 'I said no to Mom. I wouldn't talk to her.'

'Oh, sweetie,' said Hugh. 'Don't beat yourself up over it. You didn't know . . .'

'I should have talked to her.'

'This is not your fault. None of this,' Hugh said firmly.

But Eden was not looking for consolation. She was miles away. Thinking about the small, cookie-cutter-style house she had seen on the screen, where Tara had lived with her boyish husband and their son. 'Where was he?' she demanded.

Hugh frowned. 'You mean . . .'

Eden turned and looked straight into her father's sad eyes. 'Yes. Flynn. Where was he when it happened? Is he dead too?'

Hugh hesitated, and shook his head. 'No. He wasn't there. I don't know why. I don't know all the details.'

Eden felt a sudden fury flash through her like an electric shock. 'He wasn't there?' she asked. 'How lucky for him!'

'Eden, his wife and child are gone,' Hugh admonished her gently. 'I wouldn't call that lucky. He's lost his family.'

Eden's eyes suddenly filled with tears, but not for Flynn Darby. For herself. For her own mother, who had once been the glowing center of her world. 'Now he knows how we felt,' she whispered.

Two

Hugh drove home, his grim gaze fixed on the road, while Eden shivered, blanketed with both his coat and her own, in the seat beside him. The crowded buildings of the Bronx gave way to the scenic towns and villages of Westchester County. The town of Robbin's Ferry was a mere twenty miles from New York City, but it might have been a thousand miles away. There were plentiful trees and parks, and old houses in the village which had been beautifully, elegantly restored. Robbin's Ferry, a working-class suburb when Eden's parents grew up there, had become, over the years, a high-end place to live. Now, real estate prices were sky high, and most of the old family businesses downtown had given way to sleek furniture and clothing stores, and upscale florists, bakeries, delis and restaurants.

For many, living in Robbin's Ferry was an impossible dream, but for Eden it was just home. She had grown up here and the sight of Robbin's Ferry was always balm to her spirit. Well, not always, she reminded herself. After Tara left them, and Hugh fell ill, home seemed a hollow word for a while. Gradually, over time, it had become dear to her again.

Hugh turned into the driveway and pulled up beside the gray-green gingerbread-style Victorian house with white trim and black shutters. Those colors had been Tara's choice, but Hugh had never wanted to change them. He parked in front of the closed doors of the garage. As soon as he switched off the engine, Gerri Zerbo appeared at her front door across the street, and came outside without a coat. She was middle-aged and doughy, her short, graying hair framing her round face with soft waves, but Eden knew well, it would be a mistake to underestimate her. Gerri had a keen intelligence, and a steely side. Today she opened the door on Eden's side of the car and gazed in at her, her blue eyes brimming with sympathy.

Eden avoided her gaze, unbuckling her seatbelt and handing her father's coat back to him. Gerri stepped aside so that Eden could get out of the car. Eden pulled her coat tight and slung her purse over her shoulder. Then she met Gerri's gaze.

Gerri shook her head sadly. 'Oh, Eden, I'm so sorry,' she said.

Eden's fragile composure collapsed. She hung her head, and tears began to spill from her eyes. She was gently pulled into Gerri's embrace, and felt a pudgy hand smoothing her hair as Gerri murmured words of comfort. Hugh came around the car, and sighed.

'How are you doing, Hugh?' Gerri asked.

Hugh shook his head. 'Terrible,' he said. 'What a terrible day.'

Gerri gathered herself up briskly. 'Come on,' she said. 'It's freezing out here. Let's go in.'

Eden stumbled up the walkway to the front steps, and followed Gerri into the house. Gerri took Eden's coat and hung it up, while Hugh ushered her into the living room. Eden sank down

19

on one of the faded sofas and pulled a throw over herself.

'I'll be right back,' said Gerri. 'I'm going to get you some snacks.'

'I couldn't eat,' said Eden.

'You never know. You might want something,' said Gerri, disappearing down the hall toward the kitchen.

Hugh sat down on Eden's right in his well-worn leather club chair, and reached out his hand to her. Eden put her hand in his. They had hardly spoken on the way home, but the understanding between them was, as always, comforting.

'Thanks for coming to get me, Dad,' said Eden, wiping her eyes again with a soggy Kleenex. 'I don't know what I would have done.'

'You never have to worry about that,' said Hugh. 'You know you can always count on me.'

'I know,' said Eden, nodding.

They were silent again for a few moments. Then Eden looked at her father. 'They said on the news that it was a murder/suicide, but I can't believe that. She couldn't have done that to Jeremy on purpose,' she insisted.

'I understand that life with Jeremy was . . . very difficult.'

Eden knew what he was saying. The terrible effects of Katz-Ellison syndrome meant that Jeremy couldn't speak, or walk on his own. His life expectancy was uncertain, but most Katz-Ellison sufferers didn't live past the teenage years. He was prone to angry, inchoate outbursts, lashing out at anyone who tried to soothe him. 'I know. But still,' said Eden.

Gerri's footsteps could be heard on the hardwood floor of the hallway, and then she came in carrying a tray of food. 'Here,' she said, setting it down on the coffee table. 'Have something.'

'Thanks,' Eden whispered, but she looked at the tray as if the sight of it made her feel slightly ill. 'I just keep thinking,' she said, 'that people die all the time of carbon monoxide poisoning. Why would they think that it was deliberate . . .?'

'I don't know all the details,' said Hugh gently.

'But why are they even considering this as a possibility?' Eden cried.

Hugh was calm, but definite. 'I spoke to a police detective this morning. I'm afraid they are quite sure this was not an accident. The detective I spoke to said that your mother closed the house up tight and left the car running in the attached garage. The door connected to the house was left wide open.'

'Maybe she forgot,' Gerri suggested stoutly. 'Sometimes when you come in with a load of groceries, and a kid who's giving you a hard time . . .'

Hugh shook his head. 'Apparently, the carbon monoxide detector had been disabled. The windows in the house were taped shut, and the other doors in the house had towels wedged beneath them to keep the gas from escaping. Barbiturates were found at the scene.'

Eden was silent for a moment, picturing it. Her stomach was churning. 'Did she . . . was there a note?' she asked.

'There was,' said her father.

'What did it say?' she demanded.

21

'They wouldn't tell me that.'

Eden looked helplessly at her father. 'Surely we have a right to know these things.'

Hugh frowned. 'As the detective put it to me, this is a criminal investigation. Maybe when it is over . . .'

'She wouldn't do this,' Eden said stubbornly. Then she faltered. 'I just don't think she would . . .'

There was a silence during which Hugh refrained from pointing out that, all the same, she did, indeed, do this. Eden drew in a breath. 'Where was he?'

'Who?' her father asked patiently.

'Flynn Darby.'

'Apparently he was away somewhere. He found them when he came home this morning.'

Eden glared at him. 'But if she was suicidal, he must have known that. Why didn't he try to get her help? Why wasn't he with them that night? Where was he? Out on the town?'

'I don't know the answer to that, darling,' said Hugh. 'Your mother probably planned this for a night when she knew he would be away. She must have wanted to spare his life.'

Eden stared down at her hands, feeling numb. She could still remember, as if it were yesterday, sitting in the front seat of the car with her mother while Tara tried to explain to her why she was going to leave them to marry Flynn Darby. 'All I can tell you is that I can't imagine life without him. He's my soulmate,' Tara had said. Furious, Eden had gotten out of the car and slammed the door shut, trying to drown out her mother's explanation. What am I? she had wondered then as she turned her back and walked away. What is Dad?

'Yes,' said Eden sullenly. 'Yes, I'm sure you're right.'

Eden felt guilty for missing work, but that evening, when she called her editorial director, Rob Newsome, he told her not to worry. She needed time to make arrangements, and time to process the shock of it all. Take the rest of the week, he said. Eden did not need much convincing.

The next day she was too numb to get dressed. She stayed in her pajamas and surfed the net addictively for any additional information, even though the reports inevitably upset her. In one account the neighbors said that they never saw Jeremy out playing like the other children. He had been seen shrieking and flailing his fists at his mother, though she never raised her voice to him. Neighbors described Flynn Darby as someone who kept to himself, and Tara as an attentive mother. Everyone insisted that there was no other sign of trouble in that house. Day turned into night as Eden searched for explanations. Finally, that evening, on the *Cleveland Plain Dealer* website, an elderly couple who lived next door to the Darbys answered at least one of Eden's nagging questions.

'I heard the boy screaming bloody murder one time, and his mother came over and asked to borrow a stepladder,' said the old man. 'She told me, "The carbon monoxide alarm is too sensitive.

It's always going off without warning. My son can't bear the sound of it."

'Her husband wasn't home, so I said I'd help her. I brought over the ladder and took the batteries out.' The old man sighed. 'I told her she should replace it with a new alarm and she said she would. But I guess they didn't.'

Eden's fitful sleep that night was filled with nightmares, and the next morning she was groggy when she was awakened by her father shaking her gently.

'You have a phone call,' he said, indicating the landline extension in her room.

Eden blinked away sleep and felt a pounding in her head as she peered at him. 'Who is it?' she asked.

'Your mother's husband. You need to speak to him.'

Eden was dumbstruck for a moment. Then she sat up, holding the covers around her, and picked up the phone. 'This is Eden,' she said.

'Eden,' said a thick, unfamiliar voice, 'this is Flynn Darby.'

'Oh. Hello,' she said.

'I'm sure you know why I'm calling.'

For a moment, Eden did not reply.

'I'm making funeral arrangements for Friday,' he said. 'Is that convenient for you?'

'Uh yes, I suppose,' she said.

'Yes or no?' he said brusquely.

'Yes,' said Eden.

'Is there anything you want included?'

'I don't know what you mean. Like what?' Eden asked.

24

'Music. A poem?'

'Offhand, I can't think of anything. All I keep thinking is that I wish it wasn't happening.'

There was a silence from Flynn's end of the line.

Eden forced herself to concentrate. 'I have to say . . . I'm sorry for your loss. Of my mother. And your son.'

'Thanks,' said Flynn brusquely. 'They are having a joint service – Tara and Jeremy. I'll email you all the details.'

'Okay,' said Eden quickly.

'Can you call Tara's sister, Jodie? That would be helpful.'

Eden felt numb. 'Yes. I'll take care of it. I'll call her,' she said. 'Are your . . . um . . . grandparents coming?' she asked. She knew from her mother that the elderly couple lived in Robbin's Ferry where they had raised Flynn after his mother's death. 'I mean, if they . . . you know . . . need a ride to the airport or something . . .'

'That's very nice of you,' said Flynn. 'But my grandmother's in bad health. They're pretty frail, the two of them. They can't make the trip.'

'Oh, I just thought . . . if they needed a ride . . .'

'Thanks. It's just not gonna happen.' There was a silence. Then Flynn said, 'Please tell your father, if he wants to come, he can.'

Eden stiffened. She realized that Flynn was being generous, but still, his suggestion seemed vaguely insulting. 'I'll tell him,' she said.

'Anyone I've forgotten?' he asked.

If Tara and Hugh had never parted, if the funeral were here, in Robbin's Ferry, there would be dozens of people. But now . . . 'No,' said Eden. 'Actually, I'll let Mom's friend, Charlene, know.'

'Okay,' he said abruptly.

Eden could tell that he was about to end the call. 'Wait,' she said. She was silent for a moment.

Flynn sighed.

'Why did she do it?' Eden said.

Flynn was silent for a long moment. Eden thought he might have hung up. 'I'm sure she had her reasons,' he said.

Three

Eden called her Aunt Jodie, and they decided to fly out and meet in Cleveland. Jodie, Tara's younger sister, was a physics professor at Georgia-Tech, and Eden had heard, from those who knew them as children, that Tara was always known as the pretty one, and Jodie as the smart one. Jodie planned to fly from Hartsfield-Jackson in Atlanta. Eden was leaving from Westchester. The two agreed on a time to rendezvous at Cleveland Airport on the morning of the funeral, and they booked hotel rooms near the airport for that night.

Eden had not seen her aunt or her uncle in quite a while. Jodie's husband, Kent, was a journalist, on assignment in the Middle East. Their son, Ben, was in graduate school in California. Eden had fond memories of them at family gatherings when she was a girl, but once Tara married Flynn

26

and gave birth to Jeremy, the family get-togethers stopped happening. Eden was glad to know that Jodie would be with her on this difficult occasion.

When Friday came, Hugh drove Eden to Westchester Airport. He embraced her at the curb outside the terminal. Eden could feel him trembling, and when he pulled away, she saw tears in his eyes. Hugh wiped them away, embarrassed. 'I thought about coming with you. I wish I could be there in a way.'

'Flynn said you were welcome to come,' said Eden. 'I probably should have mentioned it. But I didn't think . . .'

Hugh shook his head. 'No. I wouldn't have come anyway. It's better if I stay away. They had their own life.'

Eden's heart shriveled inside her, thinking about the truth of that statement. Their life with Tara had long been over. 'I probably shouldn't go either. It's not as if they wanted anything to do with me.'

Hugh gave her a warning look. 'It's your mother,' he said. 'She loved you.'

'I know, I know,' she said. 'I'm going.' She hugged him again. 'I better get on that plane.'

He waved as she entered the terminal, and kept waving till she was out of sight.

Jodie beamed at Eden when she saw her at the terminal in Cleveland. 'You look wonderful, Eden,' Jodie exclaimed, hugging her. Even though she was over forty, Jodie wore her hair as she always had, in bangs and a ponytail. It was true that she was not a beauty like Tara, but she had

27

a certain calm self-assurance which her older sister had never possessed.

Eden hugged her back. 'So do you,' she said sincerely. She was so glad to see Jodie's familiar face in this place where she felt ill at ease.

'How was your flight?' Jodie asked.

'Bumpy, but not too long,' said Eden. 'Yours?'

'About the same. Oh, it's good to see you again,' said Jodie. 'I just wish this wasn't the reason . . .'

'Me too,' said Eden.

'I'm so sorry about your mother. We didn't talk that much, but when we did, she always talked about you. She adored you, you know.'

Eden shrugged. 'Not enough, I guess,' she said.

Jodie frowned. 'Don't say that. Whatever made her do this, it wasn't for a lack of love for you. I wish I knew why, but Tara wasn't one to share her problems. In fact, she could be very . . . secretive. I had no idea.' Jodie shook her head.

She tried to call me on the night she died, Eden thought. And I blew her off. She did not mention this to her aunt, but focused on arrangements instead. 'We'll pick up the hotel shuttle,' she said. 'I reserved us a rental car, at the hotel. We can drop our bags off, and then we probably should be on our way.'

'I guess there's no avoiding it,' agreed Jodie grimly.

The day was cold and brilliantly bright. Thanks to the GPS, Eden and her aunt found their way to the funeral home with no difficulty. Eden felt slightly sick as they entered the gloomy sandstone building in downtown Cleveland where the service would be. A large information board in the foyer listed the various visitations which were scheduled. There was no mention of Tara and Jeremy.

Eden went up to one of the undertaking staff. 'Excuse me, are we in the right place? My mother and my half-brother's service is this morning and it's not posted . . .'

'I'm sorry but this funeral is invitation only. I need to have your name,' said the balding, dark-suited man in a hushed tone. He looked around, as if to be sure that there was no one listening.

'Eden Radley,' she said. 'And this is Mrs Jodie Altman.'

The man frowned over a clipboard he was holding, and crossed off a couple of lines. Then he directed them to a room that was tucked away near the back of the first floor. It was a square room wallpapered in a silver stripe, with gray velvet drapes at the windows. It had been set up with chairs for the mourners. At the front of the room were two plain, pine coffins, side by side, both closed. Behind the coffins, on an easel, was a blown-up photo of Tara and Jeremy. The photo had been taken in a field, on a summer day. There was a verdant line of trees at the horizon, and the blue flash of a lake. Tara, wearing a white, gauzy shirt, was sitting in tall grass, surrounded by yellow wildflowers, smiling into the camera, her black hair escaping a messy updo, her brown eyes sad and limpid. She held her arms protectively around Jeremy, her chin resting on the top of his head. The boy had delicate features and shiny

29

hair, but his mouth hung open in a twisted grimace and his eyes were obscured by thick glasses which sat crookedly on his face.

Eden's eyes filled with tears. She looked away.

'It's a beautiful photo,' said Jodie, shaking her head. 'I don't know how she could have done it. Taken the child's life too. I know she adored him.'

Eden nodded and wiped her eyes. 'It just seems so unlike her.'

Jodie stifled a sob, and shook her head.

'Should we sit?' Eden asked, feeling suddenly young and uncertain.

'Well,' said Jodie, 'normally, we'd go and speak to the grieving husband. But I don't see him anywhere. Do you?'

Eden looked around, puzzled. 'No. I don't.'

Just then, a pale young woman with shiny, shoulder-length brown hair and narrow, black-framed glasses approached them. She had waxy, ivory-colored skin, and she seemed lit from within, like a tapered candle. She was dressed in a dark, hipster outfit with a black pea coat, black tights and a short, lacy skirt. A handsome young black man, slim and also bespectacled, with a shaved head of perfect proportions, shadowed her protectively. Unlike most of the men in the room, he was dressed in a suit and tie.

'Are you Eden?' the young woman asked hesitantly.

Eden nodded.

The girl exhaled, and gripped Eden's hand between her lacy, fingerless black gloves. 'I thought so. Your mother always talked about you.

My name is Lizzy Jacquez. I'm a grad student in psychology. I do research for Dr Tanaka. I worked closely with Jeremy and your mother. This is my husband, DeShaun Jacquez. Dr Jacquez,' she corrected herself proudly.

The young man smiled. His teeth were perfection. 'She always says that,' he demurred. 'I'm still an intern. Nice to meet you.' He shook Eden's hand in a strong grip.

'I'm so sorry,' Lizzy said. 'Your mother was a wonderful woman. And Jeremy. He was the best boy in the world.'

Then, Eden realized that she had heard Tara mention this girl's name before. 'Oh yes. My mother said that you were a great support to her,' she said.

Lizzy covered her face with her hands. DeShaun put an arm around her. 'You okay, babe?' he murmured.

Lizzy straightened up and took a deep breath. She lifted her glasses with the back of her hand and wiped her eyes. 'I'm supposed to remain objective. Not get involved, but . . .'

'Don't blame yourself for that,' said Eden gently. 'It's only human. By the way, this is my mother's sister, Jodie.' Everyone shook hands.

'I admire the work that you do,' said Jodie. 'It must take a terrible toll on you to work with kids that have such dreadful conditions. And no real hope.'

Lizzy's face brightened with the shining faith of a true believer. 'Dr Tanaka is determined to discover the treatment that will help these children. They and their families all suffer so much. If anybody can do it, it's him. I lost my own brother, Anthony, to this disease when he was five. I decided right then and there to make it my life's work.'

'That's impressive,' said Eden.

'It's hard to explain, but, if you've been through it, you're really a part of this community. My mother volunteered as a babysitter for Jeremy, just so that Tara and Flynn could get away out once in a while. She and my dad know better than anyone how tough it is to have a child with Katz-Ellison.'

'I'm so sorry,' said Eden. 'Obviously, my mother was surrounded by a lot of very kind people.' She looked around the room, which was slowly filling up. 'Lizzy, do you know where Mr Darby is? I thought he would be right up front.'

Lizzy's eyes welled up again. 'Oh, I'm sure he is so distraught. I don't know where he'll find the strength to face this day.'

Just then, a sturdy, serious-looking Asian man of about fifty, wearing a topcoat, entered the room and looked around. A murmur went up among the mourners, and a cluster of people gathered around him. He nodded toward each of them and then he eased into a seat at the back. Eden suspected that this must be Dr Tanaka, the researcher heading the Katz-Ellison study at the Cleveland Clinic. Her suspicion was confirmed when Lizzy spotted him. 'Dr Tanaka has arrived,' she said in a hushed tone of respect. She turned to DeShaun, who said that he was right behind her, and then she rushed to greet her boss and mentor. Dr Tanaka nodded, and folded his hands. His manner was respectful, but it seemed as if he wished to keep his fellow mourners at arm's length. He showed little other emotion.

'You know, this is just rude,' Jodie fumed. 'I don't care how upset he is. Everybody here is upset. He should be here. Why even have this service if you're not going to show up?'

Eden did not have to ask whom she was referring to. 'I'm sure he intends to show up,' she said.

One of the couples who had hurried to greet Dr Tanaka conferred with each other and then hesitantly approached Eden. She recognized the well-meaning, uneasy expression on their faces. The woman was slim with an olive complexion and dark curly hair cut in a fashionable bob. She had a beautiful printed scarf draped around her neck. The man had dark hair, a mustache and lively brown eyes.

'Excuse me,' said the woman. 'I saw you talking to Lizzy. Are you Eden?'

Eden nodded.

The woman reached out for her hand. 'My name is Marguerite, and this is my husband, Gerard. I met your mom at the clinic. Our youngest daughter suffers from Katz-Ellison. In fact, a lot of these people are from the clinic. We try our best to support one another.'

'So I understand. It's nice to meet you,' said Eden. 'I'm glad to know my mom had friends here.'

'Well,' said Marguerite. 'She was a beautiful person. She and I kind of bonded over the kids at first. But then we got talking one day and realized that both of us were older than our husbands . . .'

Gerard looked at her aghast, as if she were sharing some terribly personal secret.

'Well, honey, it's true,' said Marguerite. 'And we're both . . . we both loved to read. We would exchange books. We lived only a few streets apart. It gave us a lot in common.'

'I'm sure that was comforting to her,' said Eden.

'I just feel guilty that I didn't do more to help her. She was so anxious lately but I never dreamed . . . I tried to reassure her that she would get through it. But she was a lot more alone than I am. No matter what, Gerard and I are partners in this. We both work, but Gerard's mother moved here from France when she was widowed. And my whole family is in the area. Your mom had nobody but the people at the clinic. Don't get me wrong. They are wonderful people and they really understand. But there's no substitute for having your own family nearby.'

Marguerite's words made Eden squirm with guilt. She'd known very well that her mother was struggling. Maybe she should have made the effort to come out here and get to know Jeremy. She'd rebuffed every invitation, still hurt by Tara's abandonment. Why hadn't she tried to get beyond her own anger?

'And she had her husband,' Gerard reminded his wife. His French accent was pronounced, and charming.

Marguerite rolled her eyes. Eden looked from one to the other.

34

'He tried,' said Gerard stoutly. 'It was hard on him too.'

'Well, no one knows that better than you,' said Marguerite, 'but you don't shirk your responsibilities. You step up.'

'We shouldn't be talking about this right now, chérie,' Gerard admonished her. 'Eden doesn't want to hear this kind of talk.'

In fact, Eden wanted to hear more, but it did seem like the wrong time and place. 'I'm wondering where Flynn might be right now,' she said.

Marguerite shook her head. 'I hate to say it, but this is typical. He was never there for her.'

'Eden, we don't want to detain you,' said Gerard, firmly closing the subject. 'I'm sure you have many people to talk to.'

'Thank you both for coming,' said Eden.

Tears welled in Marguerite's eyes. 'Of course we came. Tara and Jeremy were very dear to us.'

'You know, we have a café downtown called Jaune,' said Gerard.

'It's a mélange of Provençal and Middle Eastern cooking. You should come by while you're here. We'd love to feed you dinner,' said Marguerite. 'On the house.'

Eden nodded and thanked them both, knowing she would be leaving the next day, and would probably never visit their restaurant. She watched them as they went and took a seat near the back among the other families from the clinic. Eden thought that Marguerite and Gerard reminded her of the kind of friends she had in Brooklyn. Young, eclectic, dedicated urbanites full of projects and ideas. When she left this place, she reminded herself, she had a life to go back to. A life far away from all this sadness. The thought of it was steadying. She turned away and looked for her aunt, who was already seated. Eden slipped into the chair beside Jodie. She glanced around the room. People were restless. Some were conversing while others nervously glanced at the door, waiting for some kind of direction. Finally, a member of the funeral home staff approached the lectern, which was surrounded by baskets of gladioli and carnations.

'We're going to begin shortly,' he said. 'We're just waiting for . . .'

'I'm here, I'm here,' bellowed a thick, slurry voice. All eyes turned to the back of the room.

Flynn Darby appeared in the center aisle. He was wearing a long wool topcoat that looked like it had come directly from the thrift shop. Under the coat he had on an oversized, shapeless black turtleneck, jeans and engineer's boots which were unlaced. His unruly hair, which was curly and blond, looked almost stiff with dirt and grease. Eden had seen Flynn Darby before, but only fleetingly. Her mother had invited Eden to their apartment several times when they first were together, but Eden always made an excuse. She refused to sit down to dinner with this man who had torn their lives apart. Still, she had always been curious about him. Now, she gazed at him in disbelief. Beside Flynn, a young woman in a headscarf, a shapeless floor-length dress and a blazer, supported him with one arm. Her eyes were almond-shaped and hazel-colored under

36

sharply defined black brows. She wore no make-up, but her face had a kind of grave beauty.

'Who is that with Flynn?' she whispered to Jodie.

Jodie shook her head. 'Who knows?'

'What's the matter with him?' Eden whispered.

'I'm just guessing,' said Jodie, 'but I'd say he's either drunk or stoned.'

He was still a young man, in his mid-thirties, but his glittering blue eyes had dark circles underneath, and looked unfocused. He was even-featured, with high cheekbones and hollow cheeks. He had a wide, full-lipped mouth, and there was a flash of white teeth as he curled his lip and snarled, 'Whass everybody looking at? I'm here. I'm here.'

The mourners looked away, no one willing to meet his defiant gaze. Early on, before she knew anything about their liaison, Eden had asked Tara about this author, a product of the Robbin's Ferry public school system, whom Tara had recruited for the bookstore's literary series.

'Is he cute?' Eden had asked.

'I suppose so,' Tara had said carefully.

'You think I'd like him?' Eden had asked her mother playfully.

A pained expression flickered over Tara's face. 'I'm sure of it,' she had replied.

The undertaker hurried to lead Flynn and his modestly garbed companion to the front of the room. The young woman sat down and lowered her eyes. Flynn looked at the coffins in confusion, almost as if he did not know what they were doing there. He sat down heavily in a chair beside

37

the girl in the headscarf. The undertaker introduced a Unitarian minister, who was clearly a stranger to Flynn.

The minister preached a tepid homily, and said a few generic words about mothers and sons. He made some remarks about Tara's beauty and Jeremy's feistiness that sounded as if they had been supplied by someone who hardly knew them. The undertaker leaned over Flynn and spoke into his ear. Flynn used his hand to wave away the man's concerns. He rose unsteadily to his feet and lurched toward the podium. He peered out at the assembled mourners, his gaze bleary. 'So you all show up,' he said, slurring his words.

The undertaker put a soothing hand on Flynn's sleeve, but Flynn shook him off. 'I'm doin' it,' he said irritably.

He reached into his pocket and pulled out a grimy, folded piece of paper which he flattened against the lectern.

He stared at the words for a few moments, as if mustering his forces, and then brushed at his cheeks with trembling fingers. 'Shall I compare thee,' he began, faltered, and then continued 'to a summer's day? Thou art more lovely and more temperate . . .'

He took a deep breath and read Shakespeare's love sonnet in a quavering voice. The young woman in the headscarf kept her gaze lowered, and wiped tears from her cheeks. When Flynn finished, the room was silent. He folded up his paper, jammed it in his pocket, and stumbled back to his chair.

And so, it was over. There would be no burial. Both were to be cremated after the service. The funeral director announced that there would be a brief reception at the hospitality lounge at the Cleveland Clinic, and all were invited to come.

'At the hospital? Really? Why not at their house?' Eden whispered.

'I don't think he's in any condition to host,' said Jodie disapprovingly.

'That's for sure,' said Eden.

'Besides, it's a crime scene,' said Jodie. 'Probably still blocked off by the police.'

'Do we have to go?' Eden asked.

'We have to go,' said Jodie.

As they left the funeral home, the beautiful day was fading, and storm clouds had begun to gather. Eden had cried, on and off, a good deal during the day, and felt exhausted. They found their way, with little difficulty, to the Cleveland Clinic. The hospitality lounge had all the warmth of an airport gate. They seated themselves on a molded plastic version of a loveseat in front of the plate glass windows.

Lizzy had shed her pea coat and was rushing around the lounge, putting out some functional-looking trays of sandwiches and cookies. Lizzy's husband, DeShaun, brought them each a small plastic cup of wine. Eden and Jodie both thanked him for his kindness. Eden noticed that at least half of the mourners, including her new acquaintances, Gerard and Marguerite, had foregone the chilly reception. They probably had to make dinner preparations at their café.

'Is Flynn coming?' Eden asked DeShaun.

'I think he's lying down,' said DeShaun. 'Not feeling up to it.'

'And his companion?' Jodie asked.

'Oh, I don't know. I don't really know her.'

Just then Lizzy flew by, balancing a tray of deviled eggs. DeShaun hailed her. 'Hey, honey. Who was that girl with Flynn?'

Lizzy stopped, holding the eggs aloft. 'Her name is Aaliya Saleh. She's a student at the college where he teaches. She works for him part-time as an intern.'

'What does that entail?' Jodie asked suspiciously.

DeShaun raised his eyebrows. 'With Flynn? Mostly putting out fires, I suspect.'

Lizzy gave him a reproving look. 'I understand that she's very competent. Very organized.'

'Flynn always seems to have someone to come to his rescue,' Jodie said sarcastically.

'He's suffered a terrible blow,' Lizzy reminded her.

'I don't mean to sound so critical. It's very nice of you and your husband to help out,' Jodie said.

'We're glad to help,' Lizzy said coolly. She offered the platter she was holding to Jodie. 'Egg?'

Jodie and Eden shook their heads. 'I'm not really hungry,' Eden said apologetically.

Lizzy and her husband moved on to the other guests.

'My mother would have hated this,' said Eden. 'It's so impersonal.'

'I know,' said Jodie.

'Are any of these people Flynn's family?' Eden asked.

'I don't think so. From what I understood from your mother, he just has those grandparents in Robbin's Ferry.'

'Yeah. When he called me I offered to help them get to the airport. He said they were too old and sick to make the trip. Whatever happened to his parents?'

'I guess his father was never in the picture,' said Jodie. 'The mother was a drug addict who died of an overdose in some crack house in Miami when Flynn was two. They found Flynn alone in their apartment the next day, wandering around in a filthy diaper, eating cat food that he found on the floor. His grandparents came and got him. They raised him.'

Eden grimaced. 'That's a horrible story.'

'I know,' said Jodie. 'I should have more sympathy for him. But he really acted like a lout today.'

'True enough,' Eden sighed.

They sat in silence for a moment. 'When are you headed back to the city?' Jodie asked.

'Soon. I've just been . . . paralyzed all week.'

'I'm sure you have. But you need to get back to your life.'

'I'm going to,' said Eden.

Jodie nodded and shifted in her seat. 'How's your dad doing? I always felt bad about the way my sister treated him. Hugh was so good to us. He helped put me through college. Did you know that?'

Eden shook her head.

41

Jodie sipped from her plastic cup. 'I always idolized your father.'

'That makes two of us,' said Eden.

'I thought my sister was so lucky to marry Hugh Radley.'

It felt a little strange to be discussing her mother's first marriage at Tara's funeral. But as a child Eden, like most children, had no real interest in the family history. Now, as an adult, she had an opportunity to satisfy her curiosity, and she was glad to take it. Besides, it wasn't as though they were besieged with people wanting to make their acquaintance. 'She said she met him at a picnic,' said Eden.

'Oh, I remember. She was still in high school but she always had boyfriends. Even then, Tara was a beauty,' Jodie reminisced. 'She came home from the picnic that night and said that she had met the guy she was going to marry.'

'Didn't your mother object? I mean, that my mom wanted to get married so young?'

'Are you kidding? My mother was ecstatic. She was a single mother herself, barely making ends meet. This was the best thing she could have hoped for. Hugh was a little bit older, he had that masonry business. He was a catch.'

'Do you think my mother really loved him?' asked Eden.

Jodie hesitated a moment. 'Your dad? Yes, she loved him,' she said firmly. 'Tara was just a little bit too young to get married. She never went to college or lived on her own. But yes, she adored Hugh.'

Eden shrugged. 'I thought so too, but what did

I know? I was just a kid. They were my whole world.' Eden's voice caught in her throat. 'And then she left.'

'Well, your mother was a starry-eyed romantic and, over time, marriage becomes . . . something comfortable. If you're lucky. I think your mom just wanted some drama in her life. Another chapter. But, in the end, what did she really do but trade one man for another, one child for another?'

Eden was surprised by the bluntness of her aunt's analysis. 'That's a little harsh.'

Jodie shrugged. 'I know. I'm sorry. I guess I'm a little angry at her. She pretended everything was fine. She never even gave me a chance to . . . help her.'

Eden nodded. She understood, but didn't know how to reply. She tried to remember her mother's smiling eyes, gazing tenderly at her, but all she could think of was Tara taping shut the windows and stuffing towels under the doors. Was that why you were calling me? Eden wondered. Were you going to ask me for help? Were you giving me a chance to change your mind?

'Eden?' said Jodie. 'Have you had enough? 'Cause we can leave. We've made our appearance.'

'No one cares that we're here,' said Eden. 'Let's go.'

As they started for the door, Eden saw Lizzy out of the corner of her eye. She was hailing Eden, waving something at her. Eden stopped, and turned as Lizzy approached her.

'Are you leaving?' Lizzy asked.

Eden nodded apologetically. 'I'm exhausted,' she said.

'Headed back to New York?'

'Well, not directly. Tomorrow I'm flying home. My dad's picking me up at the local airport. I'll probably head back to New York the next day.'

'So you'll be going back to Robbin's Ferry,' said Lizzy.

'Briefly,' said Eden.

'I was just wondering if you could do us a favor.'

'Us?' said Eden.

'Flynn, really.' Lizzy was holding a program from the funeral service in her hand. 'I know that Flynn's grandparents wanted to be here but it wasn't possible for them to travel. They live in Robbin's Ferry. Flynn wanted them to have a memento from the service.'

'Couldn't he mail it to them?' Eden asked, and then cringed inwardly at how callous she sounded. Lizzy had done so much to help, and here she was, balking at one small errand.

Lizzy did not seem put off by her reaction. 'I think it would be nicer if you brought it to them. They may have questions about what happened. They're old and feeble, and it's strictly a mission of mercy, but, after all, Jeremy was their great-grandson.'

And my mother was responsible for his death, Eden added silently. 'Yes, of course,' she said, taking the program from Lizzy. 'I'll take care of it.'

'Do you need their address?' Lizzy asked.

'No. It's a small town. That's easy to find out.'

Lizzy thanked her profusely, and then excused herself to return to her hostess duties.

Jodie looked at Eden with one eyebrow raised. 'Really? They want you to make a delivery for Flynn?'

'It's all right,' said Eden with a sigh. 'It's little enough.'

Jodie shook her head. 'You're a good girl.' She tugged at Eden's sleeve. 'Now, let's get out of here, before they think of anything else.'

Four

Early the next morning, Eden and Jodie went to the airport and went their separate ways. Hugh picked Eden up at Westchester Airport and brought her back to the house. Eden was home in time for lunch. Gerri made sure that there were sandwiches waiting in the refrigerator. While they ate at the kitchen counter, Eden told her father about the funeral. He asked a few questions, but the pain in his eyes made Eden want to look away.

Eden brought the dishes to the sink and rinsed them. While she had her back to her father she said, 'I've actually come back with a mission.'

'What kind of mission?' Hugh asked.

'I have to take a program from the funeral service over to Flynn's grandparents. They weren't able to travel to the funeral, and one of Mom's friends asked me to bring it to them.

Hugh was silent. Eden shut the dishwasher, and turned around to look at him. He was gazing blankly out the kitchen door.

'I'm dreading it,' said Eden.

'It seems like a lot to ask of you,' said Hugh. 'Can't he just mail it to them?'

'I asked the same thing,' said Eden. 'But they're old and I'm sure they were very upset not to be able to be there. I guess it just seemed like the right thing to do. You know. Give it a personal touch.'

'I suppose,' said Hugh doubtfully.

'Would you happen to know where they live?' she asked her father.

Hugh sighed, but, in fact, there was very little about Robbin's Ferry which he did not know. He knew the Darbys' street, and described the house.

'Okay. Well, I think I'll just go and get it over with,' said Eden. 'I won't be staying long.'

Following her father's directions, Eden drove to one of the older neighborhoods in Robbin's Ferry, on a tree-lined street that ended at the river. The Darby house was, as Hugh had described it, the eyesore of the neighborhood. It was a split-level, probably built in the 1950s, and its gray asbestos shingles were covered with grime. It was surrounded by newer, or more recently renovated houses, but the Darby house sat on its immensely valuable lot, stubbornly unimproved, with a wheelchair ramp which did nothing to enhance the house's façade. There was a fanlike arrangement of small American flags in a metal holder atop the railing on the ramp. A US Marine decal, reading *Semper Fi*, obscured the small window at the top of the front door. The linings of the drawn curtains in the house's other windows were unevenly stained with yellow, like old teeth. On the top floor of the house there was a window with cardboard standing in for a missing pane. The yard was large and seemed mostly untended. Even now, in winter, Eden could see that the bushes and trees around it were straggly.

Eden steeled herself, and got out of the car. She walked up to the front door. There was a metal knocker, but it hung askew. Eden knocked on the door.

There were sounds of life coming from behind the door. Finally it was answered, the door dragged across a matted shag rug of faded, indeterminate color. The man who opened the door was old and wiry, and colorless as the house itself. He wore his white hair in a short crew cut, and his face was etched with lines. The afternoon sun reflected off his steel-rimmed glasses.

'Yes?' he demanded.

'Mr Darby? My name is Eden Radley. I . . . my mother was married to your grandson . . . that is . . .'

'I know who you are,' he said abruptly.

Eden nodded. 'I just got back from Cleveland, from the funeral. Your grandson asked me to bring you something.'

'Come in,' barked the scrawny old man, turning his back on her. He shuffled away from the door, slightly stooped, but with no other obvious physical impairment. Eden followed him into the

47

living room. The furniture was worn, and the room was hot and stuffy. A skinny old woman wearing a pink sweatsuit sat slumped in a wheelchair, an afghan over her knees. Her thin white hair was fluffy around her face.

Flynn's grandfather flopped down into a Barcalounger beside his wife. 'Company, old girl,' he said. He did not offer Eden a seat.

The old woman peered up at Eden, as if she had difficulty with her vision. 'Who is it, Michael?' she asked in a querulous voice.

Eden walked over to the wheelchair and bent over, offering the old woman her hand. 'I'm Eden Radley. My mother was married to Flynn. Your grandson. I've just come back from the funeral.'

'Whose funeral?' the woman asked in confusion.

'Her mother's,' Michael Darby shouted at his wife. 'And Flynn's kid. I told you about this. The mother killed herself. Took the boy with her.'

The old woman pressed her lips together and tears rose to her rheumy eyes.

'Oh yes. Terrible. Just terrible.' She clutched Eden's warm hand in a cold, clawlike grip.

Eden disengaged and straightened up. 'I understood that you couldn't make it because of your health.'

'We could have made it. He didn't want us there,' said Michael.

Looking at the two of them, Eden doubted very much if they could have negotiated hotels and airports. Not without considerable help. And, judging from the deteriorating condition of the house, help was in short supply for these two.

'Well, in any case,' she said, 'I brought you

both a copy of the program from the funeral service. Flynn wanted you to have it.'

'Oh he did, did he?' said the old man combatively. 'That would be the first time he ever thought of us.'

'Michael, don't be like that,' said the old woman in her thin, plaintive voice. She looked up at Eden hopefully. 'Flynn is a nice boy. He always tried his best. He had a lot of problems.'

'Nice boy, my ass. He was always nothing but trouble,' said Michael Darby.

For a moment, Eden almost felt sorry for Flynn. 'Well, he wanted you to have this.' She put the program in the old woman's hands.

The paper shook as Flynn's grandmother held it, frowning at the picture. 'Who are they?' she asked.

Michael Darby's pale cheeks reddened. 'I told you,' he cried. 'Flynn's wife and kid.'

The old woman's eyes softened. 'She's very pretty,' she said. She looked up at Eden. 'She looks like you!'

Eden did not know what to say. 'Thank you,' she said.

'How is Flynn?' asked the old woman.

Eden shrugged. 'He's . . . having a hard time.'

'Why a hard time?' Flynn's grandfather demanded.

'His wife and child are dead,' said Eden, affronted by his tone.

'Are you kidding me?' said Michael Darby. 'His wife was old enough to be his mother, and the kid was nothing but a drooling mess. It's a blessing he got rid of both of them. Your mother

49

did him a favor, checking out like that. Flynn's on easy street now. Got the life insurance for the both of them. He'll be off on a world cruise. No, we won't see him again. He won't come back here until we die and he can get his hands on this house and make a bundle selling it to some developer who will pay him a king's ransom to knock it down. You mark my words. All we sacrificed for him, and for what?'

Somewhere in the middle of this diatribe, Eden realized that this visit to the grandparents must not have been Flynn's idea at all. This was just something that Lizzy, in her innocence, thought would be nice. A nice idea in theory, Eden thought. But, in reality, completely pointless. 'Well,' she said brusquely, 'I've delivered the program to you. I'm going to go now.'

'Oh, don't go,' the old woman pleaded. 'Stay and have some cookies. Do we have cookies, Michael?'

'I don't know,' Michael grumbled, twisting forward to get out of his chair. 'I'll check.'

'Don't bother,' said Eden. 'I can't stay. I'll show myself out.'

'Please stay. Make her stay, Michael,' cried Flynn's grandmother.

'Leave her alone, Mother,' Michael said in a long-suffering tone. 'She wants to go. Let her go.'

Eden did not hesitate. She left the house without a backward look. She was shaking as she drove home. The old man was so vile, that it made her wonder what Flynn's years growing up had been like. Obviously, raising Flynn after his mother

50

died was not something they had undertaken willingly. How often did his grandfather remind him of that? she wondered. How could Flynn ever have felt at home in that house?

When she got home, exhausted by the whole ordeal, Eden went up to her room and took a nap. She was awakened by her father gently shaking her. The afternoon dusk was deepening into night.

'Sweetie, don't you think you ought to go back?' he asked.

'You want me to leave?' Eden asked plaintively.

'No,' said Hugh. 'But I know you should. You have work.'

Eden knew he was right. It was time. Even though she was eager to escape the memories which surrounded her here, she dreaded saying goodbye to her father, who looked utterly drained after the week's events. It was only his urging that forced her out of the nest.

At the train station, she kissed him tenderly on the cheek and noticed how pale and papery his skin seemed. They embraced for a long time.

'I'm worried about you, Dad. You seem . . . a little tired,' Eden said, sniffling into a tissue.

'I'm fine,' Hugh said. 'Don't worry about me. Stop worrying.'

Eden hugged him again, thanked him for everything and climbed aboard the train. She found a seat and leaned her forehead against the cold train window. Although it was only a short, thirty-five-minute ride on the train from Robbin's Ferry to New York City, the psychological distance was vast. By the time Eden had reached

Grand Central, and taken the subway out to Brooklyn, the winter day had grown dark. The subway was a short walk from her apartment, which was on the second floor of a brownstone, in the front. A bay window, nearly obscured by the branches of a London plane tree, looked out over the city street. A fabric artist who lived in the next block had come in to water her plants, and left the lights on, as Eden had requested. She couldn't bear to come home to complete darkness. There was enough of that in her life at the moment. Eden let herself in. Her friend had left a note of condolence and a little box of candy on the table. Eden felt both relieved and lonesome to be back in her own place, her own world.

She was looking glumly into her empty refrigerator when she got a call.

Her friend Jasmine, who was a waitress at the Black Cat across the street, was purring in her ear. 'You're back?' Jasmine said. 'Come over here. Right now. Have dinner with your friends.'

Eden hesitated, but only for a moment. 'Ten minutes,' she said.

Five

The dinner was a little awkward at first, but a few drinks, and universal good intentions, smoothed out the evening. Eden's friends would not allow her to pay for anything. She looked around fondly at the motley group of actors and bloggers, artists and waiters who had gathered to welcome her back, with no questions asked. The topic of her loss was avoided by tacit agreement. It was not a subject to be discussed in a large, lively group. But their banter distracted her, and their concern for her was palpable. She felt lucky to be among them. Late in the evening, Vince, the bartender from the Brisbane Tavern, came in and was immediately invited to join their table. Eden could feel his gaze on her during the evening and they exchanged a nod and a smile. He was undeniably attractive, and ordinarily she might have flirted with him, but she was too exhausted tonight, and too fragile. She sank into the supportive kindness of those at the cheerful table like a warm bath, and when she got up to leave, she quickly accepted the offer from her gay barista friend, Drew, to walk her back to her apartment.

She barely slept, and thought about calling in sick when the alarm went off, but, finally, Eden told herself that she would have to face it sooner or later, and there was no point in putting off the inevitable. She wore sunglasses on the subway to Manhattan, even though the day was cloudy, and, when she entered the building on 57th Street, she avoided eye contact with anyone she passed. In the elevator she kept her gaze straight ahead. Even though she recognized some of the people who worked at DeLaurier Publishing, she pretended not to see them. She entered the reception area and waved at Melissa without stopping to chat.

Once she was burrowed in her own office,

she felt safer, and the anxious racing of her heart settled down to a normal rhythm. A bouquet of flowers arrived from the company, and were set on her desk. Sophy came in, as she always did, and settled herself in the chair in front of Eden, ready to listen. Sophy could be a wonderfully matter-of-fact person, and she did not avoid the difficult subject of the murder/suicide. Her questions were both unabashed and tactful. Eden admitted helplessly that she could not explain it, and Sophy agreed that it was utterly baffling. Somehow, Eden felt better. She had said it out loud to someone who did not know her family, and she had not turned to stone as a result. It would be easier to say it aloud the next time.

Work had piled up on her desk and computer, and even though she had little appetite for it, she forced herself to begin working on manuscripts. Gradually, she found her interest returning. She hid out in her office for the rest of the work day, and no one tried to coax her out. When her mind wandered from the task, she chided herself into refocusing. She was lucky to have a job that interested her. Getting back to work felt like a relief.

Over the next few days, life as it was, far from Robbin's Ferry, began to resume a semblance of normalcy. Eden called her father every night, reassured by the sound of Hugh's voice. Her friends were solicitous, and invited her to dinner. She ate in someone else's kitchen, or as their guest in one bistro or another, for the better part of two weeks. Her crying jags became less frequent. Her mother's suicide had been a shock and a loss, but, in many ways, she told herself, she had grieved for her mother years ago. When Tara left Hugh for Flynn Darby, life as Eden knew it was torn apart. While Tara's death was much more final, the feeling of losing her mother was not new to her. She had survived it once, she reminded herself. She would survive again.

One day Hugh called, and asked if he could come into Manhattan and take her out to dinner after work. Eden was surprised, but glad for the opportunity to see him. After they had eaten at a Chinese restaurant on the West Side, Hugh got around to the purpose of his visit. 'I'm going to Florida for two weeks,' he said.

Eden was delighted to hear that news. 'Oh Dad, that's great. You gonna do some fishing?'

'I hope so,' he said. 'I've been a little worried about going so far away from you at such a difficult time.'

'I'll be fine,' Eden reassured him. 'My friends are looking after me. I haven't had dinner alone since I got back.'

'Are you sure you're okay?' he asked.

'I'm okay,' said Eden, and she did not allow even a shade of sadness into her voice. She wanted him to go to Florida, and rest in the sun, without worrying about her. 'Who are you going with?' she asked. 'Are you going by yourself?'

Hugh looked a little pained. 'Actually. No. Um . . . I'm going with Gerri. Her cousin has a condo down there that he's lending us for the week.'

55

'Gerri?' said Eden, taken aback. 'I thought you two were just . . . friends.'

'We are friends,' Hugh said firmly. 'And my friend asked me if I wanted to go to Florida.'

'Okay,' said Eden slowly. 'How long have you known about this?'

'Not long. It was kind of spur of the moment.'

'Dad, you're not spontaneous,' said Eden.

Hugh smiled shyly. 'Okay, okay. It's something we talked about on and off for a while. Gerri was thinking of asking her cousin, and then the cousin just called and offered. So, it seemed like . . . the thing to do.'

'Well, great,' said Eden, trying to mean it. My father is going away with a girlfriend, and I can't even get a date, she thought. But whatever.

'I'll miss you,' he said sincerely.

'It's only two weeks,' said Eden.

'I always miss you,' he said.

'I know, Dad. Listen. You have a wonderful time.'

Their parting was fond, but not sad. Eden was proud of herself for that. Part of her wanted to just climb into his pocket and stay there. But her life had to go on.

And so did his.

A few days after she bid her father farewell, Eden got a call from Rob Newsome, the editorial director.

'Eden,' he said. 'Mr DeLaurier would like us to come to a meeting in his office at four o'clock.'

'What's it about?' she asked. She had never been summoned by the publisher before. It was a family business, one of the few left in New

56

York publishing, which had been started by Maurice DeLaurier's great-uncle nearly a hundred years earlier. Maurice was widely considered to be a shrewd CEO, who had grown the business from the small house it had been when he inherited it. Eden had met him when Rob Newsome hired her, but after that she had done little more than exchange polite greetings with the impeccably turned-out executive.

'A new project. I really can't say any more than that. I'll see you at Maurice's office at four.'

'Okay,' said Eden.

At four o'clock she refreshed her make-up, straightened her form-fitting knit dress, and walked down the corridor toward the publisher's office. She got a nod to enter from his assistant. Eden tapped on the door then went in. The office had a wall of windows overlooking 57th Street, and the afternoon sun had turned the room, which was lined with bookshelves and furnished in leather and rich-looking carpets, to a blinding red gold. Eden closed the door and approached the conversation area where the two men were sitting. Maurice DeLaurier stood up politely and indicated a club chair.

'Eden, thanks for coming. Won't you have a seat?'

She glanced at Rob, and sat down in the empty chair.

'It's good to see you back at work. You've been through a difficult time.'

'Thank you for the flowers,' said Eden. Although she doubted that he even knew about the flowers, he nodded graciously.

'Little enough,' he said, 'under the circumstances. Now, if you don't mind, I'll come straight to the point. I've asked you both here because I've been having some conversations with Gideon Lendl. He has made us a most interesting proposal.'

Eden immediately recognized the name of one of the most powerful literary agents in New York. 'Gideon Lendl himself?' she asked. She knew that it was unusual for Gideon Lendl to personally represent an author. His authors tended to be quite literary but also commercial, often landing on the best-seller list. Usually, the bigger, better-known publishing houses landed Gideon Lendl's clients. She felt a little thrill of excitement at this news.

She glanced at Rob. His face was expressionless and his eyes were fixed on the publisher. Eden felt as if he was avoiding her questioning gaze. She turned back to Maurice. 'Is it a celebrity author?' she asked. They were all well aware of the clout a celebrity could bring to the sales of a book.

Maurice shook his head. 'No. Up to this point, this author has only published in small literary magazines. But circumstances conspire to make this a very interesting property. I must tell you that the situation is a little delicate, though.'

Any book which was being fronted by Gideon Lendl himself was bound to be an important property. What does this have to do with me? she wondered. She had worked closely on big books with various editors in the company, but had not handled any major projects herself.

As if he had read her mind, Maurice addressed

her. 'Eden, this particular book has . . . personal implications for you.'

'For me?' she queried.

Maurice pressed his lips together and leaned forward. 'Eden, the author wants you to be the editor of this book.'

'Me? Why in the world? Do I know the author?'

Maurice nodded. 'In fact, you do. His name is Flynn Darby. I believe he was married to your late mother.'

If Maurice DeLaurier had smacked her across the face, he could not have stunned her more effectively. Eden blinked at him, as if trying to summon her senses after a knockout punch.

'Mr Darby is a very talented writer, and the novel he has written makes for compelling reading. But, I feel I must warn you that it's . . . somewhat grim, and very clearly about his life with your mother. There's a great deal in there about their . . . marriage, and their struggles with a disabled child. Apparently, Mr Darby had been working on it for several years, and it was nearly finished when this terrible tragedy occurred.'

Eden stared at Maurice DeLaurier. The publisher was about to offer her a chance to instantly gain status in the company. In the publishing world in general. All she had to do was betray her family. She felt the old familiar hatred for Flynn Darby wash over her, and she began to shake all over. 'And now, my mother's suicide, my half-brother's . . .' She couldn't bring herself to say 'murder'. 'It would be good for sales,' she said bluntly.

'Eden,' Rob said in a warning voice.

'Sorry,' she mumbled.

'Eden,' Maurice said kindly, 'I'm the one who's sorry. I realize how difficult this must be for you. I don't have to tell you that authors cannibalize their lives rather shamelessly. Frankly, it can be a little . . . repulsive from time to time. Your stepfather is far from the only writer who has chosen to do this. No sooner does a personal tragedy occur than many an author is trying to use it to advance his or her career. Mr Darby is not unusual in that regard.'

Eden was not able to look him in the eye.

'But I have to be very honest with you,' said Maurice. 'The timing on this, while unfortunate in some ways, is very significant for us. It makes his book very topical. This book has the potential to be a major best-seller. First of all, it's very well written. I want you to know that. This isn't some hack job. Then, there is the disability angle, which he handles sympathetically. And then, undeniably your mother's tragic death and the death of their son—'

'Gives it currency,' said Eden in a dull voice.

'It's an important opportunity,' said Maurice.

She shuddered and turned to Rob. 'Did you know about this?' she asked him.

'Maurice emailed me the book last night,' Rob said evenly. 'He wanted me to know what we were wading into here. Obviously, if you choose to do it, I would be advising you. It's a lot to take on.'

'And me being the editor would also be a talking point, I suppose,' she said, trying to sound matter-of-fact.

60

'Eden, this is a business,' said Rob. 'Of course it would beneficial for publicity purposes to have you as an editor.'

'I'm sure that's why Flynn asked for me,' she said.

'Well, I asked Gideon about this,' said Maurice. 'He feels that Mr Darby sincerely wants your input on this. You know more about the people involved than any other editor could possibly know. Mr Darby acknowledged to Gideon that you might not be willing to work with him.'

'He realized that, did he?' she asked.

'He did, but he asked Gideon to put this forward to you anyway.'

Eden took a deep breath and stared at a spot on Maurice's desk. How could she possibly do this? How could she work closely with Flynn Darby, knowing that he was using her mother's death as a way to promote his career? How could she ever explain it to her father? He would be appalled. 'And if I don't agree to do it?' she asked. 'Will I lose my job?'

'Oh heavens, no,' Maurice demurred. 'Don't even think such a thing.'

Eden studied the publisher's face and body language. He was being sincere to a point, she thought. He would not fire her for refusing. But she would not soon be forgiven for her refusal to cooperate.

'It should be said,' Rob interjected, 'that if you don't take this project on, it may not stay with our company. Flynn Darby could have his pick of publishers.'

Maurice shook his head. The paterfamilias.

'Rob, don't do that. Don't try to pressure her that way.'

Eden felt as if she would explode with frustration. It seemed like a cruel double blow that Flynn had put her in this position of jeopardizing her own career if she said no to his book. 'I understand the consequences,' she said.

'Look, Eden,' said Maurice. 'We may be getting ahead of ourselves here. Why don't you read the book first before you make a decision? I think you may be surprised by it. It's really quite good. Of course, you would be looking at it from a very different perspective. But give it a read, and try to keep an open mind while you're reading. If you decide that you cannot do it, I will respect your choice.'

There was no way out of this trap, and Eden knew it. She had to at least look at the book, and respond. Or be seen as completely intransigent and unreasonable.

Once again, Flynn had given her no choice. 'All right,' she said. 'I'll read it.'

Rob stood up. Maurice followed suit.

'We'll need an answer very soon,' said Maurice.

'You'll have one,' said Eden. She got up and smoothed down her dress. 'I'll read it tonight.'

Six

By the time she got home from work, Eden's head was pounding. So this is what a migraine is like, she thought. The thudding in her head made her feel sick to her stomach. Every step was jarring, every smell sickening. She was supposed to have dinner with her friend, Shelley, a masseuse who lived and worked in a converted factory in Red Hook. She texted Shelley a message that she could not make it tonight. She pulled the shades, took about four aspirin and lay down on her bed, with all the lights turned off in the apartment, and a washrag on her forehead.

Sleep, she thought. I have to sleep. Anything to escape.

But she couldn't sleep. All she could do was think about Flynn Darby, who was now going to profit handsomely from Tara's suicide, from Jeremy's pitiful death. And what role would Eden play in this profit-taking? If she agreed to do it, she would feel like a traitor to her father, to herself, to her mother's memory. If she refused, Flynn would have another editor in no time, and she would be denied even the possibility of some influence on this very public version of her mother's life. He was a user, and he had put her into an impossible position. There was no way that she was going to be in the right.

She went over and over the same territory in her mind, and then, somehow, she was blessedly released from consciousness. She fell into a deep sleep, and was awakened by the ringing of her phone. She blinked and looked around. The ringing was coming from her bag on the floor beside her bed. The bag which contained her iPad. The iPad which contained Flynn Darby's book. She rummaged angrily in the bag, pulled out the phone and snapped into the receiver. 'Yes?'

'Eden, it's Vince. From the Brisbane.'

She was not expecting to hear from him, and wasn't sure that she wanted to. It was difficult to get enthused at the idea of getting to know someone right now. But even if it had been someone she longed to hear from, she wouldn't have been able to respond. 'Hi, Vince. Look, I can't talk,' she mumbled. 'I have a horrible headache.' As soon as she said it, however, she noted that the headache was much better after that deep sleep. Still, the only thing she wanted was more sleep.

'Oh, sorry to hear that,' he said.

'Yeah, I'm sorry too. It's been a tough day. Another time,' she said, ending the call. No sooner had she slipped the phone back into her bag and turned over on the bed than she was asleep again.

Someone pounding a nail into the wall in her dream became impossible to ignore. As soon as she began to question it in the dream, she commenced the swim to the surface of consciousness. The damp rag, which had been on her forehead, was now lodged, cold and wet, under her neck, and she could see that darkness had fallen outside. The sound of pounding in her dream was, she now realized, coming from the door of her apartment.

Eden forced herself to sit up and then stand. She touched her head gingerly, but the headache had abated, and she felt a surge of gratitude for the end of that misery. If only that hammering on her door didn't make it start up again.

'Coming,' she shouted. She shuffled to the front door in her stocking feet, a hoody pulled on over her knit dress. She glanced in the mirror by the door and saw that her make-up was smudged under her bleary eyes, and her hair looked as if someone had combed it with an egg beater.

Eden sighed and opened the door without taking off the chain. She looked quizzically at the man in the hallway through the narrow opening.

Vince, the bartender, was standing there, holding a fragrant brown paper bag adorned with the Black Cat logo. 'Hi, Eden,' he said.

'How did you get in the building?' she demanded irritably.

'Someone was going out and held the door for me,' he admitted.

'How did you even find out where I lived?'

Vince shrugged. 'I asked your friend Jasmine. I told her you had a migraine and I wanted to bring you some of those Thai spring rolls from the Black Cat. Food can really help when you have a headache like that.'

'And just like that, she told you where I lived?' Eden demanded.

'Well, I asked her for your address.'

Just then, the elevator door opened behind him, and Jasmine emerged, carrying a six-pack of Coke. Jasmine waved at the opening in the door.

'Hi, Eden,' she said. 'How are you feeling, sweetie? Vince came in the restaurant and told me you had a migraine, so we got you this takeout and I stopped at the corner and bought you some Coke. That's always good for a headache. Can we come in?'

Eden realized, a bit sheepishly, that there was no harm intended here. Vince was not trying to muscle his way into her place. He just decided to do something nice. The two of them were in collusion. They were being solicitous. Shamed by her own assumptions, she unlatched the chain and opened the door.

'Come on in,' she said. 'I'm a mess. Don't even look at me.'

'You look fine,' said Vince.

'Please, don't be gallant,' Eden said. 'Put the stuff on the table.'

Vince set the bag on the table, and Jasmine went and put the six-pack of Coke in the refrigerator, pulling out a couple and offering one each to Eden and to Vince. Eden took hers gratefully. Vince hesitated.

'Well, sit,' said Eden. She looked into the bag and began to unpack round aluminum containers with plastic lids. 'Wow, you brought a feast here.'

'We weren't sure what would appeal to you besides the spring rolls,' Vince said.

Eden was beginning to feel ashamed of her ill humor. 'Have you two eaten?'

Vince shrugged. 'I'm not that hungry,' he said.

'Well, I'm starved,' said Jasmine. 'You two sit down at the table. I'll get the plates.'

All awkwardness fled as the three of them tucked into the takeout. They chatted companionably, and Vince flirted amiably with them both. Why not? Eden thought. She was just glad to be here with them on this most trying of days. She felt as if she had never eaten a meal that tasted so good. Vince, who had professed not to be hungry, was licking his fingers in satisfaction.

'Thank you,' said Eden. 'Really. I can't thank you enough. Both of you. I really felt wretched when I got home from work. I can't remember ever feeling that bad from a headache.'

'What brought it on?' Vince asked.

Jasmine shot him a warning glance. 'She's under a lot of stress.'

Vince, belatedly, looked uneasy. 'Of course,' he said. 'Your mother's death.'

Eden sighed, and pushed back from the table. 'No, though, it was something related to it that brought it on.' She hesitated. She knew they wouldn't press her if she decided not to explain it. But she found that she wanted to tell them. She wanted to bounce it off people who weren't involved.

'My publisher called me in today,' she said. 'It seems that the house has been offered an important first novel, and the author wants me to edit it.'

'That's good, right?' said Jasmine, starting to stash the clutter of containers and napkins into the Black Cat bag.

'The author is my stepfather, and the book is based on his marriage to my mother, and about their lives with my now late half-brother, who suffered from a rare genetic disorder.'

Vince's eyes widened over the napkin he had pressed to his lips. He lowered the napkin and frowned at her. 'Okay, don't be mad at me for asking, but doesn't it seem like he is trying to capitalize on recent events?'

'Yes,' said Eden. 'Exactly. My mother killed herself and her son by carbon monoxide poisoning. My publisher insists that the book has great literary merit. But obviously, this murder/suicide gives the book built-in publicity. They gave me until tomorrow to decide if I want to go along with this.'

'That's disgusting,' Jasmine exclaimed. 'How could he even think of exploiting their deaths this way?'

'I know,' Eden agreed.

'Still . . .' said Vince.

'Still what?' Eden asked.

'I know this is going to sound cold, but, let's be realistic. Of all the books published every month, how many have this kind of . . . story attached to them? It's a public relations coup.'

'That doesn't make it right,' said Jasmine indignantly.

'I'm not saying it does. Just stating facts,' said Vince. 'Look at it this way, Eden. Someone's going to publish this book. Why should your stepfather be the only one to profit from this tragedy? If it can help your career, why shouldn't you do it?'

'Ever the businessman,' said Jasmine. 'That's why you own the Brisbane and I'm still a waitress.'

'You own the Brisbane?' Eden asked, surprised.

Vince shrugged and smiled. 'Yup. You figured I was an actor, right?'

'Or a would-be writer,' Eden admitted wryly.

Vince shook his head. 'Nope. I work there, and

I live above the store. Not exactly glamorous but it's mine.'

'That's quite a coup in this neighborhood,' Eden observed.

'I worked briefly on Wall Street, years ago. I was good at it but I hated it. So I took my ill-gotten gains and bought the building. That's why I've got all this gray hair. But never mind that. We were talking about you.'

Eden had to admit to herself that she looked at him with a new respect. He understood the problem. And he saw the big picture dispassionately. Something she was not able to do.

'What are you going to do?' Jasmine asked.

Eden frowned and was silent for a minute. 'I don't know. I'm sure you're right, Vince, but it makes me sick just to think of it. I guess the first thing I'm going to do is read the book, so I can support my position coherently.'

All three nodded thoughtfully. Then Vince stood up. 'Well, we better get out of here, Jasmine. Reading a whole book is gonna take a while. So you have to read it tonight?' he asked, looking at Eden.

She nodded. 'I have to force myself to.'

'Well, don't get another headache,' said Jasmine, ruffling Eden's hair as she passed by her on the way to the kitchen. 'I'm putting these leftovers in your fridge.'

Eden thanked them again. After they put on their coats and collected their belongings, she walked the two of them to the door. She watched, almost enviously, as they went out into the hallway, teasing one another playfully.

Jasmine punched Vince in his upper arm.

Could be something developing there, Eden thought, watching them. Part of her felt happy at that idea, and part of her felt jealous. No, she insisted to herself. If that's what happens, it's a good thing. All I know is, I just wish I were going with them. Away from here. Anywhere. Anything but the task which was facing her. The book she was going to have to read. But there was no point in resisting. Just start it, she told herself. You don't have to read the whole thing to be able to say no. Just enough to make a case for why you can't do it.

She shuffled into her bedroom, took off her clothes and put on a warm bathrobe. Then she slid into her bed. She turned on the light attached to the headboard, picked up her iPad and began to read.

Seven

Eden tapped on the open door to Rob's office.

'Come in,' he said. His graying, close-cropped head was bent over his PC. His shirtsleeves were rolled up, his jacket hung across the back of his chair.

Eden stuck her head in. 'Your assistant isn't at her desk.'

'Eden!' he exclaimed. 'Sit down. Let me finish this email and I'll be right with you.'

She went in and sat in front of the editorial

director's desk. She glanced at the framed photos of Rob's smiling family on his desktop, and then she glanced at her own reflection in his office window. She had been up all night, and there were dark circles under her eyes, and folds of exhaustion in her face. She had taken a shower and washed and blown out her hair first thing this morning after she finished the book. She had put on a charcoal-gray military-style jacket that felt like a suit of armor to her. It usually made her feel sharp and in control. However, sharp and in control were the last things she was feeling this morning.

'There,' said Rob. 'Send. Now, how are you doing? I assume you're here about Flynn Darby's book.'

'I am,' she said.

'You had a chance to read it?'

Eden nodded. 'I read all night.'

'And? What did you think?'

Eden gave the book her most valuable compliment. 'I couldn't put it down.'

Rob nodded, deliberately keeping his response noncommittal. 'That was how I felt when I read it,' he said.

Despite her positive reaction, Eden was unsmiling. She had wanted to hate it. She was prepared to hate it. Even now, she was telling herself that the only reason she found it fascinating was the opportunity it afforded to have a look inside her mother's second marriage. That had been irresistible to her.

Rob waited for her to elaborate. Finally he said, 'It's a very powerful book.'

71

'Rob, I can't help feeling resentful that he now wants to use the death of his family – of my mother and my half-brother – for promotional purposes,' she said angrily.

Rob tented his fingers and pressed them to his lips before he spoke. 'I can understand you feeling that way, of course,' he said. 'But he couldn't have known that this would happen when he was writing it.'

Eden sighed. 'No, I suppose not. He doesn't even address it in the book.'

'Well, it has to be addressed. The book may need to open with that, and then go back to the beginning,' Rob mused. 'Or maybe just a very matter-of-fact recounting at the end. It's not clear which way to go.' He peered at her. 'So, I guess, this is the big question – do you want to take a whack at it, or would you rather pass?'

'I'd rather pass,' said Eden. 'It's sickening, it's so close.'

Rob nodded, avoiding her gaze.

'But if I pass, it will just be sent somewhere else, and someone who doesn't give a damn will take it on. I don't want that. I'd rather be the one who sees it through. Gets it into print.'

Rob kept his enthusiasm tempered. 'Don't agree to this if it feels wrong to you. You don't have to do it, you know. There will be other books.'

'I know,' said Eden. Although she knew what he was not saying. There would never be another book of this significance aimed directly at her. There would never be another such opportunity. In her mind's eye, she was seeing a flashing review of those pages she had read. How this thinly disguised couple met, and both realized that they were at a crossroads in their lives. According to Flynn's account, they struggled not to succumb to their emotions. The daunting age difference between them and the female character's reluctance to leave her long marriage and her daughter made the situation seem bleak. Hopeless. And yet, they knew that they had to be together. With the birth of their son, they felt new hope. And then, their hopes were dashed. They uprooted their lives and moved to be near the doctor who offered them the best hope for their child's terrible, mystifying condition. The woman secretly blamed herself, wondering if perhaps her child's illness was some sort of cosmic retribution for the pain she had caused her first husband, her daughter.

Eden had wondered, when she read that part, how Flynn had known it. Was it just something he suspected? Or were he and her mother so open with one another that Tara had been able to tell him her most secret fears, her worst suspicions? Somehow, Eden suspected the latter. Either way, it gave Eden a guilty, but undeniable, feeling of satisfaction to think that Tara had blamed herself, had suffered because of how she had treated Hugh and Eden. And, she felt a grudging admiration for Flynn, who could have left that out, and never mentioned it. It was fiction, after all. But it was fiction based on truth, and the truth which supported it gave the book its gravity, its sense of reality.

The entire book had a feeling of impending doom which kept Eden caught up in it the whole way. She even found herself hoping that it would all work out for them. Knowing that it did not. 'I want to do it. I want this book to be mine,' she said.

'That is great news,' said Rob. 'Let me call Maurice.'

'Yes,' she said, with a certainty undermined by anxiety. 'Tell him I'm in.'

Negotiations for the purchase of the book began within a few days, and Eden was kept abreast of the process, although Rob and Maurice were at the forefront of the financial discussions. Eden never heard from Flynn in the course of the negotiations. Gideon Lendl represented Flynn's interests ably. When the purchase price was finally decided, Eden was forced to question anew her participation in this project. Flynn was going to be handsomely compensated to tell the story of his marriage, now immensely more interesting because of the murder/suicide of his wife and son.

The news of his success was to be conveyed to him by his literary agent. Gideon Lendl assured Eden that Flynn would be informed immediately.

The thought of it made Eden feel queasy. Rob invited her to Maurice's office to celebrate with a glass of champagne. Eden went, knowing that she had to share in this celebration.

Maurice lifted his glass. 'To great reviews, and great sales,' he said. 'And to Eden, for taking on this difficult project.'

'I'll do my best to do a good job on it.'

'I know you will,' said Rob.

For the next two days, she expected to hear from Flynn, thanking her, perhaps, for taking on his book. But he remained silent. Was it her place to call him? And say what? Congratulations on cannibalizing my family history for personal gain? Stop, she told herself. You agreed to this. You can no longer blame this entirely on him. Still, she could not help but feel that her acquiescence was a favor to him, and that he owed her his gratitude. She felt trapped in a standoff, and she didn't know exactly how to proceed. She felt stupid having to ask for guidance, first thing out of the gate. But she finally decided that she was in need of a little advice.

She went down to Rob's office and knocked on the door. He asked her to come in and offered her a seat. 'What's up?' he said. 'No second thoughts, I hope.'

'No. It's just . . . I'm not sure about the protocol here,' Eden said. 'Do I call Flynn and ask for a meeting, or what?'

'Yes. I was thinking about this. It probably would be a good idea for you to arrange to go out there to Ohio to meet with him. That way you can confer directly over the manuscript. There's still a great deal of work to be done and it might be best to begin the process face to face. DeLaurier will pick up your expenses for the time there.'

'Isn't this normally done electronically? I mean, that's been my experience.'

'Well, normally, yes. But this is kind of a . . . delicate situation,' said Rob. 'You two have a personal history, and you are dealing with the aftermath of a tragedy. A lot depends on the relationship you have going forward. There's going to be some publicity which might prove awkward for the two of you. No use in pretending otherwise. The more closely you work together on this, the better. We want you to have a united front when it comes to the handling and promotion of this book. How do you and your stepfather normally get along?'

'I've hardly ever spoken to him,' said Eden.

Rob looked startled. 'Really?'

Eden shrugged. 'There was a lot of bad feeling. That part of the book was painfully accurate.'

'I'm sorry. I didn't realize . . .'

'That's why I was so shocked that he wanted me to be his editor.'

Rob nodded. 'Well, in that case, I definitely think it would be best for you two to begin the work in person. Do you have a problem with that?'

'No,' said Eden, but her stomach felt queasy. 'I just wasn't sure . . .'

'The situation is a bit unusual,' Rob agreed. 'But I think you should go out there and try to . . . come to a meeting of minds.'

The memory of her recent trip to Cleveland, for her mother's funeral, weighed heavily on Eden. The prospect of repeating that trip filled her with dread. Be a professional, she chided herself. No one forced you to do this. 'All right,' she said, standing up. 'I'll get the ball rolling.'

Eight

The arrangements were businesslike, and done by email between Eden and Flynn. Eden called her father in Florida to tell him that she was going out to Cleveland to see an author she had met at her mother's funeral – one of Tara's friends – who had subsequently brought his book to DeLaurier. Her father sounded happily preoccupied and didn't question it, other than to remark that it was ironic that she was going there again, after spending a lifetime without ever setting foot in Ohio. He was proud of the way she was sometimes required to travel for business. To Hugh, it seemed a sign of her success, that her company would pay for her to fly out to meet authors. It wasn't the first time she had been on such a mission. She couldn't bear to tell him the truth of who she was going to meet.

She flew out to Cleveland from Kennedy, and picked up her rental car. She had reserved a one-bedroom unit at the Garden Suites hotel not far from the airport. When she arrived, Eden was pleased to see that the room, though unprepossessing, was, as advertised, more like an apartment than a hotel room. It had a living room and a dining area, as well as a small bedroom. The sliding glass doors, all unbreakable and safely locked, faced out onto a small courtyard which was bleak in the winter chill, with a few scrawny trees, and snow piled against the building and beneath a pair of garden benches. All the furnishings in the apartment-sized room were well worn and nondescript. Still, a layout of this size would have cost a thousand dollars a night in New York City, she thought. Here, the price was rock bottom and reasonable. Eden pulled the stiffly lined drapes closed, unpacked quickly and set up her electronics. She lay down on the plaid double bedspread and tried to take a nap, but it was no use. Her nerves were on edge.

Finally, she got up and went down to the desk to ask where she might buy a few basic supplies. The pudgy young man in his maroon Garden Suites V-neck pullover directed her to a convenience store down the block. Eden elected to walk, and was amazed at how the damp cold cut through her. The road to the convenience store was quiet, almost dead, except for the roar of planes arriving and departing overhead. The store was haphazardly stocked, but she carried back some water bottles and a few things for breakfast. She had noticed that the room had a coffee maker, and she liked the idea of having breakfast in her robe and slippers. When she came back through the lobby, the young man at the desk buttonholed her to inform her of the hours that breakfast would be served in the lobby.

'I think I'm going to have it in my room,' she said.

'No problem,' the desk clerk said pleasantly. He asked her if she wanted a free newspaper delivered in the morning, and Eden gratefully agreed.

78

Just then a stout, gray-haired man in a plaid sport coat and a parka came up to the desk. 'Can I help you with those?' he asked, pointing to Eden's plastic bags bulging with water and crackers. 'I'm in the next suite over from yours.'

Eden leaned away from him, surprised and shocked as if she had been spied on, but the young clerk laughed.

'Don't mind Andy,' he said. 'He's here so much he thinks of this place as his neighborhood.'

'I do indeed, Oren.'

Eden smiled wanly. 'Oh, I see.'

Andy, undaunted by Eden's obvious discomfort, plucked one of the plastic sacs from her hands, and opened the door to the sidewalk. 'Shall we?' he said.

Eden wasn't quite sure how to act in the face of overbearing friendliness, but the clerk was looking at them with benign amusement. She walked along beside Andy, who explained that he was on the road and away from his beloved home in Indiana, his wife and children, for almost half the year. 'Counting the days till I retire,' he said as they reached their respective doors. 'Though to tell the truth, I'll probably miss the road.' He handed Eden back her bag with a smile. 'If you need anything now, Eden, I'm right next door.'

Eden thanked him, although she did not feel totally comfortable with his familiarity. 'Good night,' she said, and hurried to lock the door behind her.

The hours until the arranged meeting dragged, but at last it was time to get into her car and go.

She left some extra time so she could negotiate her way across Cleveland, but, as she had six weeks earlier during the funeral visit, Eden found it an easy matter to get around. The city traffic was not the cutthroat affair that she was accustomed to in the New York area. People seemed to take their time, and there was usually a moment where one could peer at an address, or make a last-minute turn without the screeching of brakes all around.

They had agreed that Flynn would pick the restaurant for their first editorial meeting, and Flynn had decided on an Italian restaurant called Alfredo's. Eden was picturing an old-world sort of place, with dim lights and candles, and a shiny mahogany bar. The reality was something very different. Eden parked her car on the busy, rundown block, and walked to the storefront with the striped awning which read Alfredo's. She went in and was greeted by a pot-bellied man in a black T-shirt, wearing an apron stained with red gravy. The restaurant was filled with Formica topped tables. There were napkin dispensers and shaker jars of Parmesan on every table.

'I'm meeting . . . um, Flynn Darby. He might have made a reservation,' she said.

But before the word was out of her mouth, the proprietor shook his head. 'Sit anywhere,' he said.

Eden went to a table against the wall near the back. Along the wall was a painted mural of someone's imagined version of the Amalfi coast, with stone buildings overlooking the sea from a verdant Italian hillside. That was about it for décor. The menus were laminated and almost as big as the tabletop. Eden picked one up and felt grease on her fingers.

The bell jingled on the front door and Eden looked up to see Flynn Darby entering the restaurant, carrying a bottle in a brown paper bag. For a moment she was able to study him before he noticed her. She hoped to banish that image of a drunken lout at his wife and son's funeral. But little had changed. He was undeniably good-looking, although his hair was, again, unkempt and his engineer boots were scuffed and unfastened. He was wearing a T-shirt that was frayed at the neck, under a battered leather jacket. He seemed lonely and forlorn, and he exuded a labile sexual energy. Eden immediately recalled that moment in his book when he first met her mother. He had described their encounter, from both their points of view. For his part, he had seen only Tara's aging, but still intense beauty. But he said that her first instinct toward him seemed to be almost motherly. She saw a bad boy in him, who needed protecting. Looking at him now, Eden could imagine it. Her mother had always been attracted to outsiders, to rebels. Sometimes Tara seemed to chafe at her comfortable life with Hugh, as if it did not reflect her authentic self. And everything about this man seemed to fairly scream danger. Whatever the magnetism had been which drew them together, their meeting was an instant of soulful recognition which could not be denied. For either one of them.

Flynn murmured to the proprietor, and then glanced to the back of the room and caught sight of Eden, seated beside the wall. He handed the paper bag to the proprietor, and came to join her.

'You found it, I see,' he said.

Eden looked around and nodded. 'You could have picked something a little more . . . luxurious. You do know the company's paying for this,' she said.

Flynn looked at her through heavy-lidded eyes, bemused. 'You don't like this place?' he asked, pulling out the chair across from her.

'No, it's fine,' she said.

'I like the food here,' said Flynn, sitting down heavily. 'Nothing pretentious.'

Eden nodded. 'Whatever you think.'

'What do you want?' he asked.

'Excuse me?' Eden asked, startled. 'What do you mean?'

'To eat. What do you want to eat?'

Eden felt flustered. 'I don't know. What do you recommend?'

'Everything's good,' said Flynn. He gestured to the proprietor, who arrived immediately at their table, holding the uncorked bottle of wine. Flynn looked over at Eden.

Eden ordered pasta and a salad.

'You're being overly cautious. You've got that New York superiority thing going on. But you may be surprised.'

Eden gazed back at him coolly. 'I'm not that hungry,' she said.

Flynn tipped his chair back and looked at her through narrowed eyes. 'I feel like I know you. From your mother,' he said.

Eden did not want to hear it. She decided to

turn the tables. 'Do you like living here in Cleveland?' she said. 'Are you going to stay?'

'No,' he said bluntly. 'We only came here because of Dr Tanaka's work on Katz-Ellison syndrome. At that point, your mother was willing to try anything.'

Eden hesitated. 'So, you really just uprooted your lives for Jeremy's sake.'

Flynn shrugged as if it were of no importance.

'After all that, it just seems unfathomable to me,' said Eden, 'that my mother would just give up on Jeremy. After all she'd been through.'

'You can't possibly know what she felt,' he warned.

'But surely she had some hope for him. Why would she just . . . throw it all away?'

Flynn cleared his throat as the proprietor returned and placed their plates of food down in front of him. He poured a few inches of wine into their glasses. '*Saluti*,' he said.

Flynn lifted his glass. '*Saluti*.'

Eden picked up her glass and sipped it. She was surprised to find that the wine was full-bodied and rather tasty. 'Cheers,' she said. The proprietor nodded, and shuffled away.

Eden hesitated a minute, and then decided to be blunt. 'Did you know that she was suicidal?' she asked. 'There's no mention of that in your book. Did you realize that she was coming to the end of her rope? That she needed help?'

Flynn twisted the stem of the wine glass in his large, rough fingers, and stared into the ruby liquid. 'Let's talk about something else,' he said without meeting her gaze.

'I realize it's a difficult subject,' said Eden. 'But I can't help but wonder if a good psychiatrist or psychologist might have helped,' she persisted. 'Maybe she just needed someone to talk to.'

Flynn looked at her coolly. 'She talked to me,' he said.

'Obviously that wasn't enough,' said Eden, avoiding his gaze.

'You have no idea what you're talking about,' said Flynn bluntly, setting down his glass and picking up a fork.

Eden thought about her mother's phone call, on the night of Tara's desperate act. 'That's why I'm asking you,' she said. 'Is there something I need to know—'

'Nothing you need to know now,' he said deliberately. 'It's all over now. And it has nothing to do with the book. The book is why you're here.'

Eden sat back and stared at him. 'Why did you want me to be the editor on this book? You could have had a much more senior person at a bigger house.'

Flynn's eyes narrowed. 'It's what your mother would have wanted.'

'That's the only reason?' she asked.

Flynn shrugged. 'DeLaurier's a good house. I thought about it, and decided to mention our connection to Gideon Lendl.'

Eden kept her face expressionless. 'Perhaps you thought that my being involved might be a good talking point for interviews,' she said.

Flynn returned her gaze implacably. 'I'm not really expecting a lot of publicity. It's a first novel, after all.'

'But everyone agrees that the murder/suicide of my mother and Jeremy will attract a great deal of interest,' Eden countered. 'It's unusual. Unnatural . . . for a mother to . . . do that.' She could hear it in her own voice – she was baiting him. It was unprofessional, but she couldn't seem to stop herself.

Flynn stared back at her. 'If it does, it does. Would that upset you?'

Eden had no intention of explaining her own feelings. But he was studying her as if he could see right through her. She tried to deflect his comment. 'It just strikes me as . . . opportunistic.'

She knew she had crossed the line from baiting him, to insulting him. She felt guilty, and satisfied, all at once.

'And yet you signed on,' he observed. 'You agreed to do it.'

Eden wanted to protest that she had no choice, but she knew that was not exactly true. She had agreed, in spite of her misgivings. He would see right through her protests.

Flynn sipped his wine and studied her. Finally he shifted his weight in the chair. 'Look, let's call a truce,' he said. 'You and I have both suffered a great loss. Doing this book might be kind of a . . . healing thing for both of us.'

'I don't need any help healing,' said Eden shortly. 'I'm fine.'

Flynn peered at her. 'Really? I'm not. And if you don't mind my saying so, you don't seem fine either.'

Eden was chastened by his honesty, and ashamed of her abruptness. For a moment, she could see beyond his scruffy sex appeal to what it was that her mother had liked about this man. It was not a faux pas for him to observe that some healing was in order. And it wasn't true that she was fine. She was bluffing her way through this on every level. 'Maybe you're right,' she said, adopting a milder tone. 'Maybe there will be some . . . therapeutic value in working on this together. Many things about my mother came to mind when I was reading your book. I'm sure we both have . . . insights we can share.'

Flynn immediately bristled. 'Well, let's get one thing clear. I'm not really interested in adding your insights to the mix. You're not a co-author.'

Despite his insulting tone, Eden recognized immediately the protective author's ego in his words. This was a reaction common among authors to any mention of changes in their work. 'I'm not proposing that we change what you've said in the book. I'm just talking about some shading. And we have to address the reality of my mother and Jeremy's death.'

'I'm not sure I want to hear this,' he said defensively.

'I've given it some thought. There are a number of approaches—'

'I don't want to talk about this right now. Let's start the editorial work tomorrow. You can come to the house,' he said. 'I'm sorting through your mother's things. There may be items you want to keep.'

I'm not here to collect mementoes, she thought. I'm here to work. But she did not say it. She would look through Tara's things, though she doubted there would be anything she wanted. She pictured the commonplace little blue house she had seen on the internet news, now the scene of the crime. She wasn't really looking forward to visiting there, but it almost seemed like a penance she had to pay.

'Okay,' she said. 'Sure.'

'I teach two creative writing classes at the community college in the morning,' he said. 'Come in the afternoon.'

'That's fine,' said Eden. 'I'm hoping we can get a lot done while I'm here.'

'Do you want dessert?' he said abruptly.

'I don't think so,' said Eden. 'I've had enough.'

'So have I,' he said with a sigh.

Eden could not help thinking that he was talking about her company, rather than the food.

Nine

Eden returned to the hotel, got into her robe and pajamas, and then set to work on the editorial letter she planned to email to Flynn. He was clearly going to be one of those authors you had to fight with over every change. She was used to that. Every editor at DeLaurier, or any other house, had encountered that attitude many times. The challenge was to convince the author that her only goal was to improve the book, and that, yes, most books could survive a little editing.

Immersed in the book, she was startled by the

ringing of her phone. She knew who it had to be at this hour. Her friends all texted her. Only her dad would call her this late. She felt a surge of anxiety. She had told him a white lie in order to avoid admitting that she was editing Flynn's book, helping him to publish the story of her mother's treasonous defection from their family. Luckily, her father, though always interested in her life, was never one to pry. But sooner or later, she was going to have to face it. She cringed, knowing that her father would be angry and disappointed. Maybe as the publication date got closer, she told herself, it would be easier to explain it to him. She didn't really believe that, but she wasn't ready to grapple with it yet. She just hated lying to him.

'Hi, Dad,' she said cheerfully.

'Hi, honey. I didn't wake you, did I?'

'No, not at all. How was the trip to Florida?'

'Great,' he said. 'Just got back. We had a great time.'

Eden waited for him to elaborate, but he was guarding the details for whatever reason. Perhaps they were both holding back on their news until they could meet face to face. 'Well, good,' she said. 'I'm glad.'

'Look,' he said hurriedly, 'I know it's late and I don't want to keep you up.'

'It's okay,' she said. 'It's good to hear your voice.'

'Yours, too,' he said. 'Listen, I got a call today from a guy at an insurance company out there. Harriman Insurance. The guy's name is Barry Preston. Apparently, you are some kind of beneficiary to your mother's policy, and she put our home number as your contact number. I guess she figured I would always be able to reach you.'

'Probably,' said Eden.

'Anyway, he wants to talk to you about the insurance.'

'Oh,' she said slowly. 'Okay.'

'I gave him your number and he said he would call you, and come to talk to you at your hotel. I checked up on him after the call. He's legit. Has he called you yet?'

'No. But thanks for the heads up.'

'I don't know what it's all about, but I'm sure he'll fill you in. All right, little girl. You get some rest now.'

'Thanks, Dad. I will. Love you.'

Despite her promise to her father, it took Eden longer to finish the editorial letter than she had expected. It was nearly two a.m. before she was satisfied, and pressed 'send'. She crawled into her bed, read a page or two of an Alice Munro short story and was asleep in no time.

The first thing she did when she awoke the next morning was to check her phone. Flynn had emailed her in reply, telling her tersely that they could discuss her proposed changes but he was not convinced they were necessary. Eden took a deep breath. She had a lot of experience with authors and had learned not to take their resistance seriously, although this was a particularly difficult situation. But she'd known it would be, going in. She tried not to think about Flynn's negative role in her life. She had taken the task on, and now she had to prove that she was capable of

89

doing it. She had to figuratively put on her professional hat, and ignore the implied insult to her competence. He told her to come over at two. Eden replied that she would.

She also had a message from Barry Preston, whom her father had mentioned. He wondered if he could come to see her at four-thirty. Eden texted him back that it was okay, and she was sure she would be back in her suite by then.

She opened the stiff drapes in the living room area onto the little courtyard. It was a windy day and the straggly trees seemed to shrink against the chill. Being here in this city, isolated and far from her own life, made Eden think constantly of her mother. The bleakness of the day mirrored Eden's feelings. Here, where it had occurred, Eden had finally become acquainted with her mother's husband, and met friends at the funeral, but no one had offered her any understanding of what had actually happened. She realized that what she wanted were facts. Facts which would make her better able to comprehend it. She glanced at the time on her phone. She had hours before she needed to meet with Flynn. She hesitated, and then went to her computer and looked up the number of the Cleveland Clinic. She had a right to know, she reminded herself. It was her mother, after all. She punched in the number and got through to the operator.

'Yes,' said Eden. 'Is Dr Tanaka in today?'

'He's in, but he's on another call,' said the receptionist.

'Could you just ask him if I could possibly see him this morning? My name is Eden Radley.'

'I'm sorry, but that's out of the question. Dr Tanaka is terribly busy.'

Eden persisted. 'My mother was Tara Darby, and Jeremy was my half-brother.'

There was a brief silence at the other end of the line, and then the receptionist said, 'Wait just a minute.'

Before Eden could reply, she heard dead air. In a few moments, the receptionist came back on the line. 'Can you be here in forty minutes? He can see you then.'

'I'll be there,' Eden said.

Eden put on every warm thing she had with her, but the cold winds of Lake Erie still seemed to cut through to her bones. She hurried along the slippery sidewalk into the Cleveland Clinic and made her way to Dr Tanaka's office. She was exactly on time. She could see, by the busy waiting room, that the doctor had little time to spare. She gave her name to the receptionist and was told to sit, that she would be called. She tried not to stare at the disabled children who had been brought here, all suffering from the same condition as her half-brother, whom she had never met. But it was difficult to look at them, all behaving like cheerful, healthy children, and not think, with a leaden heart, that she had missed a chance to ever know Jeremy. She blamed herself for that, for all the good it did now.

'Miss Radley,' said the nurse at the door. 'Come through.'

Eden thanked her and went into the doctor's

office. His walls were covered with degrees and framed newspaper articles all attesting to his unique abilities and Eden studied them as she waited. She did not have to wait long. Dr Tanaka came in and greeted her, but did not extend a hand. 'Let me say, I'm sorry for your loss, Ms Radley,' he said.

'Thank you. And thank you for coming to the funeral,' she replied.

He had a mild, intelligent gaze behind steel-rimmed glasses. He seemed calm and at ease, as if his waiting room were not filled with afflicted children and anxious parents. 'Ms Radley, how can I help you?' he said in a neutral tone.

Eden took a deep breath and plunged ahead. 'My mother's death . . . the death of Jeremy . . . it's very difficult. I keep thinking there must have been some warning that she was planning this. Some signs. I've asked her husband, but if he knows anything, he's offering no explanation. Maybe he's too close to the situation to be a good judge. I've been asking myself if anyone here at the clinic had noticed her distress.'

'You were her daughter,' said Dr Tanaka. 'Did she say anything uncharacteristic in your recent conversations?'

Eden blushed. She took a deep breath. 'No, sir. Our recent conversations were perfunctory. As usual. My mother and I were . . . somewhat estranged. I regret this now, but I can't change the past.'

Dr Tanaka nodded and gazed at his folded hands on the desktop. 'First of all, let me say that your mother participated fully in our . . . work here. She was ready to go to great lengths for the sake of her child.'

Eden nodded, not knowing what to say. She discerned respect for Tara in the doctor's tone.

'Everyone who is here signs releases that they were not pressured to be here in any way. They know that there is no guarantee, and they participate willingly,' he said.

'Yes, I know they came here willingly,' Eden said, puzzled.

'Just to be clear,' the doctor said.

She gazed at him with narrowed eyes. 'Is this about . . . Are you worried about a lawsuit?'

Dr Tanaka's expression was impassive. He did not answer her question.

'Don't be,' said Eden. 'I'm not here to place blame. I just want to know why this happened. Did she ever mention to you that she felt hopeless or despondent?'

Dr Tanaka thought for a moment. 'In recent months I noticed certain changes in your mother's behavior. She seemed a bit . . . withdrawn lately. Distracted. She missed a couple of appointments, which was very unlike her. I had a feeling that there might be something wrong in her life.'

Eden felt the hair stand up on the back of her neck. 'Beyond Jeremy's condition, you mean.'

'Jeremy's condition was deteriorating, no doubt, and she was concerned about him, of course, but she knew she was doing everything she could for her child. This kind of illness takes a terrible toll on the family. Our staff is trained to seek out signs of depression or undue anxiety.'

'Did they notice those signs in my mother?' Eden asked.

Dr Tanaka nodded. 'Yes. And she was offered psychological counseling if she needed it. An offer she refused, repeatedly.'

'Did you think she seemed depressed enough that she might be considering ending her life? And Jeremy's?' she asked.

'I cannot tell you what she was thinking. But I can tell you this much. Your mother loved her son. Other people might have looked at Jeremy and seen only the difficulties. But your mother? No. Never. And no,' said Dr Tanaka gravely, 'in my opinion, she would never have harmed him. No matter what.'

His words struck her like a blow. 'Really? You seem very certain of that.'

Dr Tanaka nodded. 'I am certain of that.'

'And yet, she did harm him. She killed him. How can you explain it?' Eden asked.

'Well, I cannot explain it,' he said. 'But I'm a scientist. It's my experience that if I get an unexpected result, I have to go back over my data. I make sure that I have entered every detail correctly. That I have not missed something.'

Eden frowned at him. 'Is that what you think? That we've missed something?'

'I can't say.' Dr Tanaka stood up, signaling that their meeting was at an end. Reluctantly, Eden gathered up her coat and purse and stood up as well.

'Sadly, Ms Radley, this work never lets up,' the doctor said. 'And even though I find this situation to be baffling, I can do no more than speculate. But it does seem a question worth pursuing.' He extended his hand to her in farewell. 'And I wish you well with your inquiries.'

Eden left the doctor's office feeling ill at ease. She had come here for some answers, and all she had now was the doctor's blessing to pursue her questions.

She thanked the receptionist as she passed her desk, and then, as she was pushing open the office door, she turned back. She knew that the young girl she had met at her mother's funeral had said she was a graduate student in psychology. She was close to the situation. Maybe she could offer some answers. It was worth a try. 'Excuse me,' she said. The receptionist looked up, smiling.

'There was a girl from your office who worked closely with my mother and Jeremy. Lizzy something . . .'

'Lizzy Jacquez,' said the receptionist promptly.

'Is she here today?' Eden asked.

'No, she's not in today. She may be at the university.'

'Do you have a number where I could reach her?' Eden asked.

The receptionist grimaced. 'I'm not really allowed to give out that information,' she said.

'Never mind. Thanks.' I'll just ask Flynn, Eden thought, as she left the office and walked down to her car. She glanced at her phone. She just had time for a quick bite of lunch, then it would be time to go to their meeting.

* * *

95

Several lengths of broken yellow police tape still fluttered from different trees at the edge of the property, and there was a 'for rent' sign planted in the lawn. The blue house was a small, rectangular bungalow with a garage at one end. The house was inexpensively constructed, with several narrow windows placed just below the roofline, as if to discourage anyone from looking out, or in. It looked neglected and forlorn. Piles of bulging black plastic bags were slumped in the snow at the curb, waiting to be carted off by the trash man. Nobody was going to rush to rent this humble abode, Eden thought. Still, she was surprised to see it already up for rent. It was as if Flynn couldn't wait to get out of there. Then she chided herself for her lack of charity. She couldn't blame Flynn for not wanting to live in this house. Not after the terrible thing that had happened there. The place probably felt haunted to him.

She walked up to the front door and rang the bell. In a few moments, the door opened. Expecting to see Flynn, Eden was startled to see instead, Flynn's intern, the girl in the Muslim headscarf who had supported him at the funeral.

The girl's soulful eyes widened. She was still wearing a headscarf, though her clothes today were much less formal. She had on a loose-fitting blouse and a long, dark skirt that divided into roomy pants. She stared at Eden uneasily.

'Hello. My name is Eden. Flynn is expecting me.'

The girl lowered her gaze like a servant. 'Mr Darby is in the living room.'

'We haven't met,' said Eden. 'I'm his stepdaughter. Eden Radley.' She extended a hand, but the girl ignored it and bowed slightly.

'My name is Aaliya Saleh. It's nice to meet you.'

Just then, Flynn appeared behind Aaliya in the hallway 'Let her in, Aaliya,' he said. 'This is my stepdaughter. She's also the editor of my book.'

'So I understand,' said the girl, polite but unsmiling. She backed away from the door, and Flynn opened it for Eden to enter. She walked past him into the small, overly warm house.

'Aaliya, if you don't mind getting started on the bedrooms,' he said.

Aaliya shook her head. 'Not at all.'

Eden watched the girl disappear down the hall. Her clothes billowed around her, like dark sails. 'That's a helpful intern,' she observed skeptically.

'She has been helpful,' said Flynn, ignoring her tone. 'Come on inside.'

She edged past him in the hallway. He was wearing a stained gray T-shirt, ripped blue jeans and bare feet. He smelled tangy, sweaty. She felt slightly sick about the fact that she noticed his scent.

'In here,' he said.

The house smelled stale and there was an unfamiliar, heavy odor in the air. Eden wondered if it was some sort of residue from the carbon monoxide. She followed him into the living room, which was in a state of disarray, with half-packed boxes everywhere. There were framed photos leaning against the wall. Scribbled Post-it notes flapped on nearly every surface in the room.

'When are you moving?' she said.

Flynn ran his hand through his mop of dirty-blond waves and shook his head. 'Not sure. I have to get a place first. God, you remind me of her,' he said.

Eden froze and then glared at him. 'I don't look anything like her.'

'You can't see it,' he said.

'Let's talk about something else,' she said in a chilly tone.

Flynn shrugged. 'Up to you.'

'Where are you going to move?' asked Eden, taking the seat on the sofa that he had indicated.

Flynn rubbed his unshaven face. 'Back to New York, I guess. My grandparents want me to move back in with them, but that's not going to happen. I'd have to be a full-time caretaker. I've had enough of that to suit me. I need a little more life around me.'

Having met Flynn's grandparents, Eden doubted that they would want him to live with them for any reason. But obviously, he needed to believe that they would. 'My mother said that they raised you,' she said. She was thinking of that terrible story of Flynn, a helpless toddler alone in an apartment eating out of a cat food bowl.

Flynn shrugged. 'You probably think I ought to be paying them back by being a nursemaid for them.'

'I don't think that,' said Eden truthfully. 'In fact, I was just thinking that you've had a lot of loss in your life.'

'Happens to everybody,' he said dismissively, and sat down on the sofa beside her. From down the hall, they could hear the sound of furniture being pushed across the floor, and jostled objects thudding against one another. Flynn had spread out his manuscript and Eden's suggested changes on the coffee table in front of them. Then he reached into the pocket of his T-shirt and pulled out a crumpled packet of cigarettes. He lit one up and tossed the empty packet on the table. He reached down for an ashtray which was on the floor beside him.

'You smoke in here?' she asked.

Flynn glared at her. 'Not when they were here,' he said. 'But they're not here anymore.'

Despite the obvious truth of his words, something about the way he said it offended her. 'I wish you wouldn't,' she said. 'It's suffocating.'

'This is my last one anyway. I have to go out and get more,' he said. But he continued to smoke. 'Now about these changes.'

'Yes,' said Eden evenly.

'Most of them don't appeal to me. But I agree with you that we have to acknowledge what happened. I was thinking of this.' He pulled out a clipping from the local paper and showed it to her. The headline read 'Murder/Suicide of a Mother and Her Disabled Son'. The article detailed the deaths of Tara and Jeremy.

Eden blanched at the sight of it.

'I thought we could just run this,' he said. 'You know, in the front. As it is. Without any commentary. Just let them know, going in, what they are really reading about. That this is how the story ended. I mean, why not just put it out there?'

99

Eden tried to collect her thoughts. 'It seems a little . . . sensational, for such a serious book.'

'Sensational,' he said scornfully. 'Please. You represent a publisher. Sensational is what sells books. It's what's going to sell this book. No one but a few literature students would be interested in my pitiful life story if this,' he said, shaking the clipping, 'hadn't happened. At least be honest and admit that.'

Eden forced herself to remain calm. 'Yes, I think you're right. This . . . incident—'

'Crime,' he interjected angrily.

'This will certainly be a part of the promotion for the book. I'm not denying that. We both know it.' Eden hesitated, choosing her words. 'But don't you want to write about this? Don't you think the reader deserves, either as introduction or epilogue, to hear from you about this tragic event? Your thoughts, your feelings?'

'Are you kidding?' he cried. 'It's only been what . . . six weeks since I lost my wife and my son? It will take me years before I'm ready to write about this. Don't you know anything about this process?'

'I believe I do,' said Eden evenly.

'Well, you couldn't if you think that I could write about this so soon after.'

'No one forced you to send in the manuscript before they were even cold,' she said.

Flynn looked at her with narrowed eyes. He took a last drag on his cigarette and smashed the butt into the ashtray. Then he took a deep breath. 'That's fairly hostile,' he said.

'Sorry,' she said, though what she was thinking was quite different. How could you have married this guy? she asked her mother in her mind. She needed to calm down. Writers are like children, she reminded herself. Wayward and difficult. Everyone in the business knows that. She forced herself to be conciliatory. 'Look, let's just take it easy. I can run your idea about the clipping before the editorial director and get his reaction. Then get back to you.'

'This is not negotiable. I can't write on command,' he said gruffly.

'Understood. As for the rest of these changes—'

'Any that are grammatical are okay,' he said, trying belatedly to show how cooperative he could be. 'I can even shift a few of these paragraphs that you mention.'

There was the sound of footsteps outside in the hallway and then Aaliya appeared at the door. 'Excuse me,' she said. 'But do you have any more cartons? I have already filled the ones you gave me.'

'Down the basement,' he said.

Aaliya nodded and withdrew from the room. Eden watched her go, frowning.

'What?' he demanded.

'Well, she's a student intern. Not a servant,' she said.

'She wants to help,' he said defensively. 'She offered.'

Eden drew in her breath, unconvinced. 'We can come back to this idea about the article after I talk to Rob.'

Flynn stood up. 'Okay. Let's leave it for now.'

Obviously, the meeting was at an end. Eden stood up.

Flynn turned around and rummaged through some boxes that were piled on a chair. 'By the way, the stuff in this one's for you. Some of Tara's stuff. I thought you might want it.'

Reluctantly, she took the box. 'I hate to ask this,' she said, 'but would you mind if I went through some of her belongings? There may be some things of sentimental value to me.'

Flynn grimaced and scratched his head. 'I want to get out of here. I don't really have time for everyone to go rummaging through her stuff . . .'

I'm not everyone, Eden thought, but she didn't say it. 'I was particularly wondering if maybe she kept any diaries. She used to when I was a girl. I'm just looking for some reason, I guess. I'd like to know what she was thinking that led to this . . . tragedy.'

'She didn't have time for diaries,' he said. 'She had her hands full with Jeremy.'

For a moment, Eden saw his eyes well up with tears, and she was reminded of his loss.

'There's nothing,' he said dismissively.

'Well, that's your call,' said Eden. Cradling the box to her chest, she picked her way through the living room and toward the hallway. As she reached the door, she turned to him again. 'One more thing,' she said. 'I wanted to speak to Lizzy. Who worked with Jeremy? I met her at the funeral but I didn't have a chance to talk to her. Could you give me her number?'

'Lizzy's got nothing to say to you,' he said shortly.

Eden stared at him. 'Are you refusing to give me her number?' she asked.

Flynn shook his head impatiently. 'Don't be paranoid.' He picked up a pen and pad from a pile on the hall table. He hesitated over it a second. 'I think it's . . .'

He wrote down a number.

'You think? You're not sure?'

'That's their number,' he said.

Eden took the paper, looked at it, and folded it into a compartment in her purse. 'I'll call you when I find out what Rob thinks about using the newspaper article.'

'You do that,' he said.

Ten

Eden drove back to the motel, so distracted by her encounter with Flynn that she nearly ran a stop sign. She pulled into the parking lot beside a late-model sedan. There were two men dressed in parkas sitting in the front seat. As she got out of her car, juggling the box of her mother's belongings that Flynn had foisted on her, the man on the passenger side got out of his car and hailed her.

'Excuse me,' he said. 'Are you Eden Radley?'

Eden turned, frowning, the key to her suite in her hand. 'Yes. Why?'

The driver got out of the car as well. He was the taller of the two, trim and sleek, and wearing a Rolex watch beneath his winter gear. He reached out and handed Eden a card. 'My name is Barry Preston. I'm an investigator for the Harriman Insurance company.' He gestured to the other, stockier man. 'This is my associate, Tim McNee. We had an appointment.'

'Oh yes, of course,' said Eden. 'My father said he spoke to you.'

Andy Chisholm, the portly, gray-haired salesman in the suite next to Eden's, emerged from his room and, after he had locked his door and jiggled the doorknob, looked suspiciously at the insurance agents and Eden. 'Everything all right, Eden?' he said pointedly.

'Just fine,' she said, feeling absurdly grateful today for his concern. 'How about you?'

'Oh, fine. Calls to make,' said the salesman cheerfully. 'Making friends, I see. Sure you're okay?'

Eden smiled wanly. 'Positive.' She unlocked the door to her room and turned to the two insurance agents. 'Please come in.'

The men followed her in and looked around. Eden offered them a seat in the living room. 'Can I get you something to drink?' she asked.

Preston shook his head. 'No, I'm fine.'

'No, thanks,' said McNee. He was a well-groomed, thick-bodied guy of around forty. He flashed her an encouraging smile.

Eden sat down opposite them.

'Well, first of all, let me say that I'm sorry for your loss,' said Preston.

'Thanks,' said Eden.

'Now, Ms Radley, I'm not sure how much you

know. Are you aware that your mother had an extremely large term life insurance policy?'

'Uh. No,' said Eden. 'I was not.'

'She did,' said Preston. 'Your stepfather, Mr Darby, is named as the beneficiary. Mr Darby had a matching policy, with your mother as the named beneficiary. There is also a policy, in a much smaller amount, that they had taken out on the life of their son, Jeremy. You are named as a contingent beneficiary on your mother's policy.'

'What does that mean?' Eden asked.

'Simply put, if your mother had died after your stepfather, you would have been the beneficiary of her policy.'

'I don't know anything about . . . any of it,' said Eden.

'All three policies were purchased when your brother, Jeremy, was only eighteen months old. I'm told, by their agent, that the child had been definitely diagnosed with Katz-Ellison syndrome at that time. Mr and Mrs Darby specifically stated, in their paperwork, that they wanted to be sure, in the event of their deaths, that there would be adequate funds for Jeremy's care. For the long term.'

'Well, that makes sense, I suppose,' said Eden. She looked narrowly at the attorney. 'Wait a minute,' she said. 'I'm a little confused. My mother committed suicide. Doesn't that cancel the payout on a life insurance policy?'

Mr McNee explained. 'Only if the insured commits suicide within a year of buying the coverage. After a year has passed, it is assumed that the suicidal intentions were not formed until after the policy was purchased.'

'And that was the case with my mother,' said Eden.

The two men exchanged a glance.

'Well, okay. Then I'm not really sure why you are here,' she said.

'The total amount for the two policies on mother and son is five million dollars,' Preston said.

Eden gaped at him.

'You heard me right,' Preston said. 'Five million dollars.'

Five million dollars. 'That's a lot of money,' said Eden. She couldn't help remembering what Flynn's grandfather had said. Something to the effect that her mother had done Flynn a favor. That he would take the insurance money and be off on a world cruise.

'As you can imagine,' Preston said, 'with that amount of money involved, the company takes a very intense interest in the circumstances of your mother's death.'

Still stunned, Eden nodded. 'Well, yeah. Sure.'

'Were you aware that your mother intended to kill herself?' Preston asked.

'No,' said Eden, shaking her head at the baldness of the phrase. 'No.'

'She never said anything to you that would indicate that she planned to take her own life?'

'No,' said Eden. 'But she and I were not . . . close in recent years.'

'There is no record of her being treated by a psychologist or psychiatrist. Are you aware of any such treatment?'

Eden peered at him. 'No, she never mentioned that to me.'

'Does that strike you as strange? If she was suicidally depressed, it would stand to reason that someone would have urged her to seek help.'

'I thought the same thing,' Eden admitted, 'so I asked about that.' She recalled her conversation with Dr Tanaka just this morning. 'Apparently she was urged to seek help. But she didn't do it.'

The two men nodded, and avoided her gaze.

'I still don't understand,' said Eden. 'Didn't you say that as long as a year had elapsed between the time they bought the insurance and the time of her death, Harriman insurance has to pay?'

McNee, the smaller, stouter of the two men, frowned. 'Ms Radley, we've received an anonymous tip,' he said.

'A tip about what?' she asked.

'That your mother's death might not have been suicide.'

Eden stifled the urge to cry out. 'Not suicide?' she asked calmly. 'What else could it have been?'

McNee grimaced. 'We've considered the possibility of an accident.'

'I did think most carbon monoxide deaths were accidental,' said Eden. 'I did hear on the news, just after it happened, that the CO_2 detector had been deactivated by a neighbor at my mother's request. Is that what you think? That it was an accident?'

Barry Preston shook his head. 'No. There was a note,' he said. 'And they both had barbiturates in their systems.'

Eden shook her head. 'Then I don't understand what you're saying.'

'The tip which we received suggested that someone may have murdered your mother and half-brother, and tried it to make it look like a murder/suicide.'

Eden began to shake, in spite of herself. She stared at them. 'Are you kidding me? No . . .'

'As I said,' McNee reiterated, 'this was an anonymous tip. We have no other verification of it at this point.'

'Did you tell the police?' Eden asked.

'Yes, I spoke to a Lieutenant Burt who is in charge of the case. They received the same tip. He said they would look into it, but he hasn't returned our calls.'

Eden thought back to what they had told her. 'You said they had barbiturates in their systems? Both of them?'

'Yes, according to the police,' said Preston. 'But the coroner's report has not been forthcoming. Nor have we been able to see the suicide note.'

'Why not? Do you ordinarily have access to the police reports?'

McNee nodded. 'Under normal circumstances.'

'Did you ask the police for the reports?' she asked.

'I asked for them, of course. But, so far, the paperwork we have received is incomplete,' said McNee.

'Why? Why would they withhold it?'

'I don't know. I'm just saying that there are questions. The question of who profits from these deaths is always paramount,' said McNee.

Suddenly, Eden understood. She felt as if a cold fingertip had just been drawn down her spine. 'Flynn?' she said.

Preston interjected, answering her question with a question. 'How would you characterize the marriage between Mr Darby and his wife?'

She wanted to say that she knew very little about their relationship, but now that she had read Flynn's book, she felt as if she understood it pretty well. It's fiction, she reminded herself. They could have been fighting like cats and dogs.

'Miss Radley?'

'I knew nothing about their relationship. They . . . kept to themselves. I never met Flynn Darby before my mother's funeral.'

'Your mother must have talked about him.'

'Not really. To say the least, he was a sore subject in our family. Look, why won't the police help you with this? They're the ones who investigated it.'

'They concluded that it was a murder/suicide and that is the official version of events.'

'I guess the police have no reason to lie about it,' Eden said.

'Do you know Mr Darby's grandfather? Michael Darby?' McNee asked.

'No,' said Eden. 'I've met him once. He lives in my home town.'

'He was a police officer in Robbin's Ferry until his retirement.'

'Really?' Eden asked. She thought about the scrawny, angry man she had met. A police officer? It had to be a long time ago. 'How does this concern him?'

'It's a brotherhood, Miss Radley,' said Barry Preston. 'They protect their own.'

'Michael Darby? I don't understand. Protect him from what? What are you saying?'

'Flynn Darby, Michael Darby's grandson, is threatening a lawsuit against Harriman Insurance if we do not release the payout immediately on his policy. Harriman is considering a countersuit in federal court against Mr Darby.'

'A countersuit? On what grounds?' Eden asked.

'Well, under federal law, there is something called the slayer statute, which says that a person cannot profit from the death of someone if they were instrumental in causing that death.'

'The slayer statute?' Eden cried. She clenched her hands, which were shaking. 'Now, wait a minute. Believe me, I would rather not contemplate the fact that my mother was capable of this . . . horrible act, but Flynn Darby, no matter what I might think of him, was nowhere near that house when my mother died. Besides, the house where they lived was sealed up from the inside by my mother.'

'When you first heard about it, did it seem unlikely to you?' McNee asked. 'Uncharacteristic of your mother to do such a thing?'

'Well yes, of course. But whoever expects a loved one to do something so . . . terrible?'

'What if she didn't?' Barry Preston suggested bluntly. 'What if Flynn Darby arranged it to look as if she did?'

Eden tried to take in what they were saying. 'You think that Flynn murdered my mother? And his son?'

110

Tim McNee grimaced slightly. 'Ms Radley, we're just suggesting that there are questions. And our countersuit would be much more . . . convincing if you were to join us.'

Eden frowned at him. 'What do you mean? How could I join you?'

'It wouldn't require anything more than a few signatures from you. Harriman will absorb all the legal costs. But as the contingent beneficiary, your name would be on the suit against Mr Darby. In the eyes of the court, that would strengthen our case enormously.'

'I don't know,' she demurred.

'Look,' said Barry Preston, 'I know you'd rather not even think about the possibility, but if there is a chance that Mr Darby is going to have a huge payday after getting rid of your mother and his severely handicapped son, I'm sure you would want to . . . try to prevent that?'

'Of course,' said Eden. 'It's just . . . I can't believe he would do it.'

'Why not?'

'Well, in his book—'

'His book?' Preston asked.

Eden took a deep breath. 'Look, I may as well tell you. Mr Darby has written a novel about his life with my mother and Jeremy, and it is going to be published by the company I work for. In fact, I am going to be the editor on the project. That's why I am here in Cleveland, right now.'

'Your father never mentioned that.'

'He doesn't know,' Eden admitted. 'I haven't told him yet. I doubt he's going to be very happy about it.'

Barry Preston's eyes widened. 'And this . . . book came about recently? By chance?'

'No,' said Eden patiently. 'No, he'd been writing it for years. He brought it to my company because he wanted me to work on it.'

Barry Preston seemed to be stunned into silence by this news.

'I think he felt that I could add a unique perspective,' Eden said, knowing that was not the case. It even sounded feeble when she said the words aloud.

'That works out nicely for him,' said Preston sarcastically.

'Meaning what?' Eden asked.

Barry Preston shrugged. 'Well, you couldn't really work on his book and sue him at the same time,' he said.

Eden frowned and did not reply.

'With this contract, he has very neatly removed you from the picture.'

'You're implying that he sold the book to my publisher, and sought my advice as an editor, just to get me out of the way?'

'I'm saying that you need to consider the possibility.'

'But, there was no . . . problem about the insurance when he sent us the book. That just arose with the anonymous tip, right?'

'There's been a problem with the insurance since Day One,' said Preston. 'Your stepfather was impatient for the payout from the word go. He became extremely belligerent when we indicated that we needed to investigate the circumstances of your mother's death.'

Eden felt sick. 'Maybe . . . I don't know . . . maybe he felt that he was entitled to the money and he just wanted to . . . be paid what he was owed.'

'Maybe. But we've been in this business a long time. His attitude sent up red flags to us. And now that you tell us about this book . . .'

'Red flags how?' Eden said. 'What do you think?'

Barry Preston glanced at Tim McNee and shook his head. 'I think it's a shame you can't join this lawsuit. I think your stepfather was way ahead of us on this.'

'But he couldn't have done what you're suggesting,' Eden protested. 'He loved my mother. He loved Jeremy.'

'That's the thing about insurance, Ms Radley. People don't buy it for strangers. They buy it for the ones they love. And then sometimes, that source of protection, bought out of love . . . Well, for some, it becomes the ultimate temptation.'

Eleven

Eden closed the door on the investigators, deeply shaken by what she had heard. She surfed the net. She knew that people were capable of the most diabolical behavior. But this? The early dusk of winter had turned to darkness, and the hotel room was almost as dark as the sky. Eden turned on all the lights and tried to get warm, but she felt as if, even in the stuffy confines of this nondescript suite, she was shivering from within.

Five million dollars. Flynn seemed like a man who didn't care about money. But was there ever a man born who didn't care about money? He had seemed so bereft at Tara's funeral. Barely able to function. But he was being supported by a beautiful young Muslim girl. Not a seductive girl, but still . . . Could he have done it? And how could he have done it? He was miles away at the time. Or was he? How could you kill someone with carbon monoxide anyway? Disable them somehow, and leave them to inhale the fumes?

Disabling was not a problem for Jeremy, she reminded herself. But for Tara?

Tara would not have given up without a fight. She would have fought for her life. And for Jeremy's.

A million questions were buzzing in her head. She was supposed to call Rob and discuss the changes on the book. But part of her wanted to just call and resign. Say she could go no farther, and to get someone else. The insurance investigators had put a suspicion in her mind that was impossible to ignore. She could not stop thinking about the pitying way that investigators Preston and McNee were looking at her, as if she had played directly into Flynn's hands. No. The only thing she could do was to extricate herself from this compromising position.

And then she forced herself to be reconsider.

To think rationally. Was that, indeed, the only thing she could do? Everyone here seemed to accept the unfortunate, official version of events. The police, apparently, had closed the book on this matter. Even Eden's first impulse was to accept it. But, aside from the insurance investigators, who only wanted to deny Flynn the money, there was no one representing her mother and Jeremy. No one to speak for them. What had Dr Tanaka said? That Tara would never have harmed Jeremy, no matter what, and that something must have been overlooked.

Eden always thought of herself as a believer in fate and destiny. Maybe now was the time to put it to the test. Perhaps Flynn had inadvertently put her in a position to seek out the truth. The official version deserved to be scrutinized. To have holes poked in it, if necessary. She reminded herself that the only way for her to get the answers she needed was to stay put at this task, in this town, which gave her access, and ask questions of everyone who had known them, had lived around them.

She wavered for a moment, tempted to just walk away, and then she chided herself. No matter how unpalatable it all was, she had to continue. For her own sins, perhaps, she needed to try.

She hesitated, then dialed the number which Flynn had given her for Lizzy and waited. Lizzy's recorded voice answered. 'You have reached Lizzy and DeShaun Jacquez. Leave a message.' Eden carefully recorded her message. 'Lizzy,' she said. 'This is Eden Radley. Tara's daughter. I have a few questions, a few things I wanted to discuss with you. If you could find the time, could you call me back?' Eden left her number and hung up.

The next call she had to make, no matter how distasteful it might be, was to Rob, at the office. He seemed happy to hear from her, and hopeful that all was going well. She said that she had no time to talk but she needed to consult with him about Flynn's idea of the newspaper cutting as the preface to the story.

'Oh, Eden, I'm not . . . that idea is not appealing to me,' he said, sounding dismayed.

'Me neither,' said Eden shortly. 'But he seems intent on it.'

'You're going to have to flatter him,' said Rob. 'Make him feel that his readers will be horribly disappointed not to hear about this from him, in his own words.'

'I think perhaps he's trying to hold that back for volume two,' said Eden, unable to conceal the sarcasm in her words.

'Writers,' Rob sighed. 'Nothing would surprise me. How's the relationship? Do you feel like you have some influence with him?'

Eden thought about the insurance policy, and the investigator's suggestion that Tara's death was not suicidal. 'I'm working on it,' she said. 'I'll need to stay here a while longer.'

Rob assured her that it was no problem, and told her to keep him up to date. Eden ended the call and sat in the cheerless hotel room. Her impulse was to go to the police right now, and demand to see every bit of documentation they had about her mother and Jeremy's death. But, her phone told her that it was almost five o'clock, and this was not the ideal time for a police visit. She could go in the morning. That way she would be more likely to get results. But she couldn't just sit there, doing nothing, while this situation roiled around her.

Just then, her phone rang. She did not recognize the number. She answered. The caller was Lizzy Jacquez. 'Hi, Eden,' she said. 'DeShaun told me that you wanted to talk to me.'

'It's true,' said Eden. 'I do. Do you have a few minutes?'

'I guess so,' said Lizzy uncertainly.

'I can come to you. Where do you live?'

'Well, actually, I'm staying at my parents' house tonight.'

'I could come there,' said Eden. 'I don't need too much of your time.'

'All right. Come in half an hour,' said Lizzy. She gave Eden the address.

Eden hung up feeling vaguely hopeful. At least this was a beginning. Someone she could question. Someone who had been with Tara before her death and who knew what her mental state had been. It was a start.

The Coopers, for that was Lizzy's maiden name, lived in a house with two front porches, one atop the other. The large, old house was freshly painted and well kept, one of many on a tree-lined street, only minutes from downtown. From what Eden had seen of Cleveland, this neighborhood was somewhat unusual. Unlike the Eastern cities Eden was used to, the majority of dwellings in Cleveland

117

were not apartment buildings, but older, single family dwellings or duplexes, many of them in a sorry state of disrepair. The city had an air of dilapidation, brought on, no doubt, by the disappearance of jobs and factories in the Rust Belt. Traveling past block after block of homes which had seen better days, Eden imagined what Cleveland must have been like in its heyday. Clearly it was, at one time, a city of proud homeowners and comfortable dwellings. Now, most of the city seemed to reflect a certain depression made manifest in its rundown buildings.

She found a parking spot half a block away, and walked up the crumbling sidewalk to the chain link fence which surrounded the house. She let herself in, looking out for a large dog, which the fence suggested to her. But there was no sound of barking as she knocked on the front door, and a light appeared immediately over the transom.

The door was opened by a neatly dressed, balding man, holding a newspaper. Before Eden could identify herself, the man said, 'Come in, come in. You must be Lizzy's friend. I'm Charlie Cooper.' He stuffed the newspaper under his arm and extended a hand to her.

Eden shook it. 'I'm Eden Radley. Nice to meet you.'

'Come in, Eden. Make yourself at home. Lizzy called me to say that she would be here soon, and for you to wait.'

'Oh, okay,' said Eden. She came into the cozy living room, filled with overstuffed furniture grouped around a brick fireplace. A delicious smell was coming from the kitchen.

'Something smells great,' she said.

'Pork chops. My wife is a wonderful cook. Sit down,' he said. 'Lizzy tells us you are related to Tara Darby.'

'She was my mother,' Eden said, perching on the edge of a comfortable club chair.

'She was a lovely woman,' said Charlie, shaking his head. 'What a terrible thing.'

A voice from the kitchen called out, 'Who was at the door, Charlie?'

'Someone here for Lizzy,' he called back. At that, a bespectacled woman with short, graying hair appeared in the kitchen door, wiping her hands on her apron, which she wore over plaid slacks and a shapeless sweater.

'This is Eden,' said Charlie. 'Eden, this is Lizzy's mom, Phyllis.'

The woman frowned at Eden. 'I know that name,' she said.

'This is Tara Darby's daughter, from back East,' said Charlie.

Phyllis blanched. 'Oh my goodness. You're Tara's daughter. I'm so sorry for your loss. Your mother talked about you often. Such a terrible loss.'

'I'm glad to meet you, Mrs Cooper,' said Eden. 'I heard from a number of people that you helped my mother out by staying with Jeremy sometimes.'

'Well, I worried about her. A person needs a break from all that,' said Phyllis Cooper. 'I know what it's like. I just wanted to help.'

'I really appreciate it,' said Eden. 'Everyone here has been so kind.'

'Have you had dinner?' Charlie asked. 'Why don't you stay?'

Eden recognized the look of alarm on Phyllis's face. It was the look of a cook who had made three pork chops and now a fourth had been spontaneously invited to dinner.

'Oh no,' she said. 'I couldn't possibly. I'm just here to talk to Lizzy. You have a lovely home,' she said sincerely. It was indeed a lovely home, decorated in warm colors, the furniture comfortable, every surface covered with framed family photos.

Phyllis smiled, clearly relieved. 'Thank you,' she said. She pointed to the kitchen. 'I've got to get back . . .'

'I'll help you, darling,' said Charlie. 'Eden, you just put your feet up. Lizzy will be along any minute.'

'Thanks,' said Eden, as the couple retreated into the kitchen. They seemed like nice people, but Lizzy was coming here without her husband. She wondered if these two Midwesterners were really on board with an interracial marriage for their daughter. Social attitudes had changed, but sometimes, Eden thought, not all that much. Maybe DeShaun Jacquez wasn't really welcome in the Cooper household. Eden sat back in the chair, and her gaze roved among the family mementoes and photos in the room. There was a wedding picture of Lizzy and her husband, the two of them dressed in their formal best. It wasn't front and center, but it wasn't hidden either. So maybe everything was fine. Maybe DeShaun just had to work tonight. Doctors had notoriously terrible hours.

Eden's gaze roved over the other photos. There were numerous photos of a disabled child, some in a wheelchair, some seated among the members of his family, all smiling.

Eden got up to look closer. She studied the photos of the Coopers' lost son, Anthony, and wondering if Jeremy had looked like that. Once again, she was reminded that she never knew her half-brother. Never would know him. Tara had given her opportunities, but Eden had avoided them, not wanting to confront the emotional turmoil. That opportunity would never come again. Jeremy, who was, in fact, her only sibling, was gone forever.

The front door opened and shut, and Lizzy rushed in. Eden hurriedly turned her attention to a different photo. As Lizzy came in and saw her, Eden pointed to the picture. It was a photo of a dreamy-eyed young girl with an abundance of dark hair spilling across the shoulders of a peasant-style dress.

'Eden,' Lizzy exclaimed, hanging her coat on a clothes tree in the hall. 'You found us.'

Eden smiled. 'Just looking at your family pictures. Is this you?'

'Oh hell, no,' Lizzy scoffed, as she came in, rubbing her hands. She gazed fondly at the photo. 'That's my mom when she was young.'

'Beautiful,' said Eden.

'I was never that pretty.'

'You are too,' said Eden kindly, although, in truth, Lizzy was plain by comparison. But there was a spirit and a kind of shining integrity about her that was irresistible.

'Well, thank you,' said Lizzy. 'What is it you wanted to talk about?'

'Can we talk privately?' said Eden.

'Sure. Come in the den. I'm home,' she called out as she led Eden down the hallway to a door on the right.

'Hi, darling', 'Hi, sweetheart' came the voices of her parents from the kitchen.

Lizzy indicated a leather couch. Eden sat on one end, and Lizzy settled herself in the far corner.

Eden took a deep breath, and began. 'I appreciate your talking to me, Lizzy. I know you were close to my mother in the last months of her life. How long did you work together?'

'Well, I started my internship at Dr Tanaka's office in September. So, about . . . four months,' said Lizzy. 'She would bring Jeremy in every week for an evaluation. Some people think it's overkill, but we like to think of it as being thorough, and amassing as much information as possible.'

'At their house?'

'Occasionally I went to the house to observe. But mostly it was in the office.'

'Did you see any signs that my mother was in that desperate a mental state?'

Lizzy frowned. 'No, I wouldn't say desperate. But I think she had changed recently. She had lost some of her . . . I don't know, her hopefulness. I mean, I was mainly there for Jeremy, but I did notice that.'

'Did you ever ask her about it?'

'Of course. Because that was my job. To help deal with the stress. You know. It can be . . . debilitating.'

'What did she say?' Eden asked.

'She said it was personal. That she had some personal issues. But she didn't want to talk about it. She never . . . never expressed any impatience or anger with Jeremy. No matter the toll it took on her, his life was so precious to her. I went through this in my own family. The strain on the parents is terrible.'

'I'm sure of that,' said Eden sincerely. 'I guess people have low points in the course of it.'

Lizzy frowned and looked at the door to the den which stood ajar. She got up from the sofa, and quietly shut it to prevent being overheard. Then she resumed her seat and leaned forward toward Eden. 'Raising a child, knowing that they won't survive. This is one of the hardest things there is. My mom actually had a breakdown. She had to be hospitalized for a while. That's why she was so worried about Tara. She'd been through it.'

'I'm so sorry,' said Eden sincerely. 'That must have been awful for you. For all of you.'

'It was,' said Lizzy. 'It really was. Luckily, we had my father. And my dad is one of those people who always looks on the bright side, no matter what. He stepped right in and took care of us both. He took a leave from work and tried to make it seem like a wonderful adventure for us. He never faltered. When Mom got home, she was much better, but Dad continued to pitch in.

They're a team. And I have to say, my brother was a great kid. He was able to speak. He had a good sense of humor. Jeremy had a lot more . . . issues. He couldn't speak. He was very sensitive to noise, and light, and . . . every other thing. He tended to scream a lot. It was very difficult for your mother.'

'But you said what a wonderful boy he was,' Eden said almost accusingly. 'The best boy in the world, you said!'

Lizzy looked at Eden, somewhat bemused. 'I'm guessing you haven't spent a lot of time around children.'

Eden squirmed uncomfortably. 'Is it that obvious?'

Lizzy smiled. 'Well, when you deal with children, even children with difficulties like Jeremy's, you love those children, and you stay on their side. You feel for them, and that helps.'

Eden felt like the younger of the two of them, being schooled by someone older and wiser. 'You're right. I know nothing about this. I feel like I am still in the dark. Can I ask, how was Flynn with this whole thing? Did he and my mother . . . work together with Jeremy?'

Lizzy frowned. 'Oh yes,' she said. 'Definitely.'

'If I can speak frankly,' said Eden.

'Sure,' said Lizzy.

'I was wondering if, perhaps, having my mother so involved with Jeremy wasn't . . . a problem in their marriage.'

'A problem how?' Lizzy asked.

Eden felt as if she was wading into something she might regret. 'Well, some men . . . need a lot of attention. They can become jealous of a woman's involvement with a child. Especially, you know, when their relationship is . . .'

Lizzy was watching her warily.

'Well, before Jeremy came along, he may have been used to my mother's undivided attention. But I'm sure that in recent years she was preoccupied with Jeremy . . .'

'Of course,' Lizzy said. 'It was a difficult time.'

'Yes, but, I couldn't help wondering about this intern of Flynn's. With the veil? She seems very devoted to Flynn.'

'Aaliya,' said Lizzy. 'She's a lovely girl. Very shy, but reliable.'

'Do you think my mother might have thought that something else was . . . going on between her husband and this girl?'

'You mean . . . an affair?' Lizzy asked.

Eden shrugged. 'I don't know. I'm just looking for a reason.'

Lizzy frowned and shook her head slowly. 'No,' she said. 'Aaliya is very . . . sheltered. Her parents are dead. They got killed when their car ran over an IED in Iraq. She lives with her aunt and uncle. He is an imam at a local mosque. Very important in the Islamic community. I understand that they're very strict with her.'

'Sounds like a lonely life. People do cross the line at times,' Eden persisted.

Lizzy shook her head. 'No. Not Aaliya. Not to mention Flynn. He loved your mother. I don't think that Flynn was to blame for your mother's sadness,' she said.

Sadness, Eden thought. That was a good word

for the impression she had of her mother's mental state in the last months of her life. 'I'm not trying to . . . place blame,' she insisted.

'I realize Flynn is a little . . . different than other people. He's a writer and he has that artist's nature. That sensitivity. But I got to know him pretty well in those months, and he was . . . completely involved with his family. And completely bereft when he lost them. I can tell you that for a fact.' A spot of pink appeared in each of her waxy cheeks, as she defended Eden's stepfather.

Eden realized that she had said more than she meant to. She didn't even know Lizzy. She shouldn't be speculating about her mother's marriage with this stranger. 'People have problems in their marriages. I guess I was just curious,' she demurred.

'People's marriages are complicated,' Lizzy agreed. 'You can't judge them from the outside.'

Eden thought about herself, trying to size up Lizzy's marriage through a hasty look at the family photos. No, she thought. Things were always more complicated than they seemed. At that moment, there was a tap on the den door.

'Come in,' said Lizzy.

Lizzy's mother appeared at the door. 'Darling,' she said. 'I'm sorry to interrupt. But it's time for supper.'

Lizzy smiled at her mother, who hovered in the doorway. 'Okay,' she said.

Eden looked up at Phyllis. 'Mrs Cooper, you knew my mother. You babysat for her from time

126

to time. Did you have any idea that she was . . . feeling so desperate?'

Phyllis looked at Lizzy, as if seeking her permission to speak. But Lizzy was waiting curiously for her answer. 'Well,' said Phyllis, 'I won't lie to you. I could tell she was having a hard time.'

'But this . . .' said Eden.

Phyllis shook her head. 'Everyone's breaking point is different. I did suspect that she wasn't doing well. I mean, I'm no expert like my daughter . . .'

'You're the perfect expert,' said Eden. 'You had the same experience.'

'I did mention it to her husband. That I thought she was having a very hard time.'

'What did he say?' Eden asked.

Phyllis blushed. 'Oh, he thought I was butting in where I didn't belong.'

'I'm sure he felt that protecting Tara and Jeremy was his job,' Lizzy protested, defending Flynn stoutly.

Eden nodded. Lizzy seemed to insist on her rosy view of Tara and Flynn's nuclear family. Probably projecting, imagining that they were just like her own family. There was nothing more to be gained in this conversation, she realized. 'Okay. Well, thanks. I better get going.' She looked up at Lizzy's mom. 'It must be great to have your daughter live so close by. I know my dad would love it if I lived in the same town. Especially if I were married to a handsome young doctor.'

Lizzy's mother tenderly reached out a finger

and tucked Lizzy's shining hair behind her ear. 'It's all I ever wanted in this world. And when we have our grandchildren, we won't have to get to know them on Skype. They'll be right nearby.'

'Mom,' Lizzy chided her, shaking her head.

'I'm sorry,' she said, turning to Eden. 'She's my angel.'

'I understand,' said Eden, feeling a little nagging longing in her heart. She could remember Tara saying such things about her, long ago.

'Mom, stop.' Lizzy rebuffed her mother's attentions good-naturedly.

'Thank you for talking to me,' said Eden, wrapping her scarf around her neck. 'You were very helpful.'

'You should put my cell number in your phone,' said Lizzy. 'That was my home number you called. And you should give me yours.'

'Okay, great,' said Eden, as they exchanged numbers in their phone. 'I might need to talk to you again.'

'Anytime,' said Lizzy sincerely. 'I want to help.'

Eden felt like giving the girl a hug, but it seemed overly familiar after such a glancing acquaintance. 'I appreciate it,' she said. She followed mother and daughter down the hall, and bid goodnight to them and to Lizzy's father, who was lighting a fire in the fireplace.

'Come see us again, Eden,' he said, waving to her.

Eden nodded, and steeled herself to go back out into the cold.

Twelve

The smell of the Coopers' dinner seemed to trail Eden out of the house and down the front steps. Suddenly she was famished. As she hurried toward the car, she tried to think where she might go for dinner. Her stomach churned at the idea of fast food or Chinese takeout. She arrived at the car, turned the engine over and sat shivering, waiting for it to warm up. She wished she knew some of the restaurants in this town. Not that she would go there alone, even if she did. She hated eating in a restaurant by herself. She did it when she had to, but she never liked it.

Then, she had an idea. That couple at the funeral, Marguerite and her husband – was it Gerald? No, Gerard – had invited her to their café. She had liked them as soon as she met them, and she felt that their invitation had been sincere. She had actually wished she could take them up on their offer, but she was leaving Cleveland the day after the funeral. Maybe this would be an opportunity to have a nice dinner, and, at the same time, amass a little more information. She felt as if Marguerite was much less enthusiastic than Lizzy on the subject of Flynn, and might be an excellent person to talk to next. But what was the restaurant called?

Though she had never seen it, Eden envisioned the place as having yellow walls. They had mentioned that they served some amalgamation of French and Middle Eastern cooking. It sounded a little strange, but promising. And then, suddenly, Eden remembered why she had pictured the café walls as yellow. The restaurant was named after the color. She picked up her phone and triumphantly typed in Café Jaune.

The light from the Café Jaune storefront glowed in the middle of a mostly residential block in the center of town. Eden parked nearby and hurried inside.

Now that she was here, she wondered if they would even recall meeting her. Somehow, she felt sure that Marguerite would, if she was, in fact, working this evening. Eden had started to call, but she was reluctant to get into a long explanation of why she was back here in Cleveland. At the last minute she decided to just go ahead and visit the café, and hope she would run into them.

She hesitated in the doorway of the tiny café, which was half-filled on this chilly night. The walls, as she had imagined, were yellow, but more curry colored than lemon, befitting a Provencal décor. There was an unstudied charm about the place. Moroccan lamps glowed in jewel tones above the small tables covered in patterned tablecloths of blue, red and yellow. The mismatched, straight-back chairs were wooden and well worn, with chairpads flattened by much use.

Eden was uncertain if she should just sit down, or wait to be seated. Just then, she saw a woman in a black dress coming toward her from the back of the restaurant. The woman looked at her curiously, as if she were trying to place her, and suddenly her expression cleared.

'Hey,' said Marguerite, coming up to Eden. 'Aren't you . . .'

'Tara's daughter. Eden.'

'I'm surprised to see you here,' Marguerite said. Then, she threw her arms around Eden in a friendly embrace. 'But I'm so glad to see you,' she said. 'I'm glad you found us.'

'Thanks,' said Eden, blushing in spite of herself. 'I wanted to try your cooking.'

Marguerite led her to a corner table, and Eden sat down. 'You came all the way from New York to try our cooking?' Marguerite asked.

Eden sighed. 'It's a long story.'

Marguerite handed her a menu. 'Pick out what you want for dinner. You should try the socca. They're chickpea pancakes. Our specialty. I have a few things to take care of in the back, and then I'll join you.'

'Would you? That would be great,' said Eden. She closed the menu and handed it back to Marguerite. 'And yes, I'll try the socca. And the lamb, I think. With a glass of the house red.'

Marguerite smiled broadly. 'Excellent choice. I'll be back shortly.'

In a few moments, a young, olive-skinned guy with a thatch of black hair appeared, dressed in a white shirt and dark pants, and set a glass of wine in front of Eden. She smiled at him. He nodded gravely. Eden picked up the wine and sipped it. The warmth of it seemed to radiate

131

through her. This was a good idea, she thought, even if she learned nothing further about Flynn Darby. It was just good to be in the warmth, anticipating a nice meal.

She looked around at the other tables. There were several pairs of young people who looked like students, and, at a larger, round table, a Middle-Eastern-looking family. A recording of a man singing in French was playing quietly in the background. In a few moments, Marguerite came back and joined her at the table. The young waiter brought her a glass of wine as well, and placed a basket of bread on the table. Then he retreated.

Marguerite took a sip of her wine and sighed. 'Whew. I'm tired. I'm glad to be off my feet.'

'I hate to hold you up. I know how busy your life is. With your daughter and all.'

'She's at my sister's tonight. With her family. She loves it there. And they seem to love having her.'

'That's so nice,' said Eden wistfully, thinking of her mother, with no family to turn to when things got difficult with Jeremy. Certainly not her adult daughter.

'So,' Marguerite said. 'What in the world are you doing back here in Cleveland?'

Eden frowned. Now that she was asked, she didn't really want to tell this woman that she was the editor of Flynn's book, but she realized that if she wanted Marguerite to share confidences, she had better start with one of her own. She took a deep breath and began.

'I don't know if you know this, but I'm a book editor.'

'I know all about it,' said Marguerite. 'Your mother was so proud.'

'Well, Flynn sold a book to my company, on the condition that I be his editor.'

Marguerite grimaced. 'You're kidding. What's he up to?' she asked.

Eden broke off a piece of bread. 'I do not know. That's what I wanted to talk to you about. Some investigators from the insurance company came to see me this afternoon. They are reluctant to pay out the policy and were suggesting that he chose me as his editor so that I wouldn't be free to join in their suit against him—'

'They think that he had something to do with your mother's death,' said Marguerite flatly.

Eden stared at her. 'How do you know that?'

'Well, I've thought that all along.'

Eden blushed furiously. 'You have?'

Marguerite nodded. 'Gerard thinks I'm crazy. But I swear, there is something about that guy that gives me the creeps. Always has.'

'Wow. You really don't like him, do you?' Eden asked.

Marguerite shook her dark curls, and her silver jewelry jingled. 'No, I don't. He made your mother's life miserable. And he was never there for Jeremy.'

Eden frowned, thinking about Lizzy insisting that Flynn was completely involved with his family. Completely bereft when he lost them. Which version was true? 'Still, that's a far cry from actually . . . hurting them.'

Marguerite looked around the restaurant. 'I don't want Gerard to hear me. He thinks I'm

133

terrible. But I have wondered from the very beginning. The minute I heard about it, I said no. This is not right. I knew your mother. Oh, she was upset all right. There was something weighing on her mind. She was not herself. That is true. I've long suspected that Flynn was fooling around behind her back. I mean, all those adoring college girls? That Muslim girl who is his intern sticks to him like glue. I even asked Tara about her once.'

'I was wondering the same thing,' said Eden. 'What did she say?'

'She defended him, of course. But I could tell that it was half-hearted. She was suspicious. I'm sure of it.'

Eden stared at her. 'I thought he was so crazy about her. I mentioned it to Lizzy, and she couldn't say enough about what a great marriage they had.'

'Oh, what does Lizzy know?' Marguerite said impatiently. 'She's like, twenty-two and she's been married what, three minutes? To a handsome young doctor who worships her? Those two are still in the honeymoon stage. Look, when you've been married as long as I have, you can tell by looking at a guy when his attention is wandering. Flynn's attention was wandering.'

'Is that just woman's intuition?'

Marguerite shook her head. 'I saw it with my own eyes.'

'Saw what?' Eden asked.

Marguerite sighed. 'You might as well know. One day in the fall, I was with your mother and, after I left her, I was walking home and I ran into Flynn. Well, I saw him, that is. He didn't see me. It was a rainy day. I'll never forget it. I was hurrying along with my head down and hood up, and he was on the other side of the street, sitting at the wheel of the car with a woman, obviously not your mother, in the passenger seat. I couldn't really see her, but it was a woman. I'm sure of that.'

'Could it have been Aaliya?'

Marguerite sighed. 'Is that the intern's name?'

Eden nodded.

'I don't know. There is something strange there,' said Marguerite. 'I'll give you that. But I can't say for sure. I didn't get a close enough look at the woman. She was wearing a hat or something over her head and she was weeping into her hands. He was trying his best to convince her of something and she just kept shaking her head. He was trying to pull her into his embrace, but she was resisting. He didn't look like he was going to give up. I'm sure he got his way. Those bedroom eyes of his,' Marguerite said disgustedly.

'Oh God. That would have killed my mother,' said Eden. 'She was mad about him. Are you positive?'

Marguerite looked her squarely in the eye. 'I'd bet my life on it.'

Eden frowned, and felt pained for her mother. Flynn's book had painted a picture of an unbreakable couple, but then, who would want to read about a philandering husband in such a story? 'Well, I guess that explains it then. I mean, why she did what she did. She must have found out, and was heartbroken.'

135

Marguerite put her palm down flat on the table. 'No,' she said. 'Absolutely not.'

Eden looked up at her. 'Well, I know you didn't tell her, but she might have found out some other way.'

'That's not what I mean,' said Marguerite. 'I don't care how despondent she was, she would never have done that to Jeremy. Not in a million years. She might have kicked Flynn out, died from a broken heart, whatever. But take Jeremy's life? I don't know how anyone could think that for a minute. Tara would never . . . any more than I would. I mean, think about it. She was your mother too. Would she ever have hurt you, tried to . . . take your life, for any reason? Whatsoever?'

Eden felt flummoxed. She could not reply for a moment. 'Well, I don't know. I mean, under extreme circumstances—'

'Circumstances! Oh come on,' Marguerite insisted. 'I know all about extreme circumstances. But some things are non-negotiable. This is about Tara. Would she? Ever?'

'How can I answer that?' Eden cried.

'You can answer it better than anyone, because she was your mother and she raised you. What is the answer to that question?'

Eden took a deep breath. 'No,' she said.

Marguerite nodded and slapped her palm on the table. 'Exactly.'

Thirteen

It was nearly three in the morning when Eden finally fell into a restless sleep.

She had lain awake for hours, suffering from indigestion, but not from the food. She kept thinking of all that Marguerite had said. When finally she slept, she dreamed of Tara, but the dreams were not pleasant. In her nightmares, Tara was weeping, running, trying to protect her child, but the child she was trying to protect was not Jeremy, but Eden. That awoke Eden with a start. It was only six a.m. There was no point to getting up this early. She tried to sleep again, but her racing thoughts would not permit it.

As soon as the hour was acceptable, Eden got out of bed and began to get ready. It didn't take her long. She couldn't stomach any breakfast and she didn't really care much what she wore. All she wanted was to be warm in this city which never seemed to be anything but cold. She drove downtown to the police station and parked her car outside. Even at this early hour in the morning, the police station was abuzz with activity. A bearded black man in shabby clothes and handcuffs was being led into the building, while two lawyers shivering in topcoats conversed, then rushed inside. Eden followed them in, and waited her turn. The lobby was already filled with people

137

looking either angry or afraid. She tried not to meet anyone's gaze. When her turn came, she approached the desk and cleared her throat.

The desk sergeant looked up at her impassively. 'Yes?'

'My name is Eden Radley. Not too long ago, my mother and my half-brother were killed in a carbon monoxide poisoning in their home. I wondered if I might talk to the detectives who worked on that case.'

'Names?' he said.

'I'm sorry. What?'

'Names of the victims.'

'Oh. Tara and Jeremy Darby.'

'And why do you want to see the detective?'

'I have a lot of questions about the case,' she said, and then, fearing her request might be denied, she decided to embellish a little bit. 'I've come here from New York City to discuss this.'

'Do you know the name of the detective who handled the case?'

'As a matter of fact, I do,' said Eden, wielding the name she had learned from Tim McNee, the insurance agent. 'I believe it's a Detective Burt?'

'Just a minute.' The desk sergeant picked up the phone and spoke in a low voice to the person at the other end. He nodded a few times, and then said 'Okay.' He hung up the phone and looked up at Eden.

'Wait here,' he said. 'Step back.'

Unsure if that was a yes or a no, Eden did as she was told. In a few minutes, the door from the squad room opened, and a detective appeared.

He had gray hair and a sallow complexion. His navy blue suit had dandruff on the shoulders. He looked like he could use a shave.

'Ms Radley?' he said politely. 'Come on in.'

'Hey, how come she gets to see someone?' complained a destitute-looking woman whose clothes smelled of urine. No one responded to her question.

Eden followed the detective into the squad room, passing a number of desks with computers and ringing phones, and other officers, plainclothes and uniformed, drinking coffee and getting their day started. Detective Burt directed Eden to a small office, and a vinyl-covered chair, with a seat mended in duct tape.

'How can I help you?' he said.

Eden settled into the chair. There was a pile of folders on Burt's desk, and constant beeping on his phone. A bulletin board behind him had layers of Post-it notes and forms attached to it, as if getting to the bottom of crimes in this precinct was a never-ending task. 'I . . . I'm here about my mother, Tara Darby? Do you remember her case?'

Burt nodded. 'Sure. The carbon monoxide deaths. It wasn't that long ago,' he said.

'I received a visit yesterday from some investigators at her insurance company. They don't want to pay out on my mother's policy.'

'Are you the beneficiary?' he asked.

'No,' said Eden. 'My stepfather is. They told me that they had received a tip that my mother might not have committed suicide, as it had been reported. That she and my half-brother may have been murdered. They said you received the same information.'

The detective waved a hand dismissively. 'Gossip and slander is not the same as information. There was really very little question in this case.' He tapped impatiently on his blotter. 'I'm sorry, miss, but that's how it is.'

'The insurance investigators said,' Eden persisted, 'that the police had refused to give them all the documentation about . . . my mother's death.'

Burt looked weary. 'That's not so. We gave them whatever we had. There are some reports that are not yet completed. The coroner's office gave us a verbal report, including the results of the toxicology tests. We still haven't received a hard copy ourselves. There's a backlog in all our county offices. As for the insurance companies, this is business as usual for them. They are stalling, so they don't have to pay. Is it a large amount?'

'Yes,' said Eden.

'Well, there you go,' he said. 'It was a suicide. Your mother sealed up the house and left a suicide note.'

'What did it say?'

'I don't . . . honestly remember. That she was sorry. The normal things.'

'Would you mind looking it up?' Eden said politely.

The detective sighed, as if her request was a terrible burden. But he did not protest. He turned to his computer and began to tap on it. After a few minutes he said, 'Here it is. "I am sorry. I can't go on. Please forgive me." That's what it said.'

'Who was it addressed to?'

'Her husband,' said Burt patiently.

'Handwritten?'

He shook his head. 'Printed.'

Anyone could have written that, Eden thought. It was completely impersonal. 'Thank you,' she said, then took a deep breath. 'Mr Preston, one of the investigators, said that both my mother and my half-brother were sedated.'

'That's true,' said Burt. 'We found a bottle of barbiturates. The coroner's office stated that they both had barbiturates in their systems. I mean, what else would you do but give your child something to make him sleep, so that he wouldn't suffer? Same thing she did for herself.'

'How could a small, sick child like that have swallowed a pill?'

Burt shrugged. 'He couldn't. There was a feeding tube. She probably crushed it and put it into liquid.'

'Was the tube tested?' Eden demanded.

'Ms Radley,' he said patiently. 'He couldn't have swallowed the pill, but it was in his system. It had to come through the tube.'

'But an autopsy was done?'

'Yes, of course,' said the detective. 'As I said, we're still waiting for a copy of their report. But the coroner said that they died of carbon monoxide poisoning. I saw the bodies. Believe me, they did. They were both cherry red in the face.'

Eden felt a little nauseated by this vivid description.

'I'm sure this is all very difficult for you, but I'm trying to be frank with you.'

'I appreciate that,' said Eden.

'Now is there anything else?' he asked, rising from his chair.

Eden did not budge. 'My stepfather, Flynn Darby, is filing suit against the company for refusing to pay. They said that they plan to countersue Mr Darby under the slayer rule. They wanted me to join the countersuit.'

'The slayer rule?' Burt asked in disbelief. He shook his head. 'No wonder our insurance premiums are so high. We have to pay for these attorneys to file frivolous lawsuits. My advice to you, Ms Radley, is to keep out of it. This was a straightforward homicide/suicide. Sad and terrible, but there it is. Mr Darby had nothing to do with it. He was at a writers' convention that was held at . . .' Burt hesitated and then tapped on the computer and studied the screen. '. . . the Seagate Convention Center in downtown Toledo. He had a room in a motel right there on Garfield Street, and that is where he spent the night.'

'Did someone check on that?' Eden said stubbornly.

'Of course we checked on it. We spoke to the night clerk at the motel, and to the registrar of the writers' group. They have him signed in at five o'clock for the evening's program.'

'Do you know if he actually attended that program? Did anyone see him there, after he signed in?'

'He went to the conference with a student intern. A young Muslim woman named

142

Aaliya . . .' he squinted at the papers in the folder. 'Saleh.'

Eden stared at him. 'They were there together?'

'Two rooms,' he said. 'Different floors.'

'But he brought her there? Overnight?' Eden demanded.

'Yes. I know what you're thinking, but your mother knew all about it, apparently. We spoke to the girl. She has aspirations to be an author. She's a student at the college where he teaches. Look, my junior partner spoke to several people, including the Muslim girl's uncle, who is quite strict. He's a big mucky-muck at a mosque here in Detroit.' Burt squinted at the notes on his desk. 'The Al-Aqsa Mosque. It's spelled A-Q-S-A, so I don't know if that's how you pronounce it.'

Eden made a mental note.

'Anyway, he had actually given his permission for his niece to go to Toledo with her professor. It was all on the up and up. They attended seminars. People saw them there. I can assure you, that's where Flynn Darby was on the night that his wife killed herself. He drove this Aaliya home the next morning and went back to his house, expecting to see his family, but when he went in the house, he found them both dead, the suicide note on the table, the doors and windows blocked so that the carbon monoxide could not escape. The house has an attached garage. The garage door was locked from the inside. The connecting door to the main part of the house was open, and the car was completely out of gas. It probably idled in the garage for most of the night. Anyone in the kitchen, dining, living room

143

area could have clearly seen the door open, the car running. They could have turned it off. Your mother could have turned it off. But she didn't. Mr Darby came in the front door and found his son dead in his bed, his wife in hers. And may I just say, I have seen many people react to the deaths of their loved ones over the years. Mr Darby was in a state of complete shock.'

'Can I look at the reports myself?' Eden asked.

'No,' said Burt.

'Why not? They're about my mother. Why can't I see them?'

'Because this isn't the public library,' Burt said irritably.

'The insurance investigators suggested that the police department might be shielding Flynn because his grandfather was a cop,' Eden said, realizing that this amounted to an accusation. She was risking making Burt angry. She said it anyway. 'Is that true?'

Burt looked at her with an expression more long-suffering than angry. 'Is what true? Is it true that his grandfather was a police officer? I don't know. Maybe he was. But if you're trying to suggest some Thin Blue Line conspiracy and all of that, you're overreaching, Ms Radley. I don't know Mr Darby's grandfather or anything about him.'

'He's retired. He lives in New York state.'

'So why would we be protecting him here in Ohio?'

Eden felt slightly embarrassed. 'I don't know. They suggested it.'

'Look, Ms Radley. This is a very painful thing.

Your mother committed suicide, and took her child with her. There's nothing more you can do for her. I know that suicide is hard to accept, but you just have to try. People always blame themselves when a loved one commits suicide. And then, because it's so painful, they try to find somebody else to blame.'

'I don't believe that she would do that,' Eden insisted. 'Maybe she might have killed herself. But not her child.'

'No one ever wants to believe it,' Detective Burt said in exasperation. 'This was a very sad situation, and I know it's tempting to wish that it isn't what it appears to be. But you have to accept it, and move on.'

'I don't accept it,' Eden said, and as she said it, she realized that it was true. 'I can't.'

'Well, that's your prerogative,' said the detective, standing up. 'But this case is closed.' He looked at Eden with an expression that was unmistakable. It said, *Get out of here.* Reluctantly, Eden got up from the chair.

Fourteen

Eden shivered in her idling rental car, waiting for the heat to kick in, and thinking about what she had heard from Detective Burt. She wished she could believe what the detective had said, that everything was exactly as it appeared to be.

But her conversation with Marguerite still

weighed on her. Marguerite's insistence that Tara would never have killed her son rang utterly true to Eden. And now, there was something else. To the police it meant nothing. But to Eden, it seemed the most important fact of all.

When the detective had been describing what they found at the scene, he said that Jeremy was in his bed, and Tara was in her own bed. Eden allowed herself to think about that time in her life when her mother was the source of so much warmth and tenderness. In particular, she remembered one time, when she had fallen ill. Tara and Hugh had called the doctor, who prescribed medication and told them to watch her. If her fever does not break, the doctor said, take her to the Emergency Room. Hugh had gone out to fill the prescriptions, and Tara had made Eden's room fresh and comfortable. Eden could still remember that long night, when she thrashed in her bed, suffering from feverish visions. Right beside her, all night long, Tara was there. She stayed in her clothes, in case they had to rush to the hospital. But Tara had lain down in Eden's narrow bed, her head on an extra pillow, and watched over her daughter. Even in her feverish state, Eden was aware that her mother was beside her, protecting her, unwilling to leave her side, even when Hugh urged her to come to bed and get some sleep.

If Tara had indeed decided to take her son on the ultimate journey with her, and had arranged it so that Jeremy would not live through the night, would she have gone to die in her own bed, and left Jeremy in his? It felt utterly and completely

146

wrong to Eden. If Tara had arranged for Jeremy's death, there was no way she would have passed that last night in another room, leaving him to a fate of unknown suffering alone. They would have found the child in his mother's arms. But they did find her in another room. So, Eden realized, with a sickening start, if she had gone to sleep in the other room, the only logical conclusion was that her mother could not have known what was about to befall them.

'Damn,' Eden whispered. The police were convinced that Tara had killed herself and her son. So they would have no reason to suspect anyone else. Had they really checked on Flynn's whereabouts when his wife and son died, or had they simply made a few phone calls, and accepted everything they were told, because it confirmed what they already believed? Eden was no longer willing to accept the official version of events. Starting with Flynn's alibi.

The heat had begun to warm up the car, and a weak winter sun had turned the morning sky gray and yellow. Eden picked up her phone and googled the driving distance between Cleveland and Toledo. It was less than a two-hour drive. Detective Burt had told her that Flynn stayed in a motel on Garfield Street in the area around the Seagate Convention Center. She remembered that the street was Garfield, because it made her think of that cartoon cat. How many motels could there be? It was worth a trip of a few hours to ask her questions in person, she thought, and see if the police version was thorough, or perfunctory.

Now, all she needed was a photo of Flynn to

show around the motel and find out if anyone remembered seeing him. She googled Flynn's name, but there was nothing but a blurry group shot in images. She thought of just asking him, and pretending she needed a photo for the book jacket, but she realized how unconvincing that would sound. They were a long way from a book jacket, and that was the purview of the art department anyway. They would probably arrange for a photo of Flynn to be taken when the time came. Then, she had an idea. She got the number for Gideon Lendl's agency in New York. The receptionist, who had an English accent and whose name was Rachel, was anxious to please when she learned that Eden was the editor for one of their clients.

'Would you happen to have a photo of the author which I could use for promotion?' Eden asked. 'We plan to have a photo taken of Mr Darby for the book jacket, of course, but right now I'm already getting some requests . . .'

'Of course,' said Rachel eagerly. 'I can send it to you straight away.'

'Send it to my phone, would you?' Eden asked.

'Right away,' said Rachel.

In the next minute, the photo came through. It was a medium-distance shot, not a professional job, but it was clear and in focus. There was a brooding, almost insolent expression on Flynn's face. It would definitely do.

The drive west from Cleveland to Toledo on Route 90 bordered Lake Erie for most of the way, and there was virtually no traffic to slow Eden down. She made it to Toledo in an hour and a half, and got off at a downtown exit for Garfield Street. Her search for the likely motel took very little time, as there was only one that she could find. It was a run-down place called the Stella Motel which looked like it had been erected in the 1950s. The rug in the reception area had once been burnt orange. She could still see that color underneath a chair and an end table. The rest of the carpeting was now brown and flattened with age. The desk was a huge, curved blond wood, now dirty blond, counter that may have looked rather space age when the rug was still burnt orange. But now everything about the place looked worn out.

That description also applied to the man behind the desk, a sallow man of about fifty, wearing a dust-colored shirt and brown pants that seemed to match the rug. Could Flynn really have been staying here? Even if they were weighed down with expenses, surely he could have afforded a nicer hotel a little further out of town. This motel was certainly convenient to the convention center, but it seemed to have little else to recommend it. Eden walked up to the desk and the clerk eyed her suspiciously, and did not ask her what she wanted.

'Excuse me,' she said. 'I was wondering if you could help me. I'm trying to find out if this man stayed at your hotel.'

'Name? Date?'

Eden gave him the date and showed him the photo of Flynn on her phone.

'This your hubby?'

'No,' said Eden. 'My name is Eden Radley. This man is my stepfather.'

Steve frowned at the photo. 'Your stepfather? He doesn't look much older than you.'

'My mother's second marriage was to a younger man.'

'You're not a cop?'

'No.'

'How come you're asking questions?'

'The cops seem to have lost interest in the situation,' said Eden.

The sallow-faced man sighed wearily and peered at the picture. 'Come to think of it, they did show up here a few weeks ago, asking about him. I'll tell you what I told them. He and that Arab girl checked in that night. Two rooms. Different floors. He checked them out in the morning.'

So the Cleveland police had actually made the trip to Toledo. Eden didn't know if she was gratified or disappointed. 'Did you see him here during the night?' she asked. 'Maybe coming in from dinner or . . . I don't know. Going out to a bar or something?'

'What did this guy do anyway?' the man asked. 'First the cops. Now you. They said he wasn't in any trouble, but I don't buy that.'

A heavy-set black man in a flat-brimmed hat came up to the desk, and stood, clearly waiting for Eden to be finished. Eden stepped out of the way. 'Go ahead,' she said. 'I'll wait.'

The man looked at her suspiciously, and nodded. Then he spoke to the man behind the desk. 'Hey, Steve.'

The clerk reached around and pulled an actual key off the wooden grid of mailboxes behind him. Eden couldn't remember the last time she had seen an actual room key like that. Steve handed it to his customer. 'There you go, Darnell.'

'See the Bulls game last night?' Darnell asked.

'I think they need to get that point guard from Denver,' said Steve, seeming suddenly energized.

Darnell shook his head and jingled his keys. 'Denver wants too much for him, man. Multiple first rounders!'

'Yeah, but without him . . .' said Steve.

'Trust me, that ain't never gonna happen,' Darnell predicted.

Eden waited patiently while the two men discussed their team's prospects. Finally Darnell took his keys and headed for the elevator.

Steve resumed his slump-shouldered posture at the desk, his enthusiasm over the Bulls now exhausted. Eden pressed up against the desk again. 'Look,' she said. 'I don't know what the cops told you, but my mother and my half-brother died that night when Flynn Darby was staying here. I just want to know for sure if he was here all night or if he slipped away during the evening.'

'Like I told the cops, he checked in. And he checked out in the morning. With the girl in her Arab gear. I go off at eight, so I didn't actually see him after he checked in.'

'But he left in the morning.'

Steve shrugged. 'The night man said so. He left his key.'

Eden pounced. 'So the police didn't actually know if he actually spent the whole night, or if

151

he left and came back. Just that he left the key. I think I need to talk to the night man.'

'Good luck with that. He was an African guy. He got deported.'

Eden sighed, and stared out of the hotel's plate-glass windows, nearly opaque with grime in the weak winter sunlight. 'This is a dead end, in other words,' she said.

Steve watched her warily. 'Sorry. Can't help ya.'

Eden decided to be blunt, and appeal to this man's better instincts. 'You see, the police think my mother killed herself and my half-brother, but I don't accept that. She was my mother. She was not . . .' Eden faltered. 'She was far from perfect, but she had a . . . gentle heart. She would never have taken her child's life. I was her child too. I don't believe that she would do that.'

Steve ran a hand over his stubbly face. 'That would be pretty tough to swallow,' he admitted.

Eden looked at him directly. 'You know your own mother. No matter what anybody else says, there are certain things about her that you just know.'

Steve regarded her with rheumy eyes, now alight with curiosity. 'So you think the husband killed her?'

Eden shook her head. 'I don't know about that. I just want . . . all the information. I want to know what happened.'

'But it stands to reason,' he said. 'I mean, who else would do that but a husband?'

Eden grimaced. 'Is that what you think?'

'I see a lot of bad husbands in this job, miss.'

'I'll bet you do,' said Eden.

Steve shrugged, noncommittal. 'Tell you what. Send that picture to my phone. I'll ask around if I have time.'

They exchanged numbers and Eden sent the photo of Flynn to him. Steve studied it for a minute and then set the phone down. 'All right. I'll give you a call if I hear anything.'

With a sigh Eden replaced her phone in her bag. 'I'd really appreciate it,' she said politely.

'Sure thing,' said Steve, shuffling a pile of papers on his desk distractedly. 'Do what I can.'

Fifteen

All the way back from Toledo, Eden argued with herself.

She knew that she might be jeopardizing her own position by going around voicing her suspicions about Flynn. She was Flynn's editor, and supposedly she had his best interests at heart. She had always blamed her mother, first and foremost, for what happened to their family, but now that she knew Flynn Darby up close and personal, every meeting, everything she learned, added to her dislike of him. And deep within her own heart, she felt a growing conviction that somehow he was to blame for these deaths.

He had been drunk or stoned at Tara and Jeremy's funeral, and was leaning on the arm of a modest but beautiful young girl. He had proved

153

to be an egomaniacal author. Lizzy had defended him as an artistic personality, but that was no excuse in Eden's eyes. She had often thought that people who blamed their bad behavior on their artistic natures were like spoiled children, so sure they were special that they felt entitled to be rude. Marguerite had said that she had seen Flynn consoling and embracing another woman before Tara's death. Eden reminded herself that there might be some innocent explanation for it, but, she was inclined to doubt it. Eden knew that she had nothing concrete to hold against him. Nothing she could take to the police or the insurance investigators to give weight to her theory. All the more reason to continue, she thought grimly.

By the time Eden was back in Cleveland, the afternoon light was fading. The thought of driving directly back to the motel made her feel depressed. She pulled up to a gas pump outside a convenience store and filled the tank. Then she went inside to pay. She picked up a bottle of water and some pretzels, walked up to the counter with her purchases and set them down. The clerk behind the counter had a narrow beard and was wearing a knitted hat, and a gown-like garment with a long vest over it. A Muslim, she thought, and then chided herself for profiling the man. But as he rang up her water, Eden reminded herself that presuming someone was a Muslim was not an insulting assumption.

'Excuse me,' she said. 'I'm looking for a mosque. I was wondering if you might have heard of it?'

The young man looked up at her with calm, dark eyes. 'Which one?'

'Um, it's a mosque called the Al-Aqsa? I'm not from around here and I got my directions mixed up. I'm supposed to be meeting with Imam . . .'

The young man nodded. 'Abd al-Bari?'

Eden pretended to frown at her phone. 'Yes,' she said. 'That's it.'

'It's three streets over. About ten blocks from here.'

'Really? I'm that close?' she asked.

The young man smiled. 'You're in the neighborhood. But if you're going there . . .'

Eden looked at him warily. 'Yes?'

'You better wear something on your head.'

Eden exhaled with relief. 'Thanks,' she said sincerely. 'Thanks for reminding me.'

The man nodded as Eden paid, and left the store. She got back in the car, had a few swigs of water, and rearranged her light woolen scarf over her head. She didn't know what she was going to say, but it seemed almost like an omen that the mosque was nearby. She was trying to make this picture come into focus. Perhaps the imam could be of some help.

She found the address easily and parked across the street, although the building she was looking at did not conform to her expectations. Cleveland was a low-rise city for the most part, and she had expected to find a mosque with the traditional dome and minarets. Instead, the building front was unadorned and windowless, with a sidewalk awning over the large wooden double doors.

The lack of windows gave it a closed, forbidding look, but she told herself she was just projecting. There was way too much anti-Muslim sentiment already floating around these days. She didn't want to be a part of that. She looked both ways and ran across, dodging dirty, ice-crusted snowdrifts. She approached the tall double doors and hesitated. They did not seem to invite walk-in visitors. She decided to knock. She rapped on the door several times but there was no answer. She was thinking about grabbing the square door handle and pulling it open, when the door was pushed forward, and a swarthy man emerged, scowling. He spoke to her in Arabic, but his message was clear. *Get back. Get away.*

Startled, she blurted out, 'I'm looking for Imam Abd al-Bari.'

The man's scowl lightened somewhat, but he still regarded her as if she were some sort of alien invader. 'Not here,' he muttered.

'Can I just go in and look?' she asked.

The man glared at her. 'Not here. There.' He jabbed a finger at the rundown apartment building beside the mosque. 'There.'

'Oh? He lives there?' Eden asked.

The man nodded and pushed past her, gesturing for her to follow him. She walked behind him to the apartment building next door and waited as he pushed the buzzer and barked into the intercom. A woman's voice answered, also in a language unknown to Eden.

What am I doing? she thought. Even if I meet this man, I won't be able to speak to him or his family. The man who pushed the buzzer turned away and began to return to the mosque.

'But I don't—'

'Wait,' the man commanded, and then turned and disappeared back into the mosque.

Eden hesitated, wondering why she had come, and what she could possibly hope to learn here, when suddenly, in the gloom of the building's foyer, she saw someone, loosely garbed in layers of fabric, descending the stairs. She realized, as the shrouded person approached the door and looked out at her, that it was Aaliya herself. Eden smiled at her in relief.

Aaliya looked puzzled, and did not smile in return.

'Aaliya,' she said. 'I'm Eden. We met at—'

'I know who you are,' Aaliya said gravely. 'Why are you here?'

'I wanted to talk to you,' Eden said. 'And your parents.'

The girl's expression was inscrutable. 'My parents are dead. My aunt and uncle are my guardians.'

'I'm sorry,' said Eden. 'That's right. I had heard that . . . If you could just spare a few minutes . . .'

The girl frowned and hesitated, but finally opened the door. 'Come in,' she said.

Eden entered the building, her nose instantly aware of delicious, spicy scents in the stairwell. She followed Aaliya up the stairs and through the open door of a dimly lit apartment.

The apartment was sparingly and starkly furnished, except for some worn but still colorful rugs overlapping one another on the floor.

Instead of paintings on the cracked walls, there were decals of Islamic calligraphy. The only other decorative elements were several ornately filigreed metal shades which covered the few lights in the gloomy apartment.

A woman's voice called out to Aaliya from the back of the apartment in Arabic, and Aaliya answered, but in English. 'A visitor,' she said. 'My teacher's stepdaughter.' Aaliya turned to Eden and indicated a low cushion. 'Please sit.'

Eden seated herself awkwardly.

'Would you like some tea?' Aaliya asked.

Eden shook her head. 'No, thank you. I went to the mosque first, but the man who . . . met me there . . . sent me here. He said your uncle would be here.'

'He is at the mosque,' said Aaliya. 'But you're not allowed to go in there. Why were you looking for him?'

'I wasn't specifically looking for him. I didn't expect to find you here. I just wanted to ask some questions about the night that my mother died . . .'

At that moment a woman with a deeply lined face wearing a long robe and a headscarf entered the room. She looked suspiciously at Eden.

'Khala,' said Aaliya, 'this is the daughter of my teacher's wife. Her name is Eden.' She turned to Eden. 'This is my aunt, Chandani.'

Eden did not know what the protocol might be, but she bowed her head to the woman, and that seemed to work. The older woman bowed back, unsmiling.

'Why does she come here?' the aunt asked.

158

'She has questions.' Aaliya looked at Eden expectantly.

Eden took a deep breath and plunged ahead. 'The night that my mother died, you were in Toledo at a writers' conference, I understand. With my stepfather.'

'That's right,' said Aaliya.

If her question was a revelation to Aaliya's aunt, the woman did not give any sign. But the police detective had said that Aaliya had had the permission of the imam to go to Toledo.

'The thing is,' said Eden, 'I was wondering if you could say for a certainty that my stepfather was in Toledo all that night.'

Aaliya nodded. 'Yes. I'm certain that he was,' she said.

Eden knew that she was about to tread all over the religious and cultural values of these two women. She hesitated, and wondered if she should. And then she thought of her own mother and Jeremy, and she ignored the sensibilities of her reluctant hosts and forged ahead. 'Was he with you . . . throughout the night?' Eden asked bluntly. 'Is that how you can be so sure?'

Aaliya's eyes widened, and the color drained from her face.

'What is this woman asking you?' Chandani demanded of Aaliya. So far, she had not addressed Eden directly.

'She is asking me if her stepfather and I were . . .' Aaliya hesitated, her pale face suddenly flushed. She murmured something in Arabic.

The older woman turned indignantly on Eden

and glared at her. 'How dare you suggest that of my niece?' Chandani demanded.

Eden refused to be intimidated. 'Aaliya is a beautiful young woman. My stepfather is older, and more experienced. It's the sort of thing that can happen.'

'Maybe in your culture this is normal,' Aaliya's aunt spat out, shaking her head. 'My niece is pure. She is a devout. What you say is an insult,' Chandani insisted. 'You must please leave. You are no longer welcome in my house.'

'Khala, it's all right,' said Aaliya soothingly. She turned to Eden. 'Then the answer to your question has to be no. Absolutely not. We had separate rooms. He walked me to my room after the conference and said goodnight. The next morning, we met for breakfast at a coffee shop and then he drove us back to Cleveland.'

'I'm sorry if I gave offense,' Eden said. 'But if Flynn was not actually in his room that night, I am thinking that he might have returned to Cleveland. He might have somehow . . . had something to do with my mother's death. Now, if he was with you . . .'

Aaliya's large, dark eyes studied Eden's face. 'I understand that you are upset. But what you're insinuating . . . that's not possible.'

'I'm sorry,' said Eden humbly.

'I did call his room about midnight, but there was no answer.'

'He wasn't there?' Eden hardly dared to breathe.

Aaliya shook her head. 'Then I called his cell phone. He answered it and said he was out in a bar. I could hear people and music in the

160

background. I told him that he had insulted me. Unintentionally. But all the same.'

'Did he make a pass at you?' Eden asked.

Aaliya sighed wearily. 'No. It was something else. An assumption he made about me. People who are not religious often do not understand those who are. He presumed that, because the laws and customs of his religion do not matter to him, that I would be equally dismissive of my own. When I complained, he was very apologetic. He said he was on his way back to the hotel. He wanted to come to my room, to talk face to face, but I declined, of course. But he was willing to come and have a discussion. So, he had to have been nearby. Then he asked me to meet him in a public area. I said I would see him in the morning.

'The next day, when we met for breakfast, he seemed quite sober and he apologized to me again. He did not have the demeanor of a man who had driven to Cleveland and back to commit a monstrous crime. This I cannot imagine. He is a man of . . .' Aaliya hesitated, and seemed to grope for the right word. '. . . good intentions. The best of intentions. In this crime against his wife and son, he could not have been involved. It was a tragedy to him. That I can tell you for certain.'

'Okay,' said Eden. She had a feeling that Aaliya was telling her only part of the truth, but she also felt certain that what she had said was the truth as she knew it. 'I'm sorry to have disturbed you.'

Eden bid them goodbye and went to the door.

Aaliya's aunt was on her heels and could not wait to close the door behind her.

Eden parked near her motel room and hurried to get in out of the cold. Her hand trembled as she put the key card in the door. The red light blinked several times. Goddamit, she thought. Do I have to go to the office and have the key remagnetized? She tried it again, more slowly, and this time the green light flashed.

She reached for the doorknob. Suddenly, she was aware of someone behind her. An arm encircled her and twisted the knob under her hand, pushing the door open. Even in the cold winter air she smelled cigarette smoke and the tang of sweat.

Eden cried out, as the man murmured, 'Go in.'

She turned and saw, with a sickening thud in her heart, that it was Flynn Darby. 'What are you doing?' she demanded with more bravado than she felt.

He returned her frightened gaze impassively. 'It's cold out here,' he said. 'Go inside.'

'We weren't supposed to meet here,' Eden insisted, resisting his efforts to direct her through the door and into her room. She looked around. There was not another soul in sight in this section of the suites.

'Plans have changed,' Flynn said. 'I'm here now. And I want to go inside.'

Eden shrank from his touch, and put her key back in her coat pocket. She avoided his gaze as she entered the room, instantly turning on the lights. Flynn followed her closely, and turned to lock the door behind them once they were both in the room.

Eden took her bag and hurried over to the desk near the window. She set her bag on the desk and fished frantically for her phone in the front pocket, extracting it and slipping it into her jacket pocket.

Flynn sat down heavily on the sofa. Eden pulled the chair out from the desk and sat down in it.

'Take your coat off,' he said.

'I'm fine this way,' said Eden.

Flynn shrugged. 'It's warm in here,' he said.

'Not that warm. Look, I haven't really organized my thoughts about the opening of the book, and I really would prefer it if you would call me and not just show up like this,' she said, sounding prim to her own ears.

Flynn leaned forward, rubbing his palms on the ripped knees of his jeans. Then he sat up and twisted his back, first one way and then the other. Finally, he looked directly at Eden. 'Let's talk about what I would prefer,' he said.

Eden's heart was hammering in her chest. She shook her head, but did not reply.

'I would prefer,' he said, 'if you would stay the hell out of my business.'

Eden's heart jumped, but she forced herself to keep her expression composed. 'Really?' she said. 'That's going to be a little difficult since I'm your editor.'

Flynn stared at her. He was disheveled as always. His clothes were rumpled, and his thick, blond hair stood out like a grimy halo around his unshaven face. But his blue eyes were piercing, as if he saw right through her. 'Don't fuck with me,' he said quietly. 'You know what I'm talking about!'

Eden jumped, and angry tears sprang to her eyes. 'I don't,' she insisted. 'Stop threatening me.'

Her exhortation for him to stop threatening seemed to spur Flynn on. He raised his voice. 'You've been asking people questions about me. Things that are none of your business. I know you talked to those insurance dicks. And the police. And Dr Tanaka. And Lizzy. Did I skip anyone?' he cried, red in the face.

Eden stared at him, trying to keep her expression blank. Marguerite, she was thinking. Aaliya. And who was the other woman that Marguerite saw you with? Were you cheating on my mother? Did my mother know it? Was that why she was suicidal?

Suddenly, there was a pounding on the door of the suite. 'Eden,' demanded a man's voice. 'Are you okay in there?'

'She's fine,' Flynn shouted back at the door.

The pounding came again. 'Eden? It's Andy.'

'Who the fuck is Andy?' Flynn demanded.

Eden went to the door and opened it. Her neighbor stood on the doorstep, scowling.

'I thought I heard yelling,' he said. 'Everything okay?'

Eden managed a smile. 'It's okay, Andy. I'm fine.'

Andy stuck his head into the room and saw Flynn sprawled on the sofa. Andy greeted this intruder with a glare. 'Who's he?' he demanded,

164

as if he and Eden had been neighbors all their lives.

'It's a long story,' Eden said. 'He used to be my stepfather.'

'Well he sounds like a bully,' said Andy.

'Mind your own business, Grandpa,' Flynn said.

'Mind your manners,' Andy retorted. 'Are you sure you're okay, Eden?'

'It's all right,' said Eden. 'Thanks for your concern, though.'

Andy shook his head, and shot Flynn another dirty look before retreating.

Eden returned to the living room and sat down in a chair opposite Flynn.

His flashing eyes narrowed, and his contempt for her was written on his face.

He pointed a tobacco-stained finger at her. 'You came here supposedly to work on my book. Instead, you're rummaging around in things that are none of your business.' He shook his head. 'I knew this was a mistake. I should never have agreed to it.'

'To what?'

'To letting you have anything to do with this book.'

'Oh, now you're sorry?' Eden demanded. 'It was your idea to have me work on the book.'

'Not true. I was stupid enough to mention you to Gideon Lendl. After that, it was out of my hands.'

'Good to know,' said Eden coldly.

'Why are you trying to dredge up something the police or the insurance company can hold against me? Your mother committed suicide, and took our son with her. It sounds like you want me to be blamed for that.'

'I don't believe she killed herself,' said Eden.

Flynn looked at her with narrowed eyes. 'She died from carbon monoxide poisoning. Your mother left the car idling in the garage all night. She left a note. What else do you need to make you believe it?'

'She wouldn't have left Jeremy alone in his room,' said Eden defiantly.

'What are you talking about?' he demanded.

'She wouldn't have done that,' said Eden. 'She would have stayed with him. If you knew her so well, you would have realized that.'

Flynn gaped at her. 'That's it? That's your reason?'

'She was my mother. I know that much about her.'

Flynn lifted his chin and stared out past Eden into the dreary little courtyard. Snow flurries had begun, landing gray on the ground. Eden could see that he was thinking, as if he were considering what she had said. Then he shook his head. 'That means nothing. Obviously, she was out of her mind when she did it,' he said dismissively.

'And anybody could have written that note,' Eden persisted. 'Even you.'

Flynn sighed. 'You know, I can see why the insurance company is rooting around, trying to find a way not to have to pay up. But what's in it for you? What the fuck is your problem? A little belated guilt, maybe, that you treated her so bad? Now you're going to come to her rescue?

Now that she's dead? When she was alive you were selfish and rotten to her.'

'You don't know what you're talking about,' said Eden.

'I know that when she called you, you rarely bothered to answer. It used to make her cry,' said Flynn. 'You never cared how much you hurt her. You wanted to hurt her.'

Eden wanted to protest, but it was impossible to contradict him.

'I made her happy,' he insisted.

'Some happiness,' said Eden bitterly.

Flynn glared at her, and then looked away. 'More than you know,' he said.

'Well, if she was so damn happy . . .' said Eden, 'why kill herself?'

Flynn squeezed his hands into fists. Then he shook his head. 'I can't talk to you. When I look at you, I see someone who made her suffer. Who enjoyed making her suffer.'

What about me and my father? Eden wanted to protest. What about our suffering? But she could not force herself to say the words. She wouldn't give him the satisfaction.

Flynn stood up. 'Anyway, I came here for a reason. This little experiment has obviously been a mistake and it's time we called a halt to it. So, here's what I'm going to do. I'm going to call Gideon Lendl and tell him this is not working out. I won't tell them that you're busy going around trying to dig up dirt on my life unless they give me a hard time. I'll tell him I want a new publisher.'

A new publisher. Eden's face flamed, thinking

167

of how angry Maurice DeLaurier would be. How disappointed Rob would be with the loss.

'You could have another editor at DeLaurier if you want,' she offered weakly. 'They really do believe in the book.'

'Nope. A clean break, I think.'

Eden felt sick to her stomach. She would have to endure the humiliation of being rejected by her own author, and take responsibility for the loss to the house of an important book. Hell, she would probably lose her job. They had entrusted her with this opportunity, and she blew it. She knew she should cajole him, plead with him. But there was no way on earth she was going to do that. 'Do what you have to do,' she said, avoiding his gaze.

'I will,' he said coldly.

Before Eden could reply, he was gone.

Sixteen

Eden followed Flynn to the door and slammed it, locking it behind him. Then she crept over to the couch and curled up in the corner, pulling an extra blanket from the hall closet around her. She was shivering from head to toe, though the room was warm. There was a part of her that wanted to cry. And a part of her that refused to. For years she had been working and hoping for this job, and now she was going to lose it. The man who had wrecked her family was now going to wreck her future. For a minute she hoped that he would reconsider. That he wouldn't do it. But he had really left no room for doubt.

She looked around the desolate room. It wasn't as if she liked it here.

In a way, she thought, she would be glad to leave here. She was anxious to see her father again. She could hardly wait to return to New York, her apartment, her job, for however long she would have it, and her friends. The life she understood. She would never, for a minute, miss this dreary town, and all the unhappiness she had encountered here. She set her phone down on the coffee table, expecting it to ring. Realistically, she knew it would take a day or so. Gideon Lendl would try to talk Flynn out of this drastic move. It was the sort of professional tantrum which gave authors a bad reputation. But Flynn would not listen to his agent. Eden felt pretty certain of that. Then there would be conferences between the Lendl agency and DeLaurier Publishing. At the earliest, someone would call her tomorrow. She could be relieved of her job by tomorrow night.

At least you can go back to New York, she told herself, no matter what happens. Get up. Get your stuff packed up. You're leaving this place. She forced herself to her feet. If there was a silver lining, she thought, as she pulled her suitcase out of the closet and opened it on her bed, it was this. She would never have to tell her father that she had come out here to work on Flynn's book. It would no longer be a factor in their lives, and for that reason alone she was glad to have this over with. If she lost her job, and it seemed that she would, she would make up some excuse so that her father would never have to know how it involved Flynn Darby.

She opened the suitcase and began to put a few things into it which she would not need again until she got home. Her gaze fell on the cardboard box of her mother's things which Flynn had pushed onto her the day she was at the house. She hadn't even opened it yet. She needed to open it, and discard anything she didn't really want to bring back with her. No point in paying for extra luggage if she didn't need to. She unfolded the flaps of the box and coughed at the mold and cigarette smoke which seemed to rise in a cloud as she opened it. She hated to even look inside. Putting a hand into the box, to sift through it, she riffled through a haphazard pile of photos and mementoes. Photos of herself as a child. Photos of the three of them when Eden was young. A laminated Mother's Day card which six-year-old Eden had crayoned with stick figures, sunshine and flowers. Square white gift boxes, now stained with age, of jewelry which she and her father had given Tara over the years. Programs from class trips to the aquarium when Tara had chaperoned, and concerts when Eden had sung in the choir.

Flynn had clearly tossed this accumulation into the box without a second glance. She thought about sitting down on the floor and taking out each item. Gazing at it. Making a decision. Then she shook her head. She couldn't possibly do it. Not tonight. She felt slightly nauseous at the thought. This would have to wait until she was back home.

She refolded the flaps of the box and pushed it away from her. If it cost extra to ship it home, so be it. She would take it to a UPS office tomorrow and have them pack it up for her. She would deal with it on some future rainy day.

A sudden knock at the door made her jump. 'Eden, it's Andy again. From next door.'

Relieved, Eden got up, walked to the door and opened it with the chain still on.

'Did your friend leave?' he said.

'He's no friend,' said Eden. 'He's my stepfather. No love lost there . . .'

'I got that impression. Well, at that strip mall down the street there's a Chinese restaurant that's not bad. Do you eat Chinese food?'

'I do. I like Chinese food,' she said.

'Why don't you get your coat on and we'll walk down there and have a bite. If you don't have other plans,' he added politely.

Eden hesitated. She really didn't know this man and wasn't feeling particularly sociable. 'I'm kind of a mess,' she said.

'Doesn't matter. Just some fried rice. And tea. And sympathy.'

Eden smiled, recognizing the name of a film her parents had liked, long ago. *Tea and Sympathy*. She hesitated, and then made up her mind. 'All right. Why not,' she said.

They walked along quickly, spurred on by the cold. It was only about four blocks, but the winds from Lake Erie cut right through Eden's coat.

The restaurant was narrow and three-quarters filled with people. The waiter smiled broadly at his friend, Mistah Andy, as he called him, and promptly brought over a steaming pot of tea. Andy poured. 'The usual, my good man,' he said. 'And the lady will have . . .'

Eden gave her order. The waiter nodded and withdrew.

Andy blew into his hands. 'That chills the bones,' he said.

Eden warmed her hands over the small, steaming cup. 'Kind of wakes you up, walking over here,' she admitted. 'But this feels better.'

Andy nodded. 'There's no Chinese restaurants where I live,' he said. 'But I got a taste for it, being on the road so much. Where we're from the Red Lobster is about as exotic as it gets. But my wife always says Indiana is the best place on earth, and I guess it sort of is.'

'It must be nice to feel that way about the place you live,' said Eden.

Andy nodded. 'Although I have a feeling I'm gonna miss the road when I retire. I'm used to moving around. Trying different things. Meeting new people. Where are you from, Eden?'

'New York,' she said. 'I grew up there.'

'The big city,' Andy said. 'So, you're here because your mother lives here?'

'My mother died here. Not too long ago,' said Eden, and, to her embarrassment, her eyes filled with tears.

'I'm so sorry,' said Andy sincerely.

Eden nodded and dabbed at her eyes with a paper napkin.

'If you don't mind my saying so, that stepfather of yours seems like bad news.'

'Frankly,' said Eden, 'I sometimes think he might be responsible for my mother's death.'

Andy's eyes widened. 'Really? How so?'

Immediately, Eden sensed his keen interest, and felt as if she had said too much to this stranger, no matter how kind a stranger he might be. 'The police don't think so. It's probably just me,' she said vaguely.

'The police!' Andy yelped. 'What happened to your mother?'

Eden shook her head. 'I'm sorry. I just can't talk about it. Suffice it to say that Flynn Darby is someone I really, really dislike.'

'Well, from what little I saw,' said Andy indignantly, 'I'd say you have good reason. If he ever comes by to bother you again, you let me know, okay?'

Eden sniffed, and nodded. 'Thanks. That's very nice of you.' She dabbed at her eyes again. The waiter arrived with mustard sauce, duck sauce and crispy noodles.

'Here, have some of this,' said Andy pleasantly. 'This'll make your eyes water in a good way.'

They chatted amiably through dinner, and split the check. Andy talked most of the time about his family, which Eden found pleasant and reassuring. She told him about her job as a book editor, without mentioning that her job might soon be over, or about Flynn's role in that outcome. Instead, they had a lively discussion of best-sellers. Andy proved to be quite a voracious reader. They compared favorite books and favorite authors, and by the time they walked back through the cold Eden's faith in humanity felt somewhat restored. He said goodnight and left her at her room, after she had checked inside and reassured him that all was well. Eden closed the door behind him, and exhaled. She went and sat down on the couch, and pulled her phone from her purse. She had heard the message signal a few times, but had not wanted to be rude by interrupting their dinner to answer it.

The first message was from her father. 'Eden, it's Dad. How are you doing? Did those insurance people get in touch with you? What did they want? Let me know when you're coming home.'

The second message was from Jasmine, also wondering when she was coming back. 'Vince from the Brisbane has asked me twice.'

Eden felt rather flattered by that nugget of news. Obviously, Vince and Jasmine were not an item. Maybe he was interested in Eden after all. She didn't know too much about him, but she liked what she knew. She liked his looks. She also liked that he had given up the cushy Wall Street life to work hard at his own business. He wasn't afraid to commit himself to a life he cared about. That spoke well for him. She wanted to know more about what made him tick. It seemed as if, perhaps, he felt the same way about her. For the first time in what seemed like ages, Eden felt a little bit hopeful.

Then, she listened to the third message. It was from Flynn. 'I spoke to Gideon Lendl and he put a call in to your boss at DeLaurier. Gideon agreed with me that we were better starting over somewhere else. The less you and I have to do with one another, the better. I can't work with someone who wants to sabotage me. This is the best way. Good luck and all that.'

Eden's face flamed. This is what you get, she thought. You knew better than to take on this project with Flynn Darby involved. Her chest felt like it would explode. He was right about one thing. Nothing would please her more than to sabotage him, in any way that she could. I still have a day or two before my time here runs out. There must be something I can do, she thought, with the time I have left.

Seventeen

The Cuyahoga County coroner's office was located in a huge government building with a dreary, uninviting façade. After breakfast, Eden had programmed its address into her GPS and driven over to it. She parked in the visitor's parking of the official lot and hurried, gripping her coat shut against the wind, into the vestibule. She asked at the information desk and was directed to the coroner's office at the rear of the building. All the way down the bustling corridors, she rehearsed a convincing argument for why she should be allowed to have a copy of the autopsy. Last night she had imagined several scenarios of resistance and persuasion, reminding herself not

175

to act indignant, except as a last resort. She knew that it would be nearly impossible for her to walk away with a report which the police didn't even have yet. But she had decided that as long as she was still here, she had to at least try.

The door to the coroner's office was ajar, and she walked in. A number of clerks were busy at their computers. She walked up to the chest-high counter which separated the people working there from the general public. No one looked up as she entered. Eden felt discouraged immediately.

A young black woman, her hair fashioned into elaborate cornrows, wearing glasses and a tight leather skirt, pushed away from her desk and got up. She walked over to where Eden was standing.

'Can I help you?' she drawled, as if helping someone were the last thing she wanted to do.

Eden forced herself to smile. 'Hello. My name is Eden Radley and I was wondering if I could obtain a copy of my mother and half-brother's autopsy report. They died about a month ago. I went to the police and they said they hadn't received the reports yet. The detective I spoke to said there's a real backlog and that it probably isn't finished, but I thought if I came over here maybe I could find out how long . . .'

The woman pushed a form across the counter to Eden. 'Fill this out,' she said.

Eden recognized the brush-off. Jump through a hoop, fill out a form. Get nowhere. In the end, after much bureaucratic flummery, she was pretty sure she would walk out as empty-handed as she arrived. But she was here to go through the motions. She filled out the questions on the form.

They were surprisingly few. She pushed the form back at the woman behind the counter.

'Photo ID,' drawled the clerk.

Eden rummaged in her pocketbook and produced her New York driver's license.

The woman looked at it impassively, and then picked up the filled-out form and glanced at it. She set it down and began to enter information into the computer on the desk below the counter.

'Do you actually let the public have copies of these reports when they're finished?' Eden asked.

The woman stared at the screen. 'Not the public. Immediate family,' she said.

'Really? Well, that's me,' said Eden.

The woman did not reply. She pressed several keys and then typed in some information. 'We have it,' she said.

Eden stared at the woman's bent head, the intricate, gorgeous cornrows. She could hardly believe her ears. 'You have it? But the police don't even have it yet.'

The woman looked up at Eden, expressionless. 'You want it or not?'

'Yes, absolutely. I want it,' said Eden.

The young woman ambled over to one of the printers along the wall, her back to Eden, and set the copier in motion. She gathered up a sheaf of papers and stuffed them into an official envelope from the coroner's office. She came back to where Eden was waiting, and handed it across the counter to her. 'Two fifty,' she said, pushing her glasses back up on the bridge of her nose.

Eden shook her head. 'Is that the code for this kind of report?' she asked.

'Two fifty,' the woman repeated irritably. 'That's what you owe.'

'Two hundred . . .?'

The woman shifted her weight from one hip to the other. 'Two dollars and fifty cents. And I got no change,' she said.

Eden asked no more questions. She rummaged in her purse and came up with the exact sum. The woman took it without comment and put it into a drawer.

Eden took the envelope, filled with wonder. 'This is really it?' she asked.

'No pictures,' warned the clerk. 'That's extra. And you can't get that today. That's a whole 'nother procedure.'

'I don't need pictures. Thank you so much.'

The woman smiled slightly, as if pleased with herself. 'S'all right,' she said, and sat back down at her desk, as Eden clutched the envelope and headed for the door.

The moment she left the coroner's office Eden got on her phone and called the police station. She asked the dispatcher if she could speak to Detective Burt. After what seemed like an interminable delay, the dispatcher told Eden that he could not be reached.

'Do you know where he went?' Eden asked.

'No, ma'am,' said the dispatcher. 'I do not.'

'I need to talk to him,' Eden insisted.

'Is this an emergency?' the dispatcher asked.

'It's about my mother's autopsy report,' said Eden.

'I'll take your name and number, and he'll get back to you.'

'Please tell him it's important,' said Eden, trying to convey a sense of urgency.

'I'll tell him,' the dispatcher said in a disinterested tone.

Eden ended the call, frowning. She opened the envelope and looked at the papers therein. There was no point in trying to read it. She knew it would make no sense to her. She had planned to bring it to Detective Burt and question him about it. But when she thought about it, maybe it was lucky that he wasn't there to receive it. He had already made his mind up. She needed the help of someone with an open mind. And scientific expertise.

She thought about Dr Tanaka, suggesting that they might be missing some information about Tara's death. Telling her that she should pursue it. Who better to ask? He already seemed suspicious of the official verdict. Dr Tanaka would be able to see any medical irregularities, even if forensic science wasn't his specialty. She drove directly to the clinic, and made her way up to Tanaka's office. The sympathetic young woman at reception from her previous visit was still there.

Eden could barely contain her agitation as she waited while a mother made another appointment for her son, and the two discussed the weather and the weekend. Finally, the woman pushed her son out the door in his wheelchair, and Eden had access to the receptionist.

'I'd like to see Dr Tanaka, again. I'm Eden Radley.'

The woman nodded. 'Oh yes. I remember you.'

'Can I see him? I know how terribly busy he is, but—'

'I'm afraid not. He's—'

'Just to give him something. I need his opinion—'

'Dr Tanaka is not here. He went to a conference in Seattle. He won't be back for a week.'

The news landed with a thud in Eden's stomach.

'Can I make you an appointment for when he returns, Ms Radley?' she asked.

'No,' said Eden, shaking her head. 'No. I'll be gone by then.'

The receptionist shrugged and then tilted her chin, indicating that Eden should move out of the way. She smiled at the woman who was waiting patiently behind Eden.

Eden left the office and walked numbly down the hall. She hadn't thought of that. Gone for a week. She would be back in New York by then. She took the elevator down to the first floor, and then sat down on a leather bench in the big, glass, plant-filled atrium.

Another dead end. She didn't know what to do next. She had this report, but it was meaningless to her. And, in fact, probably didn't say anything that the police didn't already know. Hadn't Detective Burt said that the coroner called and gave him his findings over the phone? What could be in here that would make any difference at all? She took the report out of the manila envelope and looked it over. It was actually two reports, one for her mother, and one for Jeremy. There were pages of test results and paragraphs of medical jargon, but the cause of death was clearly stated. Death from asphyxiation due to carbon monoxide poisoning. She stared at the words until they blurred in front of her eyes. What am I doing here? Disliking Flynn is one thing. But I am trying to implicate him in a murder that is not a murder. And why? Just because her mother had lain down on her own bed to die? It was hardly what one might call evidence. It was a perfectly normal thing for a person to do, and there could be any number of possible reasons for it. Her mother must have been despondent, and despondent people often do not act rationally.

She felt suddenly as if she had been alone too long. She was still in mourning, after all, and she was living in some second-rate hotel in a city where she knew no one. A city where her mother had died. Eden felt suddenly deflated and sorry for herself. She folded over the report and was about to stuff it back in the envelope.

A voice behind her said, 'You look like you're having a bad day.'

Eden turned around, startled, and looked up. It took her a moment to recognize him, wearing his parka over his lab coat. He looked somehow older and more grim in the face than he had when Eden met him, but the doctor speaking to her was DeShaun Jacquez, Lizzy's husband. 'Hi,' she said. 'I didn't expect to see you here.'

'I work here,' he said with a shrug. 'You're Eden, right? You left that message for Lizzy.'

'Yes, I saw your wife a couple of nights ago at her folks',' she said. 'I'm sure she told you.'

'Oh yeah,' said DeShaun dismissively. 'Were you just in Tanaka's office? Is that about your

181

brother?' he asked, nodding toward the manila envelope.

Eden peered up at him. DeShaun Jacquez might only be an intern, but he was a doctor. It was worth a try. 'No,' she said. 'Actually. Do you have a minute?'

DeShaun grimaced and looked around. 'I'm on my break. I just went out to get this.' He was holding a brown bag from Starbucks. 'What is it?'

'Here, sit,' said Eden, moving over on the leather bench. DeShaun sat down beside her. 'Have your coffee.'

'I will,' he said. He took the latte cup out of the bag, and tossed the bag in a nearby trash can. Then he took off the lid and blew across the top. 'They have coffee in our break room, but it tastes like motor oil.'

'I understand,' she said. 'I'm so glad I ran into you. Look. This is a little bit delicate. What I have here are the autopsy reports for my mother and my half-brother. As you know, the police said my mother committed suicide. But the people who insured my mother's life have received a . . . tip . . . that my mother's death was not a suicide.'

DeShaun looked at her with raised eyebrows. 'Really?' he said. 'A tip from whom?'

'They didn't say. They don't know.'

DeShaun frowned. 'Wow. That's kind of . . . sick.'

Eden nodded. 'The cops told me to disregard it. That the insurance company just didn't want to pay out on my mother's policy. And maybe that's all it is. But I found out that no one had an autopsy report for either my mother or Jeremy. Not the cops. Not the insurance people. That kind of got me angry, and I decided to go down to the coroner's office and raise some hell. But when I got there . . . well, all I had to do was ask for it. And pay two dollars fifty. I walked out with both reports. The problem is, I don't know what the hell the reports say.'

DeShaun listened thoughtfully. 'Who's the beneficiary?' he asked. 'On the insurance policy.'

'Flynn, of course,' she said.

DeShaun sipped his coffee, his eyes narrowed. 'So, they won't pay it out to Flynn. Because they think their deaths might have something to do with him.'

Eden put a hand on the arm of his down coat. 'Yes, I think that's what it means. But please do not say that to anyone. I mean, anyone.'

'You mean Lizzy,' he said.

'I mean anyone,' said Eden grimly.

'Don't worry. There's no talking to Lizzy on the subject of Flynn. She thinks he's some kind of literary genius. And now, a tragic hero as well,' he said sarcastically.

'He must have told her about his book,' said Eden. 'He wrote a book about his life with my mother.'

'Well, I'm not surprised. He was always glad to talk about his favorite subject. Himself,' said DeShaun.

'You're not keen on him, I see.'

DeShaun shrugged. 'Let's just say I'm not impressed. But I don't really know the guy. It's

183

Lizzy who was involved with the family. She's very tender-hearted, though. She always thinks the best of everybody.'

Eden nodded. 'But you don't like him.'

'He strikes me as kind of a blowhard,' said DeShaun.

'Oh, he's definitely that. I'm just wondering if he's something . . . much worse,' said Eden.

DeShaun carefully rolled his paper coffee cup between his hands. 'I'll take a look at those if you like,' he said.

Eden looked at him hopefully. 'You would?'

'I can't look at them right now,' he said. 'I'm on duty. But I'll look at them tonight.'

'I'm probably going to be leaving town soon,' said Eden, still holding the envelope.

'I'll get back to you tonight,' he said. 'I must admit, you've got me curious.'

She scribbled something on the envelope and handed it to him. 'That's my number,' she said. 'Call me when you've had a chance to look it over.'

DeShaun tucked the envelope into his backpack. Then he stood up.

'Thank you so much,' said Eden.

DeShaun looked at her with a flinty gleam in his eye. 'Anything I can do to help you,' he said.

Eighteen

The call from Eden's boss, Rob Newsome, came not long after Eden had returned to her room.

She could tell from the tone of his voice that the news was not good. But she had guessed that already. In the age of emails and text messaging, some news could not be delivered electronically.

'Eden,' he said.

'Hi, Rob.'

'We got a call today from Gideon Lendl.'

'I know,' said Eden.

'You know?' Rob asked.

'Flynn told me yesterday that he wanted to get a new editor for his book. He said that he had called his agent about it.'

Eden could tell that Rob was relieved not to have to explain everything. 'We tried to reason with him. We offered Lendl a new editor if Darby was absolutely certain he couldn't make this work with you. According to Lendl, his client wouldn't hear of it. He wants a clean break. He's going to return the advance.'

'Well, he won't need money anymore,' said Eden bitterly, thinking of her mother's insurance policy.

'Excuse me?' said Rob.

'Nothing,' said Eden. 'I was just thinking out loud.'

'What the hell happened with you two?' Rob demanded.

'I guess I should have realized that it wouldn't work,' Eden admitted. 'Too much history between us.'

'It sounded as if your author was being incredibly stubborn,' said Rob.

Eden was grateful for what almost sounded like support from her editorial director. 'He's not been easy to work with,' she said. 'But that was my job. To work it out with him. I'm afraid I wasn't able to.'

Rob sighed. 'You know you have to be very diplomatic in this job.'

'I know that,' said Eden patiently. 'But everything I said rubbed him the wrong way. I'm really sorry about this.'

There was a silence on Rob's end of the phone. 'It's very unfortunate,' he said.

'I know,' said Eden. 'Does this mean . . . I mean, I'm concerned about my future at DeLaurier.'

Rob sighed again. 'That's not up to me. I'm gonna plead your case with Maurice. I'll emphasize the complexity of the whole thing. Going in, we knew about your prior strained relationship. And this idea came from their side of the net. I hope to be able to put your situation in a better light.'

'I'm sorry to put you in that position,' said Eden.

After a short silence he said, 'I don't know what Maurice is going to do, but you might need to consider the possibility of . . .'

'Of what?' Eden asked.

'I'm not trying to tell you what to do, Eden. But let me just say this to you. In this business people do move around a lot. If you resign to look elsewhere, no one would find that odd.'

'You think I should quit my job?' she cried.

'I'm talking about a preemptive strike. You could leave with good references and possibly even improve your position. People move from one house to another all the time. Sometimes it's to their advantage.'

'In other words, quit before I'm fired.'

'I did not say that,' he protested.

'Oh, be honest, Rob. Publishing in New York is like a small town. This will create a little scandal. Everyone in the business will know what happened.'

'More publicity for Flynn Darby,' said Ron grimly.

'It's not fair. No other house will want me,' said Eden. She was glad they weren't Skyping. He would have seen her face, and she knew that her eyes were red and wet with tears of frustration.

Rob was in no mood to be reassuring. 'I'll talk to Maurice tomorrow morning. I'll let you know what he says.'

'Thanks for the warning,' said Eden.

Rob did not reply. They ended the call.

An hour later, Eden was still sitting in her chair, staring out blankly at the desolate courtyard, contemplating her imminent unemployment, when her phone rang. She did not recognize the number, but she answered it anyway.

'Hey,' said a gruff voice. 'This is Steve.'

Steve who? Eden thought. 'Steve?'

'From the motel. Put me on FaceTime.'

'Oh, Steve,' said Eden, amazed to have a return call from the desk clerk in Toledo.

'Yeah, I got somebody here wants to speak to you. Put me on FaceTime.'

'Okay,' said Eden. 'Give me a minute.' In no time, she was looking at the sallow face of Steve, peering out from the screen of her iPad.

'Oh, hi there,' he said, as if Eden was the one who had placed the call.

'Is this about my stepfather?' Eden asked. 'Do you know something?'

Steve glanced away from the screen and nodded. 'Maybe,' he said. 'You see, I just got to thinkin'. Maybe he had company while he was here.'

'Company?'

'There's a lot of gals who work the corners around here.'

It took Eden a minute to understand. 'You mean, hookers?' she asked.

Steve nodded.

Eden frowned. 'No. I can't imagine that.'

'Why? 'Cause he's good-lookin'? 'Cause he's married?'

Eden understood what he was saying. 'I guess that's naive, isn't it?'

'Pretty much,' he said. He looked up and gestured to someone on the other side of the camera. 'Talk to her,' he said.

A woman wearing a pink fur bomber jacket, her dyed blond hair a messy haystack, walked directly up behind Steve's chair. She bent over and waved at the screen. Eden could see substantial cleavage at this close distance, as well as layers of make-up and fake eyelashes. She was fortyish. She might once have been pretty.

'This is Cassie,' Steve said as he gave up his chair to the blond. The blond woman gave Eden a nod.

'Steve showed me the picture you sent him on his phone. I showed it around to the other girls. One of my girls recognized him. She's outside. Do you want to talk to her?'

'Do I . . .? Yes,' said Eden. 'Yes. Absolutely.'

'Okay. Now that you're on the line, I'm gonna go get her.'

Eden felt her heart pounding. 'All right. If you don't mind.'

'I'll be back,' said Cassie. She stood up, taking the phone with her out of the frame.

'Don't go far,' said Steve to Cassie. 'That's my phone you got there.'

Cassie's response was unintelligible.

'And hurry up about it,' said Steve. 'I can't spend all day and night doing this.'

Steve looked back at Eden almost bashfully. For a moment, they were both at a loss as to what to say.

'I just want to thank you,' said Eden. 'For calling me back. Frankly, I didn't expect this.'

Steve grimaced as if she had insulted him. 'I wasn't doing nothing else,' he said, eager to deny his chivalry.

'I have to ask. Why did you call me back?' she asked. 'I mean, you didn't have to.'

Steve looked up from the iPad. 'I got a customer,' he said. He stood up and began speaking to the person who was checking in. Eden could hear their voices, but not what they were saying.

She waited patiently. In spite of herself, she thought about her mother and how, when she was young, Tara used to delight in every story Eden brought home from school. She would always respond with such enthusiasm, wanting more details. Eden hadn't allowed herself to think about that side of her relationship with Tara in years.

But now the memories came, unbidden. It was impossible not to miss her mother when she remembered those afternoons. For so long, anger at Tara was the only emotion she would allow herself to feel. But something had changed on this journey. And this video conference with a prostitute, Eden realized, was the kind of story Tara would have relished.

Steve sat back down in front of the computer and cleared his throat. 'She ain't back yet,' he said.

'I can wait,' said Eden.

'I guess the thing was, I kept thinking about you saying how your mother wouldn't'a killed her own kid. Even if she was down. Made me think about my ma. She wouldn't'a done that either.'

'That was why you called me back?' Eden asked.

'I kept thinking about it,' he said.

'Well, thank you,' Eden whispered. It is important, she thought to herself. This man knew it. She knew it.

'Oh Lord,' Steve complained cheerfully. 'Here they come.'

Eden felt her heart suddenly thudding.

Cassie and a young girl with brown skin and long, dyed-red hair, her cleavage visible between the snaps of her jean jacket, crowded in behind Steve. 'This is Marsha,' Cassie said into the screen.

Marsha wagged black painted fingernails. 'Hi,' she said smiling, showing her gray, meth-ruined teeth.

Cassie looked at Eden over Marsha's shoulder. 'He hired her,' she said.

Eden stared.

'Tell her,' said Cassie.

'Let me get out of the way,' said Steve, ceding the chair to Marsha.

Marsha tossed her hair and then pulled long strands nervously between her shiny black fingernails. 'He told me he was a writer,' she said, snapping her gum. 'He was cute. He was like a motorcycle guy but also like a little lost boy.'

'That sounds like him,' said Eden, shuddering. 'Do you remember what time you were with him?'

'Oh, I wasn't with him. He hired me for the girl,' said Marsha, smiling.

'The girl?'

'Yeah, the raghead girl.'

'Aaliya?' Eden could barely disguise her shock.

The young hooker shrugged. 'I'm not sure. She didn't want me to know her name. The guy was her teacher. He told me she wrote a story for his class and that was how he knew that she was into girls. He said she had zero experience.' Marsha lifted her hair and tossed it. 'He got that right. She was scared as a rabbit.'

Eden shook her head. 'She didn't know you were . . . coming . . .?'

'Nope. I told her that he hired me as a present for her. I tried to get her to take a drink to loosen up, but she wouldn't drink. You know. Against her religion.'

Eden shook her head. 'I can't believe this.'

191

Marsha looked at the computer slyly. 'I tried every trick to get her to relax, to give him his money's worth, but she wasn't having any of it.'

'And what did Flynn want out of this?' Eden demanded. 'To watch?'

Marsha shook her head. 'Nah. He wasn't into the kink. I think he was just trying to help her out. I don't know. He had his own room, he said. He paid me and then he left. Left me with her.'

Flynn was being helpful, Eden thought doubtfully. What had Aaliya said? He had good . . . intentions. Maybe so, but Eden was busy calculating. Flynn could have been at a bar in Cleveland at midnight when Aaliya called him to complain about sending a prostitute to her room. He could already have been to the house, sedated Tara and Jeremy, and the car on in the garage to run all night. Aaliya was his alibi, but he had a plan to make sure that she was otherwise engaged. Engaged in something that she would rather die than admit, if it came to that. He could easily have made the drive to Cleveland and back.

'You didn't see him again.'

Marsha shook her head, examining the ends of a hank of her lifeless hair.

She looked up at Cassie with imploring eyes. 'Can I go now?'

'Sure,' Cassie said to the younger girl.

Marsha jumped up from the seat like a schoolgirl who had just completed an oral pop quiz. Steve sat back down.

'Thanks, Cassie,' he said to the woman who had left the frame.

'No problem,' she called back.

192

'Told ya she'd know,' said Steve.

'You were right,' said Eden, trying to absorb what she had just heard. Flynn was not having an affair with Aaliya. Not at all. He had hired a prostitute to introduce his bashful, religious intern to sex with another woman. Aaliya had spurned the prostitute's advances, but she had given him an alibi from which she could never retreat. How to explain this to her family?

'Looks like the bastard didn't do it after all. He was just doing that girl a solid. You know. Trying to give her a little taste of life. Them ragheads keep those girls under lock and key.'

Eden looked at him in disbelief. 'A taste of life?' she said.

'So it must have been an accident,' said Steve, trying to cross the Ts and dot the Is of this mysterious death.

'I don't think so,' said Eden.

'What do you mean?' he asked. 'You wanted proof that he was here. You got your proof.'

'I've got something,' she admitted.

'Well, that's all the information I got,' he said, sounding slightly offended.

Eden was immediately reminded that he had gone out of his way for her sake. 'I really appreciate your calling me,' she said. 'I can't tell you how much.'

'That's all right. Hey, you bitches,' Steve growled good-naturedly, 'get back here with my phone!'

Eden heard shrieks of laughter, and then the screen went black.

Nineteen

After the abrupt end of her Skyping with the denizens of the Stella Motel, Eden sat back, more confused than ever by what she had learned. That alibi of Flynn's was no alibi at all. In a gesture that was both wildly inappropriate and possibly calculated, he had tried to make sure that Aaliya would never tell what had gone on at the Stella Motel. He was not seducing his student. Perhaps he had a larger plan for her. To use her vulnerabilities against her. Of course, he had not bargained for the fact that Aaliya took her religion seriously and would not succumb.

Eden pushed away the iPad, folded her arms on the table and put her head down on them. But how could she prove it? As much as she wanted to build some kind of case against Flynn, she was never going to get Aaliya to admit what had happened to the police. If her aunt and uncle found out, they would probably forbid her to go back to college. Eden couldn't imagine herself putting the girl in such a terrible position.

I can't wait to leave this place, she thought. She sat up, pulled the iPad toward her and began to check on flights home. Tomorrow, she thought. Even if it costs more to book it at the last minute, I'm ready to go. She had just about finished her arrangements when the phone rang.

194

She looked at the screen and saw that it was DeShaun Jacquez. This was probably about the autopsy. What does it matter now? she thought. The police version was going to stand. Murder/suicide. She answered the call, prepared to thank DeShaun for taking the time to look at the report, and put an end to it.

'Eden,' he said.

'Hi, DeShaun.'

'Eden. I was wondering if you could come over to the hospital. I wanted to talk to you and I don't get off of my shift until after ten.'

'Is this about the autopsy?' she said. 'Because I've kind of . . . changed my mind about pursuing this. I mean, I'm really very, very grateful that you looked it over for me . . .'

'Look, um, I'm on the fourth floor, in pediatrics. Can you come over here now?' he asked. 'It's important.'

Eden sighed. The night was closing in. Tomorrow, she would be on her way to the airport and out of this place. But she really owed it to DeShaun, after he had spent his precious time and expertise on the report, to at least go over there and speak to him about it. 'Okay,' she said. 'I'll be over shortly.'

It was rush hour, and the traffic was terrible. A light rain had begun to fall, and it was threatening to freeze on the highways. Eden wished she had never agreed to this, but once she was en route, · it seemed stupid to backtrack. It was nearly six when she finally reached the hospital. The lobby was quite a bit quieter than it had been during the day. She got into the elevator and pushed the button for the fourth floor.

The pediatrics wing was gaily decorated with fluffy stuffed animals and balloons painted on the walls. But nothing could dispel the anxiety which was palpable in the air. What could be worse, Eden thought, than to have a child so sick that they ended up in this cutting-edge medical facility? For a moment, she thought of her mother, coming here with Jeremy, over and over again. Knowing that he would never get better. Hoping against hope. I should have tried to be a help to her, Eden thought, and, for once, there was no querulous answering argument in her mind. She should have tried, and she knew it. Being in this place had, at least, made that clear to her. It was an uncomfortable truth, but strangely, it was soothing. She accepted the responsibility for her mistake. File under an extreme case of 'live and learn', she thought.

She walked up to the nurse at the desk. 'I'm looking for Dr Jacquez,' she said.

'I can page him for you,' said the woman. 'Sit over there.'

Eden did as she was told, and tried not to glance into any rooms and stare at the tiny patients, or their suffering parents. Just then DeShaun strode up to where she sat. His dark skin made an appealing contrast with his lab coat. With his glasses and stethoscope, he might have been a guy from a hospital drama on television.

'Eden, hi,' he said. He gestured behind him with a manila file he was holding. 'Could you come in here with me?'

'Sure,' said Eden, following him down the spotless hallway. He moved quickly, and she had to rush to keep up with him. Halfway down the corridor he pushed open a door and glanced inside. Then he gestured to her.

'In here,' he said. 'We can have some privacy.'

Eden followed him into the small, private lounge and sat down. She noticed there were religious tracts on the table, and boxes of Kleenex. DeShaun sat down opposite her and riffled through the file in his hand.

'That's it?' Eden asked. 'The autopsy?'

DeShaun nodded and flipped through the pages. Then he frowned, and handed them and their envelope back to Eden.

She carefully put them back in the envelope and looked up at DeShaun. She might as well ask, she thought. 'Anything odd about this? Anything out of the ordinary?' she asked.

'For the most part, it's what you already know. They both died of carbon monoxide poisoning. Their tox screens came back positive for benzodiazepines in their systems.'

Eden shook her head.

'Drugs for anxiety. Barbiturates.'

'Yes, I did know that,' said Eden, disappointed in spite of herself. 'The detective mentioned it to me. They assumed my mother gave them to Jeremy so he wouldn't be aware of what was happening. And probably wanted to numb herself to it as well. Just fall asleep and not wake up. Detective Burt said they found a prescription bottle.'

'Yes, he was right about that,' said DeShaun. 'I don't see anything suspicious about it.'

Eden nodded. How could she tell him that she had based all her suspicions on the fact that Tara had not met her death with Jeremy by her side? What kind of evidence was that? It was speculation based on pure emotion. 'Well, I appreciate you taking the time . . .' she said.

'If you could just sit down for a minute,' he said, 'there is information in this report which is quite significant.'

Eden looked at him, surprised. She resumed her seat. 'What information?'

'Also in your mother's tox screen,' he said.

'What about it?'

'She tested positive for cholinesterase inhibitors.'

Eden frowned. 'Translation,' she said.

DeShaun winced, as if something were paining him. 'They gave you the report, so obviously you are entitled to know its contents,' he said, as if he were trying to convince himself.

'Okay. Tell me what,' Eden asked anxiously.

'Your mother was taking a drug called Aricept.'

'I've heard of that,' said Eden, trying to think why. The name was familiar as one of many drugs advertised on television.

'It's a drug that is prescribed for dementia. For Alzheimer's disease.'

Eden looked at him in amazement. 'What? No, there must be some mistake. She wasn't even fifty years old.'

DeShaun looked at her gravely. 'I'm afraid there's no doubt. Obviously, it was extremely early onset. Just a devastating diagnosis.'

'Oh my God,' said Eden. She fell back against the chair as if he had punched her in the chest.

'This may explain why Tara would have taken her life,' he said. 'That's a very grim future to face.'

'That's true. Oh God.'

'I'm sure her physician informed her of what the future held. She would become completely helpless in a short time. When the disease begins at this age, its progress can be very, very rapid.'

Suddenly, Eden felt almost sick with sorrow for her mother, who had been forced to face such a horrible fate. But why didn't she tell anyone? 'I wonder if Flynn knew . . . I wonder who knew about it?' Even as she said it, she realized that she had not known. Tara had not told her only daughter.

'Well, the doctor who prescribed the Aricept knew, for one. I did a little asking around. Your mother was diagnosed by Dr Shaw. She's an expert in this field. Her offices are right here in this hospital.'

'Yeah. That makes sense,' said Eden absently.

'I'm not sure how much Dr Shaw can reveal to you about your mother's case, because of HIPPA. You know, the medical privacy regulations.'

'But my mother is dead,' said Eden. 'Why in the world should privacy regulations apply now?'

DeShaun shrugged. 'I know it seems strange, but that's the law. That information is still considered confidential between doctor and patient, until fifty years after a person's death. But you can inquire. There are exceptions. Probably she will make an exception for you, since you're her daughter.'

Eden was distracted, and shaken by the news. 'Oh. Okay . . . Although I guess it doesn't really matter now. It does go a long way to explain . . . Oh my God.'

'What?' he asked.

Eden looked at him. 'This sounds terrible . . .' she said.

DeShaun shrugged. 'Shoot.'

Eden shook her head. 'I don't remember ever hearing about anyone in the family . . . But . . . This sounds so selfish, but, is this type of early onset Alzheimer's . . . is it hereditary?'

DeShaun shook his head. 'No. Not as far as we know. The cause of Alzheimer's is unknown, but the only identifiable risk factor is old age.'

'So it's not genetic,' said Eden.

'Well, if your identical twin had it, you'd be twenty-five per cent more likely to inherit it than the average person.'

'But I don't have an identical twin.'

'Exactly,' he said. 'Otherwise, there's no genetic risk.'

'That's a relief,' she said, exhaling.

'That's not to say that you shouldn't stay aware . . .'

'Oh, I'll always be aware,' said Eden. 'My God. My poor mother . . .'

She shook her head and suddenly she was woozy. She began to see spots before her eyes. DeShaun seemed to recognize this, and jumped up from his chair. 'Put your head between your knees,' he said.

Lightheaded and nauseous, Eden did as she was told.

DeShaun put a comforting hand on her back. 'Take deep breaths,' he said.

Eden nodded, and tried to follow his instructions. At first she thought she was going to throw up on the floor of the little lounge, but gradually, her stomach quieted and her head cleared. She sat back up.

'Better?' he said. He poured a cup of water and handed it to her.

Eden sipped the cup and nodded.

'Do you want me to call Lizzy? She could come over and get you. I know she'd be glad to. Maybe you shouldn't be driving.'

'I'm fine,' said Eden. 'Really. I'll be okay. I just need a minute.'

A nurse appeared at the doorway of the little lounge and grimaced apologetically. 'Dr Jacquez. They need you in post-op.'

'Okay, I'm coming,' he said.

The nurse backed out of the room.

'I have to be getting back to work,' he said, standing up. 'I'm sorry, Eden. I know this wasn't what you wanted to hear.'

'I wanted the truth,' she said.

'Well, I guess it pretty much answers the question,' he said grimly, 'about why your mother might have done what she did.'

'Absolutely,' Eden whispered.

'I always think it's better to know,' he said.

Eden nodded, but could not meet his gaze as she rose from the chair and groped her way, almost blindly, toward the door.

Twenty

Eden left the hospital in a daze, managed to find her rental car, and got inside. She turned on the engine but did not move. She imagined her mother, facing a future in which she would not even be able to care for herself, much less her disabled child. Eden thought about all the times she had wished her mother ill. For the first time, perhaps since Tara had walked out on them, she wished she could take it all back. She was sorry for her lack of forgiveness.

Maybe while she was at it, she thought, she needed to look at Flynn in a new way as well. He must have known about Tara's diagnosis. How much had he suffered? His wife was going to become helpless and demented, and his son needed constant care and would die anyway. He must have wondered why so much misery had been visited on him.

She recalled him telling her that she did not know everything there was to know about Tara's suicide. Was this diagnosis of dementia what he was obliquely referring to? If it was, why not just say so? Why not tell the insurance company, so that they would end their investigation and stop hounding him? Why not tell the police? The proof of Tara's condition was readily available. And anyone could understand why a woman with this laundry list of dreadful problems might want to end it all. She was already stretched thin by caring for Jeremy. Once the Alzheimer's took over her brain, she would be unable to do anything for him. Or even be certain that anyone else was caring for him.

Now it makes sense, Eden thought.

Except for that one puzzling, inexplicable fact. Tara had gone to another room and left her son to die alone. It always came back to that question. No one else seemed bothered by it.

And then, suddenly, a simple answer occurred to her.

Tara and Flynn had faced this crisis together. Surely they talked it over and considered all the terrible options. Perhaps Tara had told him that she wished she could end her life. But Tara would never have chosen to leave Jeremy alone, just as Eden surmised. Not in life. Not at the moment of death. So it couldn't have been Tara who carried out this plan. Someone else had to do it. That was Flynn. But maybe it had nothing to do with an insurance windfall, or another woman, or any other selfish scenario. Maybe it was the desperate act of a loving husband.

Eden leaned her forehead against the steering wheel and closed her eyes.

She knew that in the eyes of the law, his motive was not an issue. If he hastened their deaths, it was a crime. No matter what the circumstances, if Flynn was guilty, he had to pay the price. It was the only right thing. He should not inherit that insurance money and live a life of comfort and privilege. He should go to jail for what he did.

She knew what the law said. But was the law right?

One of Tara's last acts on earth was to call Eden. What had she wanted? Because of her own stubborn, righteous anger, Eden would never know. All she would ever know for sure was that she turned her back on her mother at the fatal hour. She had turned away and left her mother's plea unanswered. In this tragedy, she thought, who was really to blame?

Eden needed time to think. She drove back to the motel and let herself in to the garden suite. She turned on a few lights and went into the bedroom. She crawled onto the bed and pulled a blanket over herself. She was shivering, despite sufficient heat in the room. For several hours she lay there, going over it all in her mind. At some point there was a knock at the door, and she heard Andy's voice call out to her. 'Eden? It's Andy.'

'I'm not feeling well,' she called out.

'Can I get you anything?' he asked.

'No,' she said. 'I just need to sleep.'

Andy was quiet for a minute. Then he said, 'Okay. Feel better.'

After her neighbor had left the door, Eden thought about him, and his home in Indiana. A good man. A devoted husband and father. What would you do, Andy? she wondered. If it were your wife and child, faced with those insurmountable problems? What would anybody do?

Eden replayed it all, again and again, in her mind. Be honest with yourself, she thought. You were no help to your mother. You were too angry to have sacrificed for her. You weren't interested in their problems. You would have left them to suffer. Flynn loved them enough to risk carrying out her wishes.

Nonetheless, she reminded herself, Flynn had no right to seal their fates for them. Maybe a jury would be kind to him, and understand the position he was in. Maybe he would not even go to jail.

She flopped from her back to her front, as if she was being jabbed with a stick. She looked at another aspect of the situation. If there were an investigation Aaliya's secret would come out. Flynn's well-meaning but horrible plan to introduce her to the pleasures of lesbian sex would be exposed for all to see, and Aaliya's world would be torn apart.

Not my problem. Those are the breaks, Eden told herself without conviction. But she felt sick at the thought of that young woman inadvertently becoming a target. Eden flopped over again.

Finally, at nearly midnight, she made up her mind. She got up from the bed and went to the bathroom. Examining herself in the garish light above the mirror, she reapplied a little make-up. She could hear the rain pelting the windows of the hotel suite. It was a nasty night out. She couldn't let that stop her. Eden put on her coat, put up her collar and left the hotel, hurrying to avoid the sleeting rain, and let herself into her car.

Eden drove to Flynn's house and parked along the curb behind a line of other cars. Everyone in the neighborhood seemed to be home for the night. There were still lights on in the blue house, so it was clear that he was there, and awake. Eden turned off the engine and her lights, and steeled herself to knock on that door and confront him. She glanced at the house, mentally rehearsing what she would say to him when he answered her knock.

Okay, she thought. Go ahead. And at that moment, as she marshaled her forces, the front door of Flynn's house opened and someone came running out. A slightly built woman, who was wearing a coat with a hood, bolted out across the unkempt lawn and got into a car parked up the street. Light spilled out the front door, illuminating Flynn as he ran after her onto the lawn barefoot. Despite the rain on the windshield, Eden could see him, his hair plastered to his head in the downpour, his wet clothes sticking to his body, as he chased the woman to her car. He banged on the car window, but the woman drove off anyway. He watched her go dejectedly, and then, shivering, he went back into his house.

Eden's first impulse was to drive away. But then she reminded herself of her purpose. What difference did it make if her former stepfather was having female company, now that his wife and child were dead? That had nothing to do with her. Eden forced herself to get out of the car. She locked the door and walked up to the entrance of the house. She banged on the door. It only took a moment for the door to open.

Flynn stood in the doorway, his towel-dried hair standing straight out from his head, the towel still draped over his shoulders. He was wearing no shirt, a hoody hurriedly half-zipped over his torso. He looked at his visitor, his eyes soft and alight with hope. And then he saw that it was Eden. His shoulders slumped, and his gaze became opaque, disinterested. 'I was in the shower,' he lied, as if to explain his soggy condition. 'What do you want?'

Eden ignored the lie. 'I need to talk to you.'

'It's kind of late.'

'It's important,' she said.

Flynn turned his back on her and started down the hall. 'Come in.'

Eden walked into the house, which was even more disorderly, and piled high with boxes, than it was the last time she had been here. She followed him into the living room. He gestured to the sofa and she sat down. There were two half-filled beer bottles on the coffee table.

Flynn sat down cross-legged on the floor, his jeans still damp. The soles of his bare feet were fuzzy from where they had picked up lint from the carpet. He tapped a cigarette out of the pack, struck a match from the box on the table, and lit it. He inhaled deeply, let the smoke drift from his lips, toward Eden.

'So what brings you here at this hour? If it's about the book, I'm not going to change my mind.'

'It's not about the book,' she said.

Flynn narrowed his eyes. 'What then?'

Eden studied him, still baffled, despite his scruffy, sexy looks, that this was the man her mother had given everything for.

'I think I know what happened,' she said at last. 'To my mom, and to Jeremy.'

207

Flynn frowned and shook his head. 'Please,' he said. 'No guessing games. I really don't have the patience. I've had a difficult evening.'

'I saw your friend running out,' she said pointedly.

Flynn stiffened, immediately wary. 'Are you spying on me now?'

'No,' said Eden. 'It's not my business. You're free to do what you like.'

Flynn regarded her through the curling smoke of his cigarette. 'Yes, I certainly am. Now what is it that you think you know?'

Eden took a deep breath. 'Oh, I know it all right. I was able to get a hold of the autopsy report on my mother. I asked a doctor to interpret it for me. And what he had to say was very startling. Stunning, really. I found out that my mother was taking medications for Alzheimer's. Early onset. The worst kind.'

Flynn lowered his chin, and stubbed out his cigarette. Even when the cigarette was well and truly extinguished, he did not look up.

'All at once I understood,' Eden said. 'She was facing a hopeless situation. An unbearable fate. She was going to lose her mind, little by little, until she didn't even know who she was. She was going to be unable to care for herself, never mind Jeremy. It was a death sentence by slow torture.'

Still he did not look up. He shook his head, and wiped the sleeve of his sweatshirt across his eyes.

For some reason she was surprised by his obvious grief. 'You knew, of course,' she said, wondering if she had presumed too much.

208

'She was my wife!' he whispered. 'Of course I knew.'

'I'm sorry,' Eden murmured, genuinely contrite at the sight of his sorrow.

Flynn pulled himself together. He began to speak, but he did not look at her. His voice was shaky. 'It's just as well that you found out.'

'Why didn't you tell me?' Eden asked. 'Why didn't you tell the insurance people?'

'Because it wasn't any of their business. All right, I was just being stubborn. I probably should have told you. But what good would it do? And, if she didn't tell you . . .'

Once again, in a kind of agony, Eden remembered the phone call that she left unanswered, the night before Tara died. Had Tara been planning to tell her? Hoping to explain . . .

Flynn wiped his eyes again, and took a deep breath. 'It seemed to come on overnight. Suddenly she started slipping. Little things at first. Soon she was forgetting things. Getting lost in familiar places. Not knowing . . . I thought it was all the stress with Jeremy. But then, one day, she said to me, "It's not just a few things. It's starting to be everything . . ."' Flynn closed his eyes at the memory. 'I knew then, even before the diagnosis . . . But still. When it came . . . That was . . . a catastrophe.'

'It must have been,' murmured Eden. 'What a terrible thing to hear about your wife.'

Flynn shook his head. 'You can't imagine,' he said.

Yes, I can, Eden thought. I'm not an inexperienced child. She'd learned a lot about anguish during her father's illness. But, she reminded herself, this was different. She'd never had to face the loss of her soulmate, her lover. 'Well, when I learned about her condition, it made a lot of things clearer to me,' she said.

Flynn sighed. 'I'm glad you get it. This is why I had no trouble understanding it. I wasn't even that surprised. All along, with Jeremy, she had tried so hard to be hopeful. To find the positive in everything. The Alzheimer's diagnosis just destroyed her. Not for her own sake so much, as for Jeremy. She loved that child . . .'

He lowered his head again, and his voice faded. Eden waited patiently for him to recover his composure. Finally, he sniffed and looked up again, avoiding her gaze. Eden resisted an urge to reach out and put a comforting hand on his shoulder.

'She was in a panic about the future. I kept trying to tell her not to worry, even though I was in a panic myself. I told her that I would look after her and Jeremy, that we would remain here, close to Dr Tanaka, and that she didn't need to worry. But all she could think about was what would happen to him once she was unable to care for him anymore. She always said that no one could care for him the way she did.'

'I can hear her saying that,' said Eden. 'She must have been terrified. Really. It all makes sense to me now . . .'

'It was horrible. Just a nightmare.'

'I'm sure,' Eden said. 'I can't even . . . What an excruciating decision. No one can really know what they would do in the same situation. Look,

210

I just wanted to tell you that I do respect the choice you made. If I know my mother, she was the one who brought it up. That would be just like her.'

Flynn frowned at her. 'What?'

Eden grimaced apologetically. 'I'm trying to be frank here. What I'm saying is that I'm sure you didn't act unilaterally on this. You must have discussed it beforehand. And I'm sure she didn't want to know the day or the hour, so to speak. She trusted you to do this for her when the time was right.'

Flynn peered at her with a combination of wonder and horror, as if she were shapeshifting in front of his eyes. 'What are you talking about? Are you out of your mind?' he asked.

Twenty-One

Eden was taken aback by his reaction. 'I'm trying to tell you that I understand.'

Flynn gaped at her. 'Wow, I never expected that,' he said.

'What? I thought you'd appreciate the fact that I get it,' Eden said hurriedly. 'I recognize that you were in an impossible position.'

'Let me see if I have this right,' he said slowly. 'You think that your mother and I planned the murder/suicide together, and she left it to me to carry out the plan . . . what? When I felt like it?'

'I don't know what your plan was,' Eden said

in exasperation. 'All I know is that once I found out about the Alzheimer's, it all suddenly made sense to me. My mother's desperation. The fact that you two were so close, and there was no one else she could turn to. I have a lot of sympathy for you. For the terrible quandary you found yourselves in. And the choice you made . . . Anyone with an ounce of compassion would find it was understandable.'

Flynn shook his head in disgust. 'You have no fucking clue what you're talking about.'

Eden had expected him to protest, perhaps. Not want to confess it outright. But she had not expected his anger. 'Hey, sometimes people do extreme things under a lot of stress. I want you to know that I am not judging you for what . . . happened. I'm sure the letter of the law would hold you accountable. You'd probably go to jail for it. But I have given it a lot of thought, and I want you to know that no one will ever hear about it from me.'

Flynn gazed at her. 'How totally arrogant of you,' he said.

Eden's temper flared. 'I don't know where this is coming from. I'm agreeing to protect you. And I'm not doing it for your sake. I have my own burden of guilt. I turned my back on my mother, and I shouldn't have. Maybe if I had listened to her, I would have known how desperate she was. I might have been able to help her.'

'You're not going to try to incriminate me because of your own guilt,' he said evenly.

'This isn't just about you,' she said, disliking him all over again. She had offered him absolution

212

and safety, she thought, and he chose to act insulted.

'Who else is it about, I'd like to know?' he asked.

'Well, for one, Aaliya. Your alibi. I would be positively fearful for Aaliya if it all came out about the female prostitute you hired for her. Homosexuality is a stoning offense in some Middle Eastern countries. For all I know, she could seriously be in harm's way right here if this all was made public. Even though she didn't succumb.'

He raised his eyebrows. 'You know about Aaliya? My, you have been busy.'

'Yes. How could you be so disrespectful of her convictions?'

Flynn nodded and lit another cigarette, tossing the expended wooden match into the overflowing ashtray. Still sitting on the floor, he pulled his knees close to his chest and wrapped his arms protectively around them as he took a drag on the cigarette. He did not look at Eden and the silence in the room was oppressive.

Eden refused to be the first to speak. She had made what she considered to be a sacrifice, and a generous offer. It was Flynn's turn to acknowledge it.

'All right,' he said slowly. 'You're right about that. I admit it. I couldn't imagine being young and beautiful like Aaliya, and not wanting to have a . . . taste of life. So, in a completely stupid and ignorant move, I hired someone to initiate her. I thought I was doing her a favor. My mistake, I confess. I was an ass, and she let me know it.'

Eden stared at him. 'And . . .'

'As for your mother, and my son,' he said, with exaggerated patience. 'I am only going to say this once. I would never have hurt them. No matter what. Period.'

Eden gazed at him, both fascinated and repelled. 'You must have,' she cried. 'My mother could never have done that to Jeremy. I don't believe it. It had to be you.'

Flynn clambered to his feet. 'I really don't care what you believe, you little bitch. I don't care what you think or who you tell about it. I just don't ever want to see your face again. Now get out of my house.'

Eden rose slowly to her feet.

'Go,' he cried. 'Get out.'

It was still raining as Eden left the house, though it had let up somewhat. She hurried down the block under the streetlights, got in the car and drove directly back to the motel. Back in her suite, the rain pelted the locked sliding glass doors. For a while she stared out at the darkness of the courtyard, which was relieved only by the glow of small white lights which had been haphazardly threaded through the scrawny trees. Finally, she closed the curtains. She turned on the TV to keep her company while she packed. She thought about who she should call to tell them she was leaving. Lizzy and DeShaun? Marguerite and Gerard? Dr Tanaka? People here had been nice to her, and tried to help. But they had already moved on with their lives. Their concerns had diverged from the tragic deaths of Tara and Jeremy.

214

For a moment she toyed with the idea of knocking on Andy's door and telling him that she had a flight home tomorrow. But she knew that the chubby salesman would be curious to find out what she had learned about her mother's death. And what was she going to tell him? That she had been sure that her stepfather was to blame, and now she no longer believed it? The contempt, the righteous indignation in Flynn's eyes when she offered up her theory had collapsed her conviction. Eden shook her head, as if she could shake the image of those outraged eyes free from her mind. It had seemed to her that everything pointed to him. She had presented her theory with no recriminations. She had vaguely expected acknowledgement and an apology, which she would gracefully accept.

But she knew shock when she saw it. Eden had never seen anyone so clearly stunned as Flynn was by her interpretation of events. Maybe he was the world's greatest actor. It seemed unlikely. No, it was beginning to become clear that she had it all wrong. But if it was not Flynn, and not her mother . . . Stop, she thought. Stop. You have tried and failed. The case is officially closed. Perhaps there are some things you can never know. Maybe that is your punishment for being so unwilling to ever forgive.

The packing finished, Eden ate some cheese and crackers, drank some wine and took a sleeping pill. The morning would be here soon enough. She could not wait to leave this place behind. She felt as if the thought of being home again was the only thing that was keeping her sane.

The next morning she arrived at the airport with plenty of time to spare, so that there would be no question of missing her flight. At this hour, the concourse was practically deserted. She checked her bag filled with dirty laundry, and kept only her carry-on bag with her, holding some spare clothes and a few essentials. She made it easily through security. Everyone was pleasant. Almost solicitous. As if they knew that she had had a terrible time in Cleveland. As if they could tell by looking at her that everything had gone wrong, and that she couldn't get out fast enough.

Eden bought herself some breakfast at Cleveland Bagel, and sat down in a chair at the gate for her flight. Only two other travelers were seated at the gate. The ticket clerk for the desk had not even arrived. She took out a book and tried to read, but it was no use. She sat back in the chair, sipped her coffee and stared at the local news on the television at the center of the lounge.

'Good morning, Cleveland,' said a cheery black woman with a gap between her teeth, wearing a turquoise dress which popped beautifully against her dark skin on camera.

Eden closed her eyes and let the voices from the news drone over her. And then, suddenly, she let out a cry, as if she had been wakened by a bad dream.

'Police say that the victim, writer and college professor, Flynn Darby, was found lying in the street a block from his home, in the early morning hours. Police have no witnesses but are canvassing the neighborhood in an effort to find anyone who might have information about the shooting. Mr Darby was rushed to the Cleveland Clinic, where he is in a critical condition with three bullet wounds to the head and torso. Mr Darby's wife and his son died in a murder/suicide at their home only two months ago . . .'

Eden stared, frozen, at the screen as the woman continued to run down the general information they had about the Darby family. For a moment, she could not take it in. She felt as if she were seeing it through a fog. But the reporter moved on to the story of a hijacked car, and Eden knew, with a sickening certainty, that what she had just seen was real. She wadded up the waxed paper around her bagel and her empty paper coffee cup. She stood up on trembling legs, threw the trash into a nearby can and pulled on her coat.

I have to get to the hospital, she thought. For a moment she fretted about her suitcase, which she had already checked. Too late to worry about it, she told herself. It's not important. They'll deliver it to me when I get home. Checking repeatedly to see that she had all her other belongings, she started back toward the security gates, walking at first, and then running, her carry-on bag careening along on two wheels behind her.

217

Twenty-Two

Eden was directed to a waiting area outside of the double doors leading to the surgical wing. A nurse at the entrance told her that the doctors were working on Flynn, trying to save him.

As she awkwardly pulled her carry-on bag up to the designated chair in the crowded waiting lounge between surgery and the ICU, she saw that Lizzy Jacquez was there too, standing in the corner of the small lounge, engaged in a heated discussion with her husband, DeShaun. Eden thought to hail them, but held back. The glower on Lizzy's face did not invite an interruption. DeShaun, wearing his lab coat, was saying something to her close to her ear, his dark face twisted with anger. Lizzy was shaking her head, her fists clenched in front of her. DeShaun finally threw up his hands in exasperation and stormed out of the lounge. Eden did not try to catch his attention. He clearly had too much on his mind.

Lizzy flopped down into a nearby chair and buried her face in her hands. Eden could see her shoulders shaking. What were the chances, Eden thought, that she was here for anyone else but Flynn? And why would she be so distraught? She could imagine Lizzy being shocked and saddened by the news, but this reaction was way more than shocked or sad. And then she began to wonder.

Eden thought briefly about the woman she had seen leaving Flynn's house the night before. The woman had been slim like Lizzy, and Eden had had the impression of someone young, even though she had not seen the visitor's face. Was it Lizzy? Was that why Lizzy was now so upset? Eden tried to wrap her mind around the idea. Was it possible? Flynn and the young researcher who had been so devoted to Tara and Jeremy . . . In their grief, had they turned to one another?

Eden looked worriedly at the door where DeShaun had just exited. Did he suspect there was something going on between his wife and Flynn Darby? She thought back to her meeting with him just yesterday. She tried to remember how he had seemed when he talked about Flynn. Somewhat impatient. Maybe a bit disrespectful. But not angry. Not mad at all. She wondered if something had changed between now and then. Had this even-tempered intern suddenly learned something private and devastating about his wife and Flynn Darby? Something that might turn him into a would-be killer?

Eden glanced back in the direction of Lizzy Jacquez, just as the young woman lifted her face from her hands. Their eyes met across the room, and Lizzy's eyes widened in alarm. Or was it fear? Eden wondered. What does she have to fear from me? For a minute she hesitated. I should go over there and ask her.

Just then, Eden felt her shoulder gripped by a strong hand.

'Ms Radley,' said a voice behind her.

Eden turned around, trying to free herself from

219

the unwelcome grip. Detective Burt was standing there, flanked by two uniformed officers.

'What do you want?' Eden demanded. 'Let go of me.'

Burt loosened his grasp, and Eden straightened out the collar of her coat.

'Please come with me. We want to talk to you,' said Detective Burt.

'About . . .?'

'About what happened to your stepfather, obviously,' said the detective.

'I'm sure you know more about it than I do,' said Eden. 'I was in the airport on my way back to New York when I saw the report on the TV news. I grabbed a cab and came over here.'

'We can discuss this at the station,' said the detective calmly.

'I'm waiting here to find out about Flynn's condition,' she protested.

'Frankly, your concern surprises me,' said Detective Burt. 'Unless perhaps you're worried that, if he survives this, he might be able to identify his assailant.'

Eden was about to yelp indignantly, and then her dudgeon subsided. She realized that she was in no position to protest. She had gone to the police and all but accused Flynn of killing her mother, her stepbrother. Of course she was a suspect. 'Look,' she said, 'it's true that I disliked Flynn, but I had nothing to do with this.'

'Please come along with us,' said Detective Burt.

'Wait a minute,' said Eden. 'Are you arresting me?'

'We just want to talk to you,' said the detective. 'We would appreciate your cooperation.'

Eden thought about refusing. She thought about threatening to call a lawyer. But somehow that seemed to imply that she did feel guilty. And, of course, she did not. 'Okay, I'll come and speak with you. But I will need to come back here,' she said.

'Understood,' he said.

'There's not much I can tell you,' Eden warned him. She turned to see if Lizzy Jacquez was still watching her. But Lizzy was gone from the lounge. A weary-looking woman with a baby had sat down in the chair that Lizzy had vacated.

Detective Burt signaled that Eden should go out into the hallway first. She did as he directed, and the detective and two patrolmen followed her. They went to the elevator and waited for it to arrive at their floor. When the doors finally opened, Aaliya Saleh hurried out.

'Hey,' said Eden. 'Aaliya!'

Aaliya looked up and seemed shocked to see Eden there. Then she quickly recovered her composure. 'Ms Radley. How is Professor Darby?'

'I haven't been allowed to see him,' said Eden. 'They're not giving out much information.' She turned to Detective Burt. 'This is Aaliya Saleh. She was my stepfather's assistant.'

'How do you do,' said the detective formally, gripping Eden's elbow and guiding her through the elevator doors.

'She might know something,' Eden whispered.

Detective Burt nodded at one of the patrolman. 'L,' he said, gazing at the lighted buttons. The patrolman leaned over and pushed it.

As the doors began to close and the elevator descended to the lobby, Eden felt her heart sinking. She had the distinct impression that Detective Burt was not interested in any other possible suspects.

Once they arrived at the police station, Detective Burt opened the door on a small waiting room and indicated that Eden should go inside. She went in.

'Have a seat,' said the detective.

Eden sat down. Detective Burt sat down opposite her. The patrolmen filled up the doorway. Eden glanced at them, feeling faintly uneasy.

'Now Ms Radley,' said the detective. 'You say you knew nothing about this shooting until you saw it on the news.'

'That's right,' said Eden.

'May I ask where you were last night?'

Eden's cheeks flamed. 'A number of places. Why?'

'Did you pay a visit to your stepfather, Mr Darby, around midnight, last night?'

How would he know that? Eden wondered. Who told him that? Someone had seen her and reported it. Burt clearly wasn't just fishing. He knew it. It seemed pointless to lie. 'Yes. I went to see him.'

'For what purpose?' asked the detective.

Eden licked her lips and looked away from Detective Burt. 'I went to say goodbye. I knew

I was leaving today. I felt as if it was the right thing to do.'

'After the suspicions that you expressed to me in my office? That he had arranged for your mother and half-brother's murder/suicide? You made a courtesy call to say goodbye? I find that a little strange, frankly.'

Eden hesitated. She thought about her encounter with Flynn and the imagined scenario that she had presented to him. How outraged Flynn had been, even in the face of her absolution. It was better, she thought, not to put her discredited theory on the table. But someone had shot Flynn today, and the detective was looking directly at her. The important thing was to remove any idea of her own possible motive from his mind. She could feel the weight of his suspicions bearing down on her like a wet rug. She chose her words carefully.

'In the time that I've spent here in Cleveland, I had an opportunity to learn a lot more about my mother. After digging around into the circumstances of her life, I found out that my mother was suffering from a terrible illness. An incurable, inevitably fatal condition, which made me realize that the idea of her suicide was completely understandable.'

It was Burt's turn to be surprised. 'What illness? What are you talking about?'

'Didn't you read the autopsy report?' Eden asked.

'It still hasn't been delivered. What do you know about it, anyway?'

'I went down to the coroner's office and for

two dollars and fifty cents I was able to obtain a copy,' she explained pointedly.

Burt looked irritated. 'Really? They still haven't sent it to me.' He sighed and shook his head. 'How am I supposed to do my job?' he asked, to no one in particular.

'Didn't the coroner mention this when he talked to you about his results? It was in her toxicology screen. My mother was taking medication for early-onset Alzheimer's. Apparently, the deterioration had already begun, and with early onset it's known to be swift. Her prognosis was grim. Hopeless, in fact.'

Burt sat back in his chair, and placed his hands on the armrests as if he were on a plane, coming in for a rough landing. 'Who told you that?'

'I asked a doctor to explain the report to me. The coroner never mentioned it to you?' she asked.

'Well, no one doubted it was a suicide . . . I suppose he didn't think it was important,' Burt grumbled.

'Still,' said Eden.

Burt nodded. 'Right. It might have been useful to know.' He rubbed his face absently. 'So your doubts were . . . allayed by this information. You no longer suspected your stepfather was involved.'

Eden knew she was shading the truth, but so be it. 'No, I no longer suspect him,' she said.

'So you're saying that you no longer had any reason to want him to come to harm?' he asked, his voice saturated with doubt.

'No. None,' she said.

'Can you think of anyone else who might want to harm your stepfather?'

Eden thought immediately of the scene she had witnessed in the lounge. DeShaun and Lizzy Jacquez. Lizzy was so distraught. Was it possible that Flynn and Lizzy had grown unacceptably close? That her husband had just found that out? Eden felt as if she owed DeShaun some loyalty for deciphering the autopsy for her. She was not going to bring up his possible involvement to this detective. It certainly was not her place to voice her suspicions. Besides, there were probably many other suspects. Flynn Darby was, at best, a self-absorbed, difficult man, but she wasn't going to implicate anyone else in shooting him. 'I really don't,' she said.

'Of course, thanks to your mother's death, he's a rich man now. You probably wouldn't have minded being the beneficiary of some of that money.'

Eden stared at him. 'I'm not even going to answer that,' she said.

'His grandparents inherit the lot if he dies,' said Burt. 'But they're both ill and housebound. I called to explain to them what happened a little while ago. I also spoke to the home healthcare person who looks in on them. They were sound asleep in their beds when Flynn Darby was shot. They hadn't spoken to him in quite a while. I doubt they even know about the insurance money.'

'I have no idea,' said Eden.

Burt frowned. 'Still. It's a lot of money. People have killed for a lot less. Let me ask you something. What do you know about guns?'

Eden shook her head. 'Nothing, really. I've never fired a gun.'

'I'm inclined to believe you, Miss Radley. But I need to have your fingers checked for gun residue, just in case.'

Eden started to protest, and then reminded herself that she was in no danger from a gun residue test. 'Of course,' she said.

'I'm hoping the gun will lead us to the shooter. When we find it.'

'You don't know where it is?'

Burt shook his head. 'We are searching for it. The shooter probably thought Darby was dead when he fell, and ditched the gun somewhere. Nobody likes to keep evidence of their crime around the apartment.'

'Well, in that case, I hope you find it,' she said.

'We will,' said Burt grimly. 'In the meanwhile, Officer Welch will accompany you down to the lab for that test.'

'Fine. They won't find any gun residue on me.'

'Purposes of elimination,' he said.

Twenty-Three

Eden waited patiently at the windowless police lab, in the dank, cinder-block basement of the building, which smelled of antiseptic. When the gunshot residue test was completed, she spoke to the technician, a young man in a lab coat with thick black hair and tobacco-colored skin, who

226

had performed the test. He wore a name tag that said Rishi Vasu. 'How did I do?' she asked him.

The young man looked at her warily and shook his head. 'Can't tell you that. You'll have to wait for the results.'

'I don't have to wait,' she said firmly. 'I know I haven't fired a gun.'

The young technician avoided her gaze, concentrating on his notes. 'I just do the test,' he said.

'Right. Never mind,' said Eden. 'So am I finished here?'

Rishi Vasu nodded. 'Yes. Thank you for your cooperation.'

'Thanks,' said Eden, getting up from the chair and gathering her belongings. Her suitcase was becoming a positive nuisance to wheel around. She wondered how long it would be until she could rebook her flight home. As soon as she had checked on Flynn's condition, she intended to be gone from here. Part of her wanted to stay long enough to find out who Flynn's assailant was, but, given her recent experience with the police, she knew that their investigation could take a while. The important thing was that they would soon realize, when they saw the results of the gun residue test, that whoever had shot Flynn, for whatever reason, it had nothing to do with her. When she had rushed from the airport to the hospital this morning, propelled by the shock of the news, she had not realized that it was a decision she would come to regret. But now, she had no car, no place to stay, and no business being here any longer. When she thought about it, she could imagine many people who might want to take a crack at Flynn. She did not intend to stick around until she found out which of the many it was. She was weary and discouraged, and all she wanted to do was to get on a plane back to New York.

'Oh, by the way, I have a message for you,' the lab technician said. 'You are asked to return to the office of Detective Burt. Follow Officer Welch.' He nodded toward the sturdily built, good-looking black patrolman in uniform who had escorted her to the lab.

'Why?' asked Eden, balking at the request.

'Don't know,' said the young man, edging away from her, his gaze still on his clipboard.

Eden sighed but she did as she was asked, following Welch to the elevator and returning with him to the detective's office. Detective Burt hailed her as she entered. 'I just got a call. They think they've found the weapon,' he said. 'In a storm drain, about a half a mile from the scene. They're bringing the gun in to forensics now.'

'Good,' said Eden. 'I hope this will lead you to whoever shot him. I don't like the man but still . . . I'd like to know that myself.'

'I must caution you,' said the detective, 'that while you are not under arrest, you have not been ruled out as a suspect.'

'This is ridiculous,' Eden said. 'I don't even know how to shoot a gun. I had nothing to do with this. Why are you focusing on me?'

'Do I have to remind you, Ms Radley? You had motive, and opportunity. You came here and volunteered the fact that you suspected Mr Darby of killing your mother to collect her insurance money.'

Eden hesitated. 'I no longer believe that,' she murmured.

Detective Burt was not interested in her professed change of heart. 'Ms Radley, I'd appreciate it if you would stay in Cleveland for the time being. I may have some more questions for you once we have given the gun a good going over.'

Eden shook her head in exasperation. 'Stay where? For how long?' she asked. 'I already dropped off my rental car and checked out of my hotel.'

'I'm sure you'll work it out,' he said, uninterested.

'Why don't you call down to the lab? I'm sure, if you ask, they'll tell you that I was not the one who fired the gun. I've never fired a gun. It simply wasn't me. There is no possible way.'

'This is about more than the gunshot residue. There are other considerations,' he said stubbornly. 'Our investigation is ongoing.'

What considerations? she wanted to demand of him. But she did not. Eden had never had anything to do with police in her life, other than the occasional motor vehicle stop for a broken taillight, or an expired registration. But she knew that there was no way that arguing was going to serve her purposes. 'How long do I have to stay?' she asked.

'Until we have answered a few questions for the purpose of our investigation.'

That's enlightening, she thought. But she kept

her opinion to herself. 'Look, right now I need to go back to the hospital.'

'Thank you for coming in,' Burt said.

Eden nodded. 'Can someone drive me?' she asked.

Burt looked at her in surprise. 'We're stretched a little thin around here,' he said.

'When we left the hospital you said someone would bring me back,' Eden reminded him. She knew she was being nervy, but she didn't care. They had made her come in here. They could now go out of their way to take her back.

Burt's expression was unreadable. 'Someone will,' he said.

Officer Welch was tagged to drive her back to the Cleveland Clinic. On the ride he was pleasant, and even a bit flirtatious, or so it seemed to Eden. She thanked him for the lift as they reached the front entrance to the clinic.

'Anytime,' he drawled, smiling at her. Eden smiled back in spite of the fact that she was not, at that moment, feeling very friendly toward the police. Once inside the front doors, she headed for the elevator and made her way to the fifth floor. She walked down the clean, characterless hallway to the surgical wing and pushed open the double doors. She bypassed the hallway which led to the recovery room and went up to the desk, then waited patiently for the nurse to get off the phone.

Finally, the pony-tailed woman in scrubs finished the call and looked up at Eden. 'Yes. Can I help you?'

'I was here earlier,' she said, 'but I was called away.'

The nurse nodded, but her gaze was indifferent.

'My . . . stepfather was in surgery this morning. His name is Darby. Flynn Darby. He suffered gunshot wounds.'

'Oh sure. Mr Darby,' she said.

'I assume he's out of surgery by now.'

'You assume right,' said the nurse pleasantly.

'How is he?'

'He's in guarded condition, but he came through the surgery all right.'

'Good,' said Eden, exhaling. 'Good. I wonder if I could go in to see him.'

'He's not conscious,' said the nurse.

'From the anesthetic?' Eden asked.

'He's in a comatose state right now.'

'Oh. Is he going to come out of it?' Eden asked, alarmed.

'I don't know any more than that,' said the nurse. 'Will you excuse me?' Eden nodded and stepped away from the desk. The nurse began handling several matters at once, between visitors, paperwork and the phone, but finally she looked up and gestured for Eden to return to the desk.

'Why don't you go home and get some rest?' she said. 'We'll call you if there's any change. Do we have your number?'

Eden hastily wrote down her cell phone number on a slip of paper and handed it over. She stood there, looking helplessly at the nurse.

'You can always call the nurses' station,' the nurse said kindly. 'We'll let you know how he's doing when you call.'

231

People behind her were forming a queue, anxious for news of their loved ones. Her time was up. 'Thanks,' Eden mumbled. She maneuvered her suitcase out of the way, then walked over to the waiting area and sat down, keeping her suitcase close by.

Go home? she thought. Get some rest? Where could she go? How could she rest? She felt suddenly overwhelmed by the situation she was in.

'Eden?'

She looked up and saw a woman in Muslim garb bending over in order to search her face. Her beautiful, dark eyes were full of concern.

'Aaliya, hello,' Eden said, surprised.

'What are you doing here? Are you waiting for news of Flynn?'

'I just heard that he got through the surgery all right, but he's in a coma.'

Aaliya nodded gravely. 'I have heard the same thing.'

Eden moved her leather bag off the seat beside her. 'Here, please. Sit down.'

Aaliya sat, arranging her flowing hijab around her. 'I'm a little surprised you are here. I must be honest with you. I know you were not on the best of terms with Flynn, after what happened with his book. Did you lose your job because of it?'

'My boss recommended that I try looking elsewhere for work.'

'Oh, I'm so sorry,' said Aaliya. 'I'm sure that was never Flynn's intention.'

Eden sniffed. 'Maybe. I don't know.'

'What will you do now? Will you go home?'

'I'd love to,' said Eden. 'No offense, but I'm so over this place. Once I leave here I will never look back. But the police won't let me leave Cleveland. Not yet. They are treating me like a suspect in the shooting because I expressed . . . concerns about Flynn's role in my mother's death.'

Aaliya looked at her, wide-eyed. 'Surely not. You couldn't really suspect him. Your mother committed suicide. She took her son with her to Paradise. Flynn would never have hurt them.'

'I no longer know what to think,' Eden sighed. 'But I suspect you're right. I don't think he had anything to do with their deaths.'

Aaliya looked consoled by this admission on Eden's part. 'So you will be staying in our city for a while.'

'Oh yes,' said Eden. 'I'm stranded here. I just don't know what to do next. I turned in my rental car and checked out of my hotel. I only came back to the hospital because I heard the news while I was waiting for my plane at the airport. I'm wandering around Cleveland with this suitcase like the ancient mariner.'

'You mean like in the poem. By Samuel Taylor Coleridge,' Aaliya exclaimed.

'Exactly,' said Eden, smiling at the girl's obvious pride in her literary knowledge. 'I'm adrift.'

'Hmmm . . .' said Aaliya thoughtfully, and Eden assumed that her attention had shifted back to thoughts of Flynn. Or her own complicated family problems. Then she said, 'I have an idea.'

233

'What?' Eden asked.

'Well, there is no one at Flynn's house. That was also your mother's house, as you know. So, you are family. And Flynn is not leaving this hospital anytime soon. Why shouldn't you stay there? The house is in a state of disarray, but you can probably find a bed that's still made up. And you can use his car. You might as well. I have all the keys.'

'Are you sure Flynn wouldn't mind that?' said Eden. 'I don't want you to get in any trouble.'

Aaliya smiled bashfully. 'He's always telling me, "Aaliya, you have to be bold in this world. You have to make choices." I'm sure he would be in favor of it, if he were able to give his opinion.'

The thought of Flynn's place, piled high with boxes and stinking of cigarettes, was not the most appealing prospect to Eden. But she was not awash in prospects. It would mean a free roof over her head and access to a car. She figured she could open a window and find a chair and a place to sleep. Right now, that seemed like a lot. 'Well,' she said. 'That would really be a help.'

'I'm sure it's what he would want me to do,' said Aaliya.

Eden tried not to grimace. Aaliya saw Flynn differently than she did. Eden was beginning to understand why, but she still had a long way to go. 'I would really appreciate it,' she said.

'We just have to pray that he recovers,' said Aaliya.

'I will,' said Eden.

I will try, she thought.

234

Twenty-Four

The wind had picked up, and it whipped Aaliya's hijab around her neck as they arrived at the street. Eden followed her across the street and down the block until they reached a bus stop.

'Wait a minute,' said Eden. 'We're taking the bus?'

Aaliya looked confused. 'Of course.'

'Look, if you don't have a car,' said Eden, 'why don't you take Flynn's car and use it while he's in the hospital? Why should you leave it for me?'

Aaliya shook her head. 'I don't drive,' she said.

'Oh,' said Eden.

'Flynn is always promising to teach me, but I'm a coward. Anyway, I think I'd rather take the bus. I like to make my way across the city, looking out the window.'

'Okay.' Eden shrugged, and shivered in the biting wind. They did not have long to wait. The city bus pulled up and the doors opened. Eden followed Aaliya up the steps. Eden's suitcase was a nuisance and she had to apologize to the other passengers for the whole length of the bus. They found a seat together near the back. Eden gave Aaliya the window seat so that she could look out. Eden threw the suitcase in the rack overhead and sat down beside her.

'Is it far?' Eden asked.

'Not too far,' said Aaliya. 'I'll tell you when we get there.'

The bus groaned and edged out into traffic. It was overheated, and Eden suddenly grew sleepy from the warmth of it. Her eyelids felt heavy, and then they closed. She was jerked awake by a stop, and looked around in confusion. Outside the window, the tall buildings in the densely packed downtown had given way to rows of modest houses, some well-kept, others shabby. Aaliya smiled at her. Then they rode in silence for a while, Aaliya's gaze taking in the passing city life, while Eden studied the girl surreptitiously.

'You know,' said Eden, 'I have to admit I find your loyalty to Flynn rather . . . surprising. I know what he did in Toledo.'

Aaliya looked at her, startled, then looked away. 'I don't know what you mean.'

'Aaliya, I spoke to the person he hired. I know what happened. Flynn was so far out of line by anyone's lights. You were lucky you were able to extricate yourself from that situation. You could have had him fired for doing that.'

'I had no wish to have him fired,' she said calmly.

'Well, he's lucky that you are such an understanding person.'

Finally Aaliya said, still gazing out the window, 'He was not wrong about me, you know.'

Eden looked at her in surprise. She thought she should feign shock, but the girl's frank admission deserved better. 'Oh. I'm sorry. I . . . didn't know.'

Aaliya's nod was so slight as to be almost unnoticeable.

'Still, it was beyond . . . presumptuous,' Eden observed.

Aaliya turned her face from the window and looked at Eden thoughtfully. 'Sometimes it's a relief. To have one person from whom you do not to have to hide,' she said.

Eden nodded, chastened. 'I guess that's true.'

Aaliya looked out the window again. 'We're almost there,' she said softly.

She reached up and pulled the cord to indicate that they wished to get off at the next stop.

They descended from the bus. The neighborhood looked dreary in the twilight. The blue house was dark. Flynn had left no lights on when he departed this morning, expecting to return in daylight. Not expecting to be shot. To be in a coma. To be at death's door.

Eden followed Aaliya up the walkway to the house and waited while she unlocked the door. Aaliya went in first, turning on the hall light. She turned around to Eden and said, 'Mind the boxes. Don't trip over anything. Everything is torn apart.'

'I'll be careful,' said Eden, picking her way past the tower of cardboard cubes with the contents written on them in magic marker. She could smell the odor of stale cigarette smoke in the air.

Aaliya made her way through the house, turning on other lights as well. When she had the place sufficiently lit, she came back to Eden. 'This way. Bring your bag to the guest room.'

Eden did as she was told. The guest room was a sliver of a room halfway down the hall with a neatly made bed, covered by a faded red corduroy bedspread, and a closet thrown open, as if to prove that it no longer held anything inside.

Aaliya turned on the bedside lamp and looked around. 'This room is pretty well cleared out. You can use the dresser if you want.'

Eden put her suitcase on the bench under the window. 'I'll leave it here,' she said.

'As you wish,' said Aaliya. 'Let me show you where everything is. Come this way.'

Eden followed Aaliya down the hall, past the master bedroom and the bathroom next to it, past the room which had been Jeremy's. The room smelled moldy and there was still medical equipment scattered across the rug, though it was piled haphazardly, as if the room were in an abandoned field hospital in the jungle somewhere.

They went back down the hall and through the galley kitchen to the dining area. The dining table was stacked with newspapers. Eden looked around curiously. 'Doesn't Flynn have an office?' she asked.

'It's a little room at the back of the garage,' said Aaliya.

'Is that where you worked with him?' Eden asked.

'Yes,' said Aaliya. 'It was the only quiet place.' She picked a set of keys from a bowl on the table. 'These are for the office, although I don't imagine you'll need them. These are the car keys, and these are the spare keys to the house. Front door. Back door.'

Eden nodded, trying to keep all the keys straight. 'Is there anything I should know about the house?'

Aaliya frowned. 'I can't think of anything offhand. If you have a question, you can call me. Here is my number.' She wrote a number down on a piece of paper. Eden put it into her pocket.

'Well, now that you're settled, I had better be going,' said Aaliya. 'My aunt needs me. There is a service tonight at the mosque. The women will come to our apartment for refreshments.'

'How are you getting home?' Eden asked.

'On the bus,' said Aaliya.

'No. Let me drive you home,' said Eden. 'That's the least I could do . . .'

Aaliya shook her head, smiling. 'I'm used to the bus,' she said. 'It's no problem. But I must be on my way. Make yourself at home. As much as you can.'

'I can't thank you enough. For thinking of this. For coming out here . . .'

'That's all right,' said Aaliya. 'It's a way of making myself useful to my employer, even if he can't give me instructions. I'm sure this is what he would want me to do.'

I'm not so sure, Eden thought. But she nodded in agreement as she followed Aaliya to the front door. As Aaliya walked briskly to the bus stop, Eden waved after her, calling out her thanks, and warning the girl to stay safe.

A bus pulled up and Aaliya disappeared inside. Eden watched until it had pulled away and then, reluctantly, she went back inside and closed the door. She looked around. Was it possible that her

239

mother, who loved flowers, and rooms neat and orderly, had ever lived in this house? It looked like a dilapidated warehouse with boxes piled in every room. It would certainly have been very different when she lived here, Eden thought. But that did little to dispel the gloomy feeling which came over her as she looked around.

She went into the living room, thinking she would sit down, but there were canyons of cardboard boxes on every side. She glanced at the overflowing ashtray and thought about emptying it, but it seemed like too much trouble altogether. She went into the dining area and looked at the array of keys on the table. She could take the car and go somewhere. But where? It was like being a prisoner without a cage. This city was her cage. This house was her cell. She had no idea how long her incarceration was going to last.

She put the car keys into a pocket at the front of her pocketbook, and slipped the house keys inside the bag. The keys to the office in the garage were still lying there on the scarred dining room table. She picked them up and dangled them thoughtfully from her thumb and forefinger. Flynn's retreat, no doubt, from the day-to-day struggle of his life with his dying wife and son.

Flynn. Someone had been angry enough at him that they had gunned him down early this morning and left him to die in the street. It was true that he had a talent for giving offense, but who could he have offended so much that they wanted to execute him for it? And did it have something to do with the deaths of Tara and Jeremy? No, it couldn't. Even she, who had the most reason to dislike him, no longer suspected Flynn for that.

She looked around at the chaotic house. There was nothing appealing about staying in here, she thought. There was nowhere to even sit down that wasn't already blocked by a cardboard box or two. Perhaps, in Flynn's private lair, she mused, there was an empty chair. A desk, and a computer. Perhaps there were answers as well. It wouldn't hurt to take a look.

She opened the kitchen door which led into the attached garage. This was the door which had been left open the night that Tara and Jeremy died, she thought. Now, Flynn's car was parked there. Eden peered at it, thinking about Flynn being gunned down in the street. He obviously had not been in his car at the time. And he hadn't been in the house. Apparently he was out walking in the neighborhood. Why? There was nothing odd about that, she reminded herself. Lots of people took walks. To stretch their legs. To clear their heads. But at that hour of the morning?

She went down the few steps into the garage and walked over to the office door. She inserted the key and opened it, turning on the lights from the switch that was on the wall. She gazed in at the cramped, windowless room.

There were three empty boxes piled in the corner, but the office had not yet been dismantled. The Mac sat on the desk, the printer on a cart beside it, along with piles of books. It looked like a no-nonsense workspace. Eden sat down in the swivel chair, and imagined Flynn sitting there.

241

She reached over to the mouse and tapped it. The desktop came alive, with dozens of documents, as well as a photo file, which had a photo of Tara as its icon.

Eden was a little surprised that the computer was not locked with a password, but obviously Flynn had gone out expecting to return in a short time. He had certainly never expected to end up in a coma.

She began to peruse the icons on the desktop. All the documents were named with abbreviations, and she was not surprised to find that some of those abbreviations were impossible for her to decipher. She opened a few files at random and found business correspondence and lesson plans. There was nothing illuminating about the documents which Flynn had saved. There was a master file with chapter documents from Flynn's book. There were critiques of students' work, and she came across a short story that Aaliya had written. Ashamed of her own curiosity, she read the story. It was written very delicately. Very poetically. But Flynn had not been stretching the point when he presumed that it revealed the author's attraction to her own sex. Even if it was fiction. Then she came across a file entitled T. Alz. It only took a second for her to realize that the file name referred to Tara and her Alzheimer's diagnosis.

Eden opened the file and looked through it. The file was filled with research on Alzheimer's Disease. One page had been highlighted by Flynn. It referred to the short amount of relative normalcy that Tara could expect after her diagnosis. One report suggested six months to two years. It was painful to read.

Eden shook her head. How could Flynn have faced that? She knew how people were supposed to feel. They were supposed to be willing to care uncomplainingly for their loved ones for as long as it took, and never waver. But who actually felt that way in their secret heart? Who wouldn't feel dread, and horror and depression, at the prospect? It was only human.

She exited the file and clicked on the photo file, just so that she could see pictures of her mother and Jeremy. It seemed as if they might be consoling to look at. And indeed, there was a raft of such photos. Tara holding Jeremy. Tara waving her son's limp hand at the camera and beaming. Jeremy smiling through his pain. Love abounding. Tears came to her eyes as she looked through the pictures. There were photos of Flynn as a young man, full of swagger and defiance. Pictures of him in sexy poses with various young women, or hanging out with a few guys who were not his equal in terms of attractiveness. Several of him with Tara, when they were first together, gazing rapturously at one another. In among these were several photos from long ago. Eden could tell that they were from Flynn's childhood, because they had the vanishing quality of Polaroid pictures which someone had attempted to save. An elderly couple, watching a toddler at play. She looked at it more closely. It was Michael Darby and his wife. Flynn's grandparents. So the child must be Flynn. Eden mused that people used to look so much older in their fifties and sixties than they did today. Flynn's grandfather was unsmiling, his arms crossed over his chest, his eyes filled with something that looked very much like loathing.

There were several folders of photos, organized by date. She clicked on the folder entitled 'S' with the most recent date. The folder opened like a blossoming flower into an array of photos, all ivory and flesh tones on a gray background. The photos were curved compositions, shadows and light, bunched fabric, and dark hair. In one glance, Eden realized what she was looking at.

Lizzy Jacquez was in a bed, nude, asleep, partly covered by the folds of a sheet, stripes of light falling across her glowing flesh, shifting from one shape to another as Flynn chronicled her slumber. Toward the end of the series, Lizzy's eyes are opened, and she looks back at the camera, surprised at first, then grave, her gaze softening to tenderness.

Beside her, her cell phone on the desk rang. Eden cried out and jumped. Her heart pounded as if she had been caught spying, which, of course, she had. She looked around, half expecting to see someone in the room with her. But she was alone. Lizzy, she thought. Her mother's champion. Eden struggled to compose herself before she picked up the phone. It was her father. 'Hello,' she said, her voice shaky.

'Hi, sweetheart!' said Hugh.

'Hi, Dad.' Eden averted her gaze away from the sensuous photos.

'You texted me that you were coming home. What happened?'

What happened? Eden thought. She thought about all that had happened in the last twelve hours. In the last week. Could she make up enough lies to cover it all? Suddenly, she felt completely sick of lies. There was nothing that she needed to cover up. She had done nothing wrong. 'I was. I was at the airport when I had to come back.'

'Why?' he asked.

She hesitated. Now was the moment when she could equivocate. Say that she would tell him when she got home. He wouldn't harass her about it. He would trust her. Enough, she thought. 'Flynn,' she said.

'Flynn?' Hugh demanded, a real note of shock in his voice.

'Flynn's been shot. He's in the hospital. He's alive, but it's very touch and go at the moment. The police insisted that I had to stay here, since they knew I had a grudge against Flynn.'

'What? I thought you went out there to help a writer with his book?'

'I am. I was. The writer was Flynn. It was Flynn's book. Before you get mad, I didn't have much choice. He wrote a book about his life with Mom, and his agent sold it to my company, with the caveat that I had to be the editor. That's why I was here.'

Hugh was silent at his end of the phone.

'It did not go well. And by the way, I've now been fired—'

'Eden, no—' he cried.

'I'm afraid so. But while I was here, I have been asking around, trying to find out more about Mom's death. The police thought that I blamed it on Flynn.'

'Did you?' he asked.

'Okay, that is a long story,' said Eden. 'Yes and no. I will tell you everything when I get back. But, suffice it to say, I had nothing to do with shooting the man.'

'Why didn't you tell me the real reason you were going back to Cleveland?' Hugh said.

Eden hesitated, then confessed. 'I was ashamed. I thought you would be angry at me. For even agreeing to help him with this. After all he did to us.'

Hugh was silent again.

'Are you angry?' she asked.

'Not at you. No,' he said.

'It seemed to me that I had no choice. But, of course, there's always a choice.'

'Do you want me to come out there?' Hugh said. 'Do you need an attorney?'

'No, I'm all right for the moment. They found the gun which shot Flynn today, so that should exonerate me completely, since I have no idea where a person would even get a gun, never mind know how to shoot it.'

'Oh, I wish you'd never gone back there,' Hugh said vehemently.

'So do I,' said Eden. She felt her eyes well up, but she forced herself not to cry. 'I'll be back soon.'

'I hope so,' he said.

'Are you okay, Dad?' she asked.

'Yes, I'm fine,' he said. 'Just worried about you.'

'By the way, I sent a box to our house. By UPS. I used the hotel as a return address. It's got some of Mom's things in it. Just keep it for me.'

'I will,' he said. 'You just get out of there, and get back home.'

'Don't worry. I'll be fine,' she said, with a bravado she did not feel.

'Where are you now?' he asked. 'At the hotel?'

One little lie, she thought. 'Yes. I better go.'

'Okay,' he said.

Eden hung up, and sat back for a minute. She was lucky when she thought about it. She had a father she could always count on. Not everybody could say that.

She turned around and looked again at the photos of Lizzy on Flynn's computer. They made her feel sick to her stomach. She quit the file and turned off the program. Tara would be heartsick if she knew. Eden couldn't stand to look at the file anymore.

She picked up her phone and the keys, and turned off the light in the office.

She walked through the garage, and then up into the kitchen where a single light was burning over the sink. She ran a glass of water, and turned around to lean against the cabinets.

She choked, and spat the water out. Lizzy Jacquez was standing in the doorway facing her, holding a carving knife.

Twenty-Five

'Oh my God,' Eden cried out, clutching her chest.

Lizzy stared at her, still wielding the knife.

For a moment they stared at one another, each one shocked by the encounter.

'I heard noises from the office,' said Lizzy. 'I thought someone had broken in the house. What are you doing here?'

'I'm staying here,' said Eden coldly. 'Aaliya let me in earlier. I guess I don't need to ask you what you're doing here.'

Lizzy looked at her warily. 'What do you mean by that?'

'I mean, I know about you and Flynn,' Eden said bitterly. She found herself unexpectedly furious at the girl. It was the photos. Somehow, she had had no problem thinking that Lizzy and Flynn might have bonded over their grief about Tara and Jeremy. But those photos told another story.

Lizzy set the knife down carefully on the counter, and lowered her eyes. 'How did you find out?'

'There are photos on his computer. Very indiscreet.'

'What were you doing on his computer?' Lizzy asked.

'Oh no, no,' said Eden. 'You don't get to act indignant with me. I want to know something. Was this going on while my mother was alive?'

Lizzy sank down into one of the kitchen chairs as if she were deflating, like a punctured tire. 'I'm sorry, Eden. I'm so sorry. The answer is that it has only been . . . going on, as you say, for a couple of days.'

'Really?' said Eden. 'Do I look like I was born yesterday?'

'The actual . . . deed, I meant,' she said apologetically.

'I'm guessing there was a fair amount of . . . foreplay.'

Lizzy shook her head. 'I can't . . .'

'What? Deny it?' Eden cried. 'You know, I was beginning to feel sorry for Flynn, but he has a way of turning sympathy into hate. I guess you haven't noticed that yet. Did my mother know about this?'

Lizzy shook her head. 'There was nothing to know. Not when she was alive. Neither one of us even acknowledged the attraction. I swear it.'

'Oh come on. You expect me to buy that?'

'I swear,' said Lizzy. 'I mean, I felt something drawing me to him. He felt the same way. But we never admitted it, even to ourselves, until after Tara . . .'

'Maybe she could see it,' said Eden. 'Maybe that was one reason she was so depressed.'

'There was nothing to see,' said Lizzy. 'I avoided him. He avoided me.'

'You think my mother was a fool?' Eden asked.

'No! I loved your mother. I respected her. I was . . . perfect. She never knew how I felt. I would never have willingly hurt her. I don't expect you to understand,' said Lizzy. 'I don't even understand

249

it. I love my husband. I've broken his heart with this. But this thing with Flynn . . . It's unlike anything either one of us . . . have ever known.'

'Oh wait,' said Eden dramatically. 'Where have I heard that before? Oh, that's right, when Flynn convinced my mother that she needed to leave my father and me.'

Lizzy did not protest.

'What's going to happen when DeShaun finds out?'

'He already knows,' said Lizzy. 'I couldn't do this behind his back. It would have been . . . disrespectful. I told him two days ago.'

Eden shook her head in disgust. 'You tanked a perfectly good marriage for that loser? DeShaun didn't deserve this.'

'I know that,' said Lizzy in a small voice.

'So now what?' Eden demanded.

'I don't know. I came here because I can't go home. DeShaun wouldn't have me there. And I didn't want to go to my parents because I don't want them to find out yet. So I thought I'd just come here and stay. Now I just pray that Flynn survives this attack. I don't know how I could go on otherwise.'

'Well, I hate to state the obvious,' said Eden, 'but did you ever think that maybe your husband was really, really angry at Flynn?'

Lizzy shook her head. 'Believe me, that was the first thing I thought of. But I checked. Luckily, he was in surgery when it happened. He didn't even know about it until Flynn arrived at the hospital. When I told him that I was afraid he might have shot Flynn, he said he wished he had.'

Eden sighed. 'He'd have to get in line.'

'You sound like you're blaming him for being shot,' Lizzy cried. 'That's so completely unfair!' Spots of color danced, like faint flames, in her pale cheeks.

'Do you think DeShaun is the only wronged husband in Flynn's life? He did the same thing to my father. And who knows how many others?'

'He's not like that,' said Lizzy. 'Our love is something so powerful . . . it's a once in a lifetime thing. We both feel it.'

'I pity you,' said Eden. 'You believe that. You'll see.'

The two women stared at one another, and then Lizzy looked away, her shoulders slumped. She knows I'm right, Eden thought. But she didn't say a word.

'I don't suppose . . .' said Lizzy. 'I guess you wouldn't want me staying here while you're here.'

'You've got that right,' said Eden.

'All right. I'll leave. Although I don't know where to go,' Lizzy lamented.

'Surely you have a friend,' Eden said.

'I'll just go back to the hospital,' said Lizzy. 'I'd rather be near Flynn anyway.'

'You do that,' said Eden. 'Sleep in a chair.' She followed Lizzy through the maze of cardboard boxes to the front door of the house.

Lizzy turned, as she opened the front door. 'It's more complicated than you think, Eden. I adored your mother. And your stepbrother. So did Flynn. Believe me, neither one of us would ever—'

'Pardon me, but I could never believe you,' said Eden. 'Now please go.'

She watched the girl disappear into the evening gloom, then locked the door behind her. No, you can't stay here, Eden thought, reliving her conversation with Lizzy in her mind. How could you even think anything else? she wondered. She went back into the dining area and sat down at the table in the dismantled room. She was hungry, but didn't want to eat. Thirsty, but she thought she might gag on anything she tried to swallow. She knew she should get up and try to find herself something in these cabinets, but instead, she sat, rooted in place.

Suddenly, her phone rang, startling her again, and she hurried to answer it.

'Ms Radley?'

'Yes,' said Eden.

'This is Detective Burt. Where are you?' he asked.

'I'm at Flynn's house. I'm staying here tonight.'

'Well, I have something I want to discuss with you. I wonder if you could come down to the station? I'd come out there, but a lot of things are happening, all at once,' he said apologetically.

Eden thought about it for a moment. She did not know if it had any bearing on Flynn's attempted murder, but she wanted Detective Burt to know what she had found out about Flynn and Lizzy. And she did not want to spend any more time than necessary in this gloomy house. She could stop somewhere and buy herself a sandwich while she was out. 'Okay, sure. I'll be right down.'

'I'll be waiting,' he said.

* * *

The police station was abuzz, as if it were the middle of the day. Eden announced herself to the desk sergeant, and then took a chair to wait. She did not have to wait long. Detective Burt came out the doors leading to the offices, and greeted her.

'Thanks for coming in, Ms Radley,' he said, offering her a chair in another room, not his office. This room was unfurnished, except for a square table and a few chairs. A laptop computer sat on the table, along with a half-empty bottle of water. The windows had bars.

'Eden,' she said.

'Please, sit, Eden,' he said.

Eden sat down, and Burt sat down across the table from her. The detective was in his shirtsleeves, though he still wore his tie. His face looked haggard, and his eyes, weary. But he seemed to still have plenty of energy for his investigation.

Eden looked across the desk at him. 'So why did you want to see me?'

'Ladies first, Ms Radley. Eden. Tell me what's on your mind.'

Eden took a deep breath. 'Well, since you insisted that I remain in Cleveland, I decided to stay at Mr Darby's house in his absence. I figured that while I was there, and had the opportunity, I'd take a look at his computer.'

Detective Burt raised his eyebrows. 'Really? Do you even have permission to be there?'

'His assistant let me in,' said Eden.

'The Iranian girl?' he asked.

'I don't know that she's Iranian, but yes, Aaliya. In fact, it was her idea that I stay there.'

'I don't want you doing anything illegal,' he warned.

Eden ignored his caution. 'On Flynn's computer I found photos dated a couple of days ago. They don't leave much to the imagination. It seems that Flynn Darby is having an affair with a researcher from the Cleveland Clinic who often worked in my mother's home while she was alive.'

'What's her name?'

'Jacquez, Lizzy Jacquez. Her husband is an intern at the Cleveland Clinic, named DeShaun. It occurred to me that he may have found out about them, and decided to go after Flynn. Mrs Jacquez insists that her husband was in the hospital doing surgery when Flynn was shot. I hope that's true, but . . .'

Burt frowned, and tapped his pen against his lower lip. 'We can easily check on that. And you think this affair was going on while your mother was alive?' he asked.

'Lizzy gave me some song and dance about them not acting on it while my mother was alive. She seemed sincere. But so did Flynn when he insisted he had nothing to do with my mother's death. Honestly, I don't know what to think anymore. I just know that I'm not satisfied with the answers I've received.'

Detective Burt sighed. 'And I admit I feel a bit badly about that. More and more I'm beginning to wonder if I was hasty in dismissing your concerns about your mother's death. That case is still closed. Technically,' he said. 'Although, in fact, the shooting of Flynn Darby now casts

254

everything into a different light. My experience tells me that this murder attempt on Flynn Darby is related to the deaths of Tara and Jeremy Darby. It would just be too coincidental that the crimes are unrelated.'

Eden nodded. 'That makes sense, doesn't it?'

Detective Burt shrugged. 'Luckily, as long as the victim is still alive, we have an eyewitness. Flynn Darby himself. We will question him as soon as he regains consciousness in hopes that he can identify his assailant. In the meantime, we were expecting the gun to tell us much of what we need to know.'

'And did it?'

He reached over to the laptop and tapped on it. Then he turned it to face Eden. 'I'll show you something. Take a look at this,' he said.

Eden frowned as the screen was suddenly filled with a blank-walled, nondescript room much like the one she was sitting in. There was the sound of coughing, and much rustling and throat clearing.

A man dressed in a dark windbreaker and gray pants, his head cut off by the frame, was led to a chair and told to sit down. He did so, and his wrinkled, bespectacled face came into view. His crewcut white hair made the top of his head look as if it was melting into the dingy white wall behind him.

'That's Michael Darby,' she exclaimed.

'Yes, it is,' said Burt.

'This is Detective Armand Fabian of the Robbin's Ferry, New York police department. We are conducting an interview with Mr Michael

Darby as a courtesy to the Cleveland, Ohio Central Police. All right now, Mike . . . Mr Darby . . .' said the disembodied voice outside the screen. 'As I said, we have asked you to come here as a courtesy to the Cleveland Police. They have recovered a gun, suspected to be the weapon in the shooting this morning of your grandson, Flynn Darby.'

Eden studied the aged face. It showed absolutely no emotion at the mention of Flynn's name as a shooting victim. The old man sniffed, and blinked behind his glasses. Otherwise he was impassive.

'Had you heard that Flynn was the victim in a shooting?'

'They called the house after it happened. So yeah, we heard.'

'How's he doing?' asked Detective Fabian, a note of sympathy in his voice.

Michael Darby looked back at him belligerently. 'Still living,' he said. 'Otherwise, I don't know anything.'

'Okay now, Mr Darby. A few hours after the shooting, the gun which was used to shoot your grandson was recovered in a storm drain.'

The old man gazed at the detective coolly.

'We were surprised to discover that the weapon was registered to you, sir. Can you explain how that gun, which was your service revolver when you were on the Robbin's Ferry police force, turned up in Cleveland, Ohio, this morning?'

Michael Darby stared at the detective who was questioning him. His complexion, pale to begin with, turned ashen. He blinked rapidly, but his gaze was not fixed on Detective Fabian. He seemed to be looking into the past, or into his memories, trying desperately to make something in his memories compute.

'Mr Darby? Did you hear what I asked? How did your gun end up in Cleveland?'

'Well, I certainly didn't bring it there,' said Michael gruffly.

To Eden, it sounded like an excuse. It sounded as if he was playing for time. But why? As if in answer to her question, the detective spoke again.

'No. We know that you were not in Cleveland this morning, sir. The home health aide who comes in to care for your wife twice a week reported to us that she saw you and your wife in your home at the time of the shooting.'

'Like I said. I didn't shoot him,' said the old man bluntly.

'No, sir. We're not accusing you of that. What we want to know is how that weapon came to be in Cleveland.'

'I don't know,' Michael Darby cried. 'Why are you asking me? How would I know?'

'It's your weapon, sir. Of that, there is no doubt. Who better to know its whereabouts?'

'Jesus,' he murmured, as if stunned, and trying to absorb this piece of news. Then he looked at the detective defiantly. 'He musta took it with him.'

'Who took it, sir?' asked the voice of Detective Fabian patiently.

'Flynn. My grandson. I haven't seen that thing in over twenty years. Maybe twenty-five.'

'We have paperwork here signed by you saying that you turned it in when you retired. But the weapon was never actually recovered.'

'I might have meant to but I forgot,' he said in a wheedling tone.

'So you're saying that you failed to turn in your weapon when you retired, and you have not seen it since.'

'I have not seen it. That's right,' said Michael Darby, nodding.

'Did you report it stolen?'

Michael Darby screwed his face up angrily. 'You know I didn't. Why are you asking me these questions? Everybody knows me here. Anybody here can tell you, when I say I haven't seen it, that means I haven't seen it. I didn't report it stolen because I didn't know it was stolen. I had no reason to look for it. But that would be just like Flynn. To steal something like that. Just to bust my chops.'

'Did you ever ask him if he took it?'

Darby seemed to be gathering his customary bluster. 'I told you. I didn't know about it. If I had, I woulda asked him. I woulda hit him in the head if I thought he took it.'

'Could anyone else have taken it?'

'Like who?' the old man demanded.

'I don't know. Was your house ever broken into? Anyone staying with you who might have taken it? You have an aide who comes in twice a week.'

Michael Darby looked at the detective warily. Then, he smiled, though his eyes remained cold. 'That cow wouldn't know which end the bullet comes out of.'

'So you're certain it was your grandson who took it?'

'Who else could it be? How else would it get to Cleveland?' he cried defiantly.

'Let me remind you, Mr Darby, that you are responsible for that firearm. You never returned it to the Robbin's Ferry police, so you were in possession of it illegally. Now, that weapon has been used in the commission of a felony.'

Michael's belligerence seemed to dwindle away. 'I know, I know,' he said. 'I'm an old man. I'm forgetful, all right. It was an oversight.'

'Nonetheless, you could be charged—'

'You can't do that,' Darby yelped.

'We certainly can,' said the detective.

The old man contorted his face into an aggrieved expression. 'Look here. My wife and I are trying to make do on a cop's pension. Someday you'll find out what that's like. If I'm not there at the house, somebody has to come in full-time and help her out. She can't manage on her own.'

'I'm sure it's difficult,' said Detective Fabian.

'It's way more than difficult,' Michael Darby insisted. 'I can't afford to be separated from her.'

'All right, Mr Darby. You're free to go today. But we may call on you again for further information. Thank you for coming down to the station.'

The old man shook his head and muttered something unintelligible.

The video feed abruptly stopped.

Eden sat back in her chair and stared at the blank screen. 'That's just the way he was when I met him. What a horrible old man.'

'There's something not right in his story about the gun,' said Burt. 'He strikes me as the kind

259

of guy who would take his gun out every day and admire it. I find it hard to believe that he didn't know his gun was gone. Did you notice how uneasy he seemed? I don't think he was saying all that he knew.'

'I had the same impression,' said Eden, surprised that the detective seemed to be soliciting her opinion.

'So did Fabian. But, for the moment, that's where it stands.'

'Do you think that Flynn had the gun?'

'He must have. For whatever reason, his grandfather decided not to report him for stealing it.'

'That seems like the kind of thing he would enjoy. Reporting his grandson for that,' Eden observed.

Detective Burt shook his head. 'There's no love lost between those two. But why he didn't report him . . . I don't know . . . yet.'

'So whoever it was that shot Flynn must have taken the gun from him,' said Eden.

The detective shrugged. 'He might have given the gun to someone. Or someone stole it from him. Someone he knew.'

Eden immediately thought about the people who visited Flynn in his house recently. Lizzy. Aaliya. Herself.

'He never reported it missing either. Did he ever mention a burglary to you? A break-in?' the detective asked.

Eden shook her head slowly. 'No . . . But then again, we're not exactly close.'

'Did your mother ever mention him having a gun?'

'She wouldn't have said that to me. But I can't picture her welcoming a gun in the house. That just wasn't her style.'

'A lot of questions,' Burt admitted.

'So he was shot with his own grandfather's gun,' Eden said.

'Yup.'

Eden shook her head. 'You're right. None of this seems like a coincidence.'

'No. I just need to figure out how these crimes are connected. By the way, in light of this information, and the results of the gunshot residue test, we no longer consider you a suspect, and if you wish to return home we won't stop you.'

'Okay,' said Eden. 'Thanks for letting me know that I am free to go.'

'Thank you,' said Detective Burt. 'Thanks for bringing me this information about Mr Darby. When there's a sexual affair involved, you automatically have new suspects.'

Eden immediately thought of DeShaun Jacquez, who was a victim in all this, and had been kind of her. She hoped his alibi would hold up. 'I hope it will help.'

'The more information the better,' he said.

'I just wish . . .' said Eden.

The detective looked at her with raised eyebrows.

'I wish you would reopen that investigation. Into my mother's death. There are so many questions. I no longer think that Flynn was responsible, but I still don't believe it was a suicide.'

Detective Burt smiled at her. 'I promise you, I

will go over everything again, with what we now know in mind. And I will let you know.'

'Thank you,' said Eden. 'That's all I ask.'

'Your mother has quite a champion in you,' he said admiringly.

Eden marveled at the irony of this, given her long estrangement from Tara. 'Maybe so,' she said. She got up from the chair and slung her pocketbook over her shoulder. 'I'd better get going.'

'Will you leave right away?' he asked.

'I'll spend the night here. Leave in the morning.'

'Try not to get in any trouble between the time you leave here and the time you get to the airport,' said Detective Burt.

'I think I can manage that,' said Eden.

Twenty-Six

Before she even opened the door, Eden could smell something delicious being prepared in the bistro. She was starving when she left the police station, and on her way home she was trying to decide what to do about dinner when she received a call from Marguerite.

'I heard about Flynn being shot. How is he doing?'

'Holding his own, apparently,' said Eden.

'Any progress since we talked?' Marguerite asked.

'Quite a bit has happened.'

'Have you eaten? Come over here and tell me about it.'

'Are you at the restaurant?' Eden asked.

'Yes.'

'I'll be over right away.'

As she drove to Jaune, Eden realized that she had several reasons for wanting to go there, not the least of which was the wonderful food. She was glad that Marguerite had called. She was still plagued by a nagging question which arose from her last conversation with her. She waited at the front of the restaurant for Marguerite to appear, but this time she was greeted by a pale young girl with long, dark hair and a perfectly oval face. 'Can I help you?' she asked.

'Actually, I'm looking for Marguerite. She's expecting me.'

'She's in the kitchen tonight. My dad is home with the flu.'

'You're Marguerite's daughter?'

'Amalie, her oldest,' she said, nodding. 'I can tell her you're here.'

Eden frowned. 'I don't want to disturb her.'

'It's okay. We're slow tonight. Come with me.'

Eden followed the girl in her long, swaying skirt and boots, to the swinging door with its porthole-like window at the back of the room. Amalie opened the door and yelled in. 'Mom, someone here to see you.' She turned back to Eden.

'What's your name?'

'Eden.'

'Her name is Eden,' Amalie called out.

Marguerite appeared at the door, wearing a

long, lavishly stained apron over jeans and a tank top. 'Eden!' she exclaimed. 'It's good to see you.'

'It's good to be here,' said Eden truthfully.

'Come in. Come through,' said Marguerite. 'Thanks, chérie,' she said, smiling at her daughter, who headed back to the front of the restaurant.

'I didn't realize you were cooking tonight,' said Eden.

'It's all right. I need a break. Come outside with me. I'll have a smoke. Here. Take this.' She threw together a plate of delicious-looking food and handed it to Eden. Then she picked up two glasses of wine. 'Bring it with you.'

Eden took the plate, while Marguerite juggled the wine and shrugged herself into a parka which was too large for her and had seen better days. She headed back through a storage area, passing a door on her left, and going to a door at the end of the room. Eden had the terrible thought that they were headed out to where the garbage was stored. She should have known better. Even casual and al fresco, it was, after all, a French meal.

Marguerite set one of the glasses down on a small, café-style table, and gestured to Eden to join her. Eden followed her hostess and found herself on a long, narrow screen porch along the back of the building, which looked out on a dark parking lot. Marguerite closed the door to the storage room behind her and rummaged in the pocket of the parka, pulling out a box of matches and a cigarette. Eden sat down on the small, wrought-iron chair and placed her plate on the table. Marguerite took her cigarette to the opposite end of the porch and lit it, taking a sip of wine from her glass. She exhaled with a sigh of relief or contentment or both.

Then she looked at Eden. 'Go ahead. Eat. Use your fingers.'

Eden needed no further encouragement. She picked up a spear of asparagus and dipped it in a creamy, garlicky sauce that tasted heavenly. 'Mmmm . . .' she said.

'My smoke doesn't bother you?' asked Marguerite.

'No,' said Eden, and, strangely, it was true. 'This is delicious.'

'Thanks. So, what's going on?'

Eden hurriedly chewed and swallowed the bread and garlicky sauce in her mouth. 'I just came from the police station. The detective wanted to talk to me about the shooting.'

Marguerite nodded. 'Surely they don't think it was you that shot him?'

Eden smiled and shook her head. 'Nope. For my sins. It wasn't me.'

'Do they know who did it?'

'No. They know he was shot with his grandfather's gun. Service revolver. Apparently, Flynn had taken it from him long ago.'

Marguerite looked surprised. 'You're kidding. So that means that whoever shot him . . . it was someone close to Flynn. Someone who could have taken his gun . . .? Do they have any suspects?'

Eden shook her head. 'Well, I don't know about that. But I told them what I found out. That Flynn was having an affair with Lizzy.'

'Lizzy,' Marguerite cried. 'I don't believe it.'

'Oh, you can believe it. I saw the pictures.'

Marguerite shook her head. 'But Lizzy? She's married. She and her husband were so in love.'

'Not any more. She and Flynn are now crazy about one another.'

'Good God. I just . . . I can't . . . She's such a good girl. I would never expect this from her. Flynn, yes. Certainly. But Lizzy?'

'She tried to convince me that this just started a few days ago. But I have my doubts,' said Eden. 'She spent a lot of time with the family.'

'Yes, she did. God, I always knew he was a cheater.'

'Well, you were right,' said Eden.

Marguerite frowned and inhaled another drag on her cigarette, gazing out into the darkness. 'What a mess. Do you think it was a lover's quarrel? Do you think Lizzy shot him?'

'No, I don't. She's completely distraught.'

'Oh no. Tell me it's not DeShaun . . .' Marguerite said sadly.

'I don't know who shot Flynn,' Eden said. 'DeShaun seems to have an alibi. The police are working on it.'

Marguerite shook her head. 'Wow. I didn't know about any of this.'

'But you saw them together, right? While my mother was alive?'

'Who? Lizzy and Flynn?'

Eden nodded.

Marguerite took another drag on her cigarette, frowning. 'I saw them in the same room from time to time . . . Why?'

'Lizzy swears that they never acted on their feelings while my mother was alive. But now I am wondering if my mother suspected there was something between them.'

Marguerite shook her head slowly. 'I know what you're asking. But no. I never saw anything going on between them. No. I didn't.'

Eden felt vaguely disappointed. 'Well, you probably weren't expecting to see anything so you didn't.'

'Your mother only had the nicest things to say about that girl. Always.'

Eden thought about that. It seemed unlikely that her mother would be singing the praises of her rival for Flynn's affections. Unless she really didn't know.

'I don't know,' she said. 'Maybe it's true that they didn't consummate it when my mother was alive. But Flynn isn't known for his self-restraint. Or his moral fiber.'

'Well, you know how I feel about him. I told you the last time we talked . . .' Marguerite crushed her cigarette with the toe of her boot. 'In fact, I never told you this, but I was so suspicious of him that I called the insurance company and the police and suggested they ought to look into whether he might have . . . helped your mother and Jeremy on their way.'

'That was you?' Eden exclaimed. 'You were the source of the tip?'

Marguerite glanced at Eden, and nodded sheepishly. 'Believe me, I have never done anything like that before. I did it anonymously. It wasn't as though I knew anything concrete.

267

But I just had such bad feelings about that guy. I hope you're not angry I did that . . .'

'No . . .' said Eden, although, in truth, the anonymous tip now smacked of innuendo, and not actual facts.

'When I heard about all that insurance money. The thought of him getting that when your poor mother . . .'

'I understand,' said Eden. 'I suspected him too.'

Marguerite peered at her. 'You say that like you don't anymore.'

Eden thought of Flynn's outraged eyes when she accused him. 'No, I don't. Not anymore.' She sipped her wine. It gave her a warm glow despite the chilly seat on the porch. 'But I did want to ask you about something. You told me that story about seeing Flynn in a car with a woman. You said she seemed to be crying, and he was consoling her. Do you think that was Lizzy?'

Marguerite frowned. 'No. I don't think so.'

Eden was surprised. 'No? Why not?'

'Because . . .' Marguerite was searching her memory. 'No. I don't know why. I'm just sure it wasn't Lizzy.'

Eden was dissatisfied with that response. 'How can you be so sure?'

'It's a gut feeling. I'd have to think about it.'

'Is it possible that he had somebody else before Lizzy?' said Eden.

'Are you kidding?' Marguerite exclaimed. 'Of course it's possible. I don't think Flynn has any scruples. Let me think.' Her brow was furrowed as she tried to remember the sequence of events. 'Wait. I remember this now, Eden,' she said, jabbing the air with a fresh cigarette. 'I was coming from your mother's house that day. I was on my way to my house when I saw him in the car with the weeping woman. I have no idea who she was. But when I walked in my house, Lizzy was there. She was halfway through the interview with my husband, Gerard, and the children. In fact, she had my middle one on her lap. She was already there at my house. Had been there for some time. They got tired of waiting and started without me.'

Eden stared at her. 'So it couldn't have been Lizzy,' she said, half in disbelief.

'Flynn is worthless. But no. It wasn't Lizzy.'

'Maybe he threw this other woman over for Lizzy, and she shot him.'

Marguerite shook her head. 'That guy should learn to keep it in his pants.'

'Maybe this will teach him,' said Eden. 'If he pulls through.'

Twenty-Seven

Eden let herself into Flynn's quiet house and closed the door behind her. She had thought about stopping by the hospital to check on him, but what she felt was more curiosity than concern. So it didn't seem to be the right thing to do. She felt sorry for Lizzy, sitting by his bedside keeping watch over him. He had come into Lizzy's life with the same whirlwind force for destruction with which he had once entered Tara's life. And it would probably have the same result, she thought. Lizzy's carefully ordered life would be in ruins. Flynn was good at that.

But was it any more than that? she wondered. Now that she knew the tip had come from Marguerite, she had less reason than ever to accuse Flynn. She kept thinking of the look in his eyes when he denied having anything to do with Tara and Jeremy's deaths. She found it impossible not to believe him.

Not your problem, she reminded herself. Flynn could sort out his own life, if and when he recovered. Tomorrow you can leave this city, and hopefully nothing will pull you back here this time. Last-minute flights were expensive, and she had already blown off one flight this morning. DeLaurier Publishing had paid for that one, but she would have to pay her own fare this time. She was going to have to be more frugal in the future, since she was now without a job, she reminded herself. But in this one instance, price was no object. She wanted to get out of Cleveland, no matter the cost. She would worry about the cost of it later.

Eden wasn't satisfied with the results she had achieved while she was here, but at least she had the consolation of knowing that she had convinced Detective Burt to reopen the case surrounding her mother's death. For now, she would have to be satisfied with that. She agreed with the detective that the attempt to assassinate Flynn had to be related to Tara and Jeremy's deaths, and part of her was desperately curious to know who it was that shot Flynn, but she told herself that she would know in time. Right now, the important thing was to reclaim her life.

She got a beer from the refrigerator, and then went down the hall to the tiny bedroom where she was supposed to stay the night. She looked into her suitcase, and realized that there wasn't much packing to be done. She had not yet taken anything out. She got her toiletries out and put them in the bathroom across the hall. Then she got out an outfit for travel, and hung it up on the closet door, so it wouldn't be utterly wrinkled for the trip.

That done, she went back to the dining area, still clutching her beer, and sat down at the dining table. She pushed the newspapers and unopened mail aside, and set up her iPad. She rubbed her hands together in anticipation. Now, she thought. The ticket home.

But her efforts were stymied. In the hotel she had been instantly able to access the Wi-Fi. It did not take her long to realize that she could not access the server here without a password, and she had no idea what the password in Flynn's house might be. She thought about her mother, and the dates which were important to her. For a few moments she tried combinations of logical passwords, but felt completely frustrated when none of them had the effect of unlocking the stubbornly frozen computer and putting her online.

I can't buy my ticket, she thought. A feeling of panic swept over her, but she forced herself to remain calm. Try your phone, she told herself.

She had never used her phone to buy a ticket, but of course it could be done. She got out the phone and had begun to punch in airline names and schedules, squinting at the small print, when she suddenly reminded herself that there was another, simpler option. Flynn's computer was still open, still online, out in his office. She could do it there. Easy, she thought. She slipped her phone into her pocket, went through the house to the attached garage and into his office, making herself comfortable in front of his monitor. This is more like it, she thought, as she quickly pulled up the information she needed and bought her ticket. She could not ever remember a time when she was more eager to get home. She texted her father, asking him if he could pick her up at the Westchester County Airport tomorrow at two p.m. His response was almost instantaneous, as if he had been sitting, waiting to hear from her. Knowing her father, she didn't think that was out of the question.

Eden sat back in the swivel chair and sighed. That's done. I am out of here.

Now that she was finished with Flynn's computer, she knew that the polite thing to do would be to avert her eyes and not meddle any more in his business. But the photo file seemed to entice her to look again.

She decided not to snoop any further into the file with the photos of Lizzy. Any further looking was just prurient, and she was repulsed by the thought of going down that road. But she was curious to see more recent photos of her mother, and her stepbrother, whom she had never really known. She opened the file with her mother's picture on the icon, and began to look through them.

There were a lot of photos of Tara, and of Jeremy. She recognized the photo of the two of them in the field on a blue-sky day which Flynn had enlarged for the funeral. She clicked on photos, one after another, of holidays, birthdays complete with candles on the cake, and ordinary days. Changes of season. There were photos of gatherings at the house, where Aaliya was ever present, serving cake and minding the children who were visiting. Marguerite and other parents with afflicted children appeared. Eden marveled at the fact that everyone looked so cheerful, all of the time. As if they didn't realize that their children were facing almost certain doom. How did they do it? she wondered.

There were even several photos of Jeremy with Flynn's grandmother fuzzy in the background, wearing a proud and happy smile, the light reflecting off her glasses. She must have been in better health then, Eden thought. They must have made a trip out here to see them. There were, however, no pictures of Michael Darby. No doubt he was off sulking somewhere, thinking of ways to make everyone feel bad.

Eden felt as if she had seen hundreds of photos by the time she quit the file and picked up the boarding pass she had printed. She was almost dizzy with exhaustion, and all she wanted was to take a quick shower and go to bed. She was packed, she was ticketed, and she was ready. She turned off the light in the garage, and went back through the garage and into the house. As she closed the garage door behind her, she was suddenly overcome with the feeling there was something in what she had just seen on the computer which troubled her. Something that seemed . . . wrong somehow.

Never mind, she thought. It's not your problem. Everything is in order. Time to get ready to go. She slipped her phone back into her pocket and went along to the guest room to grab some clean clothes.

She was in the shower, rinsing the conditioner out of her hair, when she heard her phone ringing in the pocket of her pants, which were hanging on a hook behind the bathroom door. Eden turned off the water and climbed out of the shower, carefully, so as not to end up a victim of her own clumsiness. She grabbed a towel and wrapped it around her as she rummaged for the phone.

'Hello?' she said.

'Eden Radley? This is Nurse Thomas. I'm calling from the Cleveland Clinic.' The nurse's voice sounded fresh and cheery.

'Yes,' said Eden warily.

'You left me your number earlier today in case your stepfather awakened.'

'I did,' said Eden.

'Yes, he just regained consciousness about a half an hour ago.'

'Oh,' said Eden. 'That's . . . that's great.'

'If you want to come down and see him, you can. Just for a very brief visit. Only a few minutes. He's in room 1229.'

'Um . . . okay.'

'I thought you'd want to know,' said the nurse, more guarded now that she had heard Eden's lukewarm response.

'No, I appreciate the call,' said Eden. 'I may . . . just wait. Until tomorrow.'

'Well, that's probably a good idea,' said the nurse. 'He really needs his rest.'

'Do the police know that he's awake?' Eden asked. 'I know they want to talk to him.'

'I'm sure someone will tell them,' said the nurse coolly.

'Well, thank you very much,' said Eden. 'Thank you for calling me.'

'Just doing my job,' said the nurse, and hung up.

Eden sat down on the closed toilet seat. She was still wrapped in a towel, and she was shivering with the cold. The steam from her shower had begun to escape the bathroom. I should call Detective Burt, she thought.

Put your pajamas on first, she told herself. You need to get warm. She forced herself to stand up and dry off. Then she put on her pajamas, and a bathrobe she had found. She pulled a pair of woolly socks on her bare feet. Then she picked up her phone. She dialed the police station and asked for Detective Burt.

'Gone for the day,' said the dispatcher. 'Is this an emergency?'

Eden hesitated. 'Not exactly,' she said.

'I'll give you his voicemail. You can leave him a message. He'll be checking them this evening, I'm sure.'

Eden thanked the dispatcher, and waited through

275

the detective's identifying message. 'Detective Burt,' she said. 'This is Eden Radley. I just got a call from the hospital. Flynn is conscious, if you want to question him.' She thought about telling him that she knew where the tip came from, but then she reminded herself that she did not need to get anyone else involved. 'Okay, that's all,' she said. 'Have a good evening.'

She padded down to the dining table and gathered up her iPad. She took it with her to the guest room to pack it in her bag, since it was pretty well useless here without the password. She switched off all the lights in the house as she went. All the while she was thinking of Flynn.

Now that he was awake, she wondered if he was safe at the hospital. Someone had made a serious attempt to kill him this morning. Surely there would be a guard on his room. There had to be security at the hospital so that no one could come and go without being seen. There was, after all, someone who was intent on ending Flynn's life.

Well, if Flynn knew who it was, he would surely tell the police. She would call Detective Burt as soon as she was back in New York, and find out. And then, she had a brainstorm. Why wait?

She rang the hospital and asked for room 1229. In a moment, she was connected. A woman answered the phone, saying just the room number.

Eden hesitated. 'Lizzy?' she asked.

'Who's this?' Lizzy asked.

'It's Eden. I heard that Flynn is awake. Can I speak to him?'

Lizzy hesitated. 'I'm not sure he's up to it.'

Eden heard the rumble of a male voice.

'It's Eden,' Lizzy said. Then she returned to the phone. 'He wants to talk to you. Here. Don't talk too long. He's very weak.'

Eden did not reply. She heard Lizzy say that she was going out to the nurses' desk to complain that the painkillers had not arrived. She heard the low rumble of Flynn's reply. Lizzy promised to be right back. Eden waited patiently. In a few moments, she heard Flynn's voice, weak and slurry. 'Hi, Eden.'

'How are you feeling?' she asked.

'Like shit,' he said.

'I'm sure. I want you to know that I called the police to tell them you were awake. They want to talk to you about the shooting. Do you know who did this to you? Did you see them?'

Flynn cleared his throat. 'Can't,' he said.

'Can't what?' Eden asked.

'Can't say,' he replied.

'Does that mean you don't know who it was?' Eden asked. 'Was it someone you knew? Why would they want to shoot you?'

There was a silence. Then Flynn said, 'Never mind. I have to . . .' He was silent again. And then Eden heard him gasp.

'Are you in a lot of pain?' she asked.

He did not reply.

'Flynn,' she asked, more gently. 'What's going on with you? If you know who did this, you have to tell the police.'

'Stay out of this,' he said in a soft voice.

'Was it DeShaun? Because of Lizzy?'

'No,' he said sharply. 'Leave it, Eden. You have to leave it. You don't know what you're talking about.'

Exasperated, she cried, 'I can't leave it. Does this have to do with my mother? Does it have something to do with her death? Or Jeremy's? Do you know? Because if you do . . . You have to tell the police if you know something. Your life could still be in danger.'

There was another long silence, and Eden thought Flynn might have ended the call. Then suddenly he said, in a voice that was thick and raspy, 'Yes. I know. I know everything. But you have to stop asking. Just don't even bother. I'm sorry, Eden.'

'Here's the nurse,' Lizzy caroled as she returned to the room. 'He needs some medication. NOW!'

'Goodbye,' Flynn said. The phone went dead.

'Flynn,' Eden cried. 'Flynn!' But the call was ended.

For a few minutes she stared at the phone. Part of her was tempted to throw on a coat over her pajamas and rush down to the hospital, but she forced herself to think clearly. That would not accomplish anything. Still, her mind was racing. Did Flynn, in fact, recognize his assailant? Or was he just confused and incoherent due to drugs and today's surgery? He sounded lucid enough. Maybe he just didn't want to talk to Eden. It wasn't as if they were close. It just seemed impossible that he might know, and not tell. In any case, he had made it clear that he was not going to tell her anything. Leave this to the police, she told herself. If Flynn knows something,

Detective Burt will know how to get it out of him. You need to get some sleep. Tomorrow you go home. Her heart lifted at the thought.

Eden pulled back the covers of the narrow bed and climbed in. She was still shivering, and it felt good to be under the covers. She set the alarm on her phone, so that she would be up and out in plenty of time to make her flight.

She had expected it would be difficult to fall asleep, but the upheavals of the day had worn her out, and she fell almost instantly into a deep sleep. Her dreams were the usual chaos of images, residue from the day, and an underlying feeling of anxiety that pervaded every repetitive situation, and every unresolvable difficulty that arose in her dreamscape. Eden moved from one jangled dream to another, until, abruptly, she was dreaming of her mother, here in this very house where she had lived and died. Tara was speaking to Eden while ministering to Jeremy, who was suspended in some painful-looking, medical contraption which was set up in that empty room down the hall. Tara was trying to free him from the equipment without any success. Eden was offering to help, but Tara insisted that she did not need any help. And yet, she kept performing the same repetitive actions which did nothing to alleviate the boy's suffering.

In the dream, Eden was imploring her mother to listen to her, that she knew how to fix it, if only Tara would listen. Finally, Tara turned away from Jeremy and looked directly at Eden. 'I am his mother,' she said, a look of warning in her eyes. 'I will decide what happens to him.'

279

Eden awoke, her heart hammering, her fingers clenching the covers. She lay in the bed, trying to breathe deeply, to calm her thudding heart. She did not understand why the dream had the feeling of a nightmare, but it had. So much so, that it had awakened her from a sound sleep. And as she breathed deeply, trying to calm her heart, her nerves, she inhaled something strange and out of place. Something that made her heart race again. She smelled the odor of gasoline. It was strong, and it was in the house.

Twenty-Eight

Immediately, Eden thought of her mother. Was this what Tara, incapacitated by barbiturates, had inhaled with her last breath? Tara and Jeremy had died from carbon monoxide poisoning, which is said to have no scent, but the carbon monoxide was created by the running car. Perhaps the house did smell of gasoline fumes on the night that they died.

It's not real, she told herself. You're imagining it. You are just anxious because of this business with Flynn, and because you are sleeping in this house where your mother died. Besides, she remembered closing the door between the garage and the kitchen. And she certainly would have noticed if she had left the car running. The car was turned off. She knew it. She had just been dreaming of her mother. She wondered if perhaps she was having some empathic experience, some bizarre reliving of the event, because of her vivid dream about Tara.

Or maybe it was nothing quite that psychological. Maybe it's coming from the neighbor's driveway, she told herself. She forced herself to get out from under the warmth of the covers. She padded in her stocking feet over to the window and looked out. All the lights were out next door, but there was no sign of a visitor, or of anyone coming or going. No car running in the driveway. Okay, she thought. Not that. She felt a little shudder of apprehension. She did her best to convince herself that she was having some sort of olfactory hallucination.

But it was no use. She was wide awake now. Go out and check in the kitchen, she thought. Go and look. You're never going to get back to sleep unless you go out there and check.

With a sigh of exasperation meant to conceal her anxiety, she pulled on her bathrobe. Luckily, she was still wearing socks. She had no slippers to put on, and the floors were cold. She opened the door of her room and stepped out into the hallway, silently heading down the hall toward the living room and the kitchen.

Moonlight filtered in through the windows, bathing the rooms in a grayish light. She could still smell the gas. If anything, it was more pronounced, the closer she got to the front of the house. She walked into the living room. As she entered the room, stacked with cardboard boxes, she was not only assaulted by the smell of the gas, she thought she heard a sloshing noise. She picked her way past the boxes toward the dining area, half expecting to find the garage door open. Instead, she gasped at what she saw.

There was someone at work in the kitchen. A slight figure, dressed in a parka and hood, was wielding a large plastic gas can, splashing the gas in an arc around the room.

'Hey! Stop!' Eden exclaimed.

The figure whirled around to face her, and the hood slipped back from her face. Eden saw the shock of gray hair, the steel-rimmed glasses, and the woman's face, but she felt as if she was looking at it through a prism. It was the woman on Flynn's computer. Flynn's grandmother. And then, as she looked closer she realized her mistake. She recognized this woman. They had met.

The woman stared back at her, stunned.

Eden stared back at Lizzy's mother, Phyllis Cooper. 'What the hell are you doing?' she cried. 'Is that gasoline?'

Phyllis Cooper was nonplussed. She gazed at the gas can in her hand. 'I thought the house was empty.'

'Jesus,' Eden cried. 'One spark and this whole place will be an inferno.'

Phyllis looked around the room as if she were confused. 'Oh no. I'm sorry.'

'Sorry? What are you thinking?'

'I don't know what I'm doing sometimes,' Phyllis apologized.

'Why would you want to burn this house down?'

'I didn't know anyone was here,' she insisted again.

'I get that,' said Eden. 'But that's not a reason.'

Phyllis grimaced, as if the question was painful to consider. 'I was worried,' she whispered at last.

'Worried about what?' Eden demanded.

Phyllis looked around at the deserted house. 'They would find something here. Something damning.'

Immediately, Eden thought of the photos of Lizzy. 'Is this about Lizzy?' she asked. ''Cause I can put those computer pictures in the trash, if that's what you're worried about.'

'What pictures?' Phyllis asked.

She doesn't know, Eden thought, somewhat surprised. 'All the pictures. Any pictures . . .' she said vaguely.

Phyllis sighed and looked around at the piles of boxes. 'He's all packed up. Ready to go.'

'Who?' Eden asked. 'Flynn?'

Phyllis sighed, and nodded. 'Such awful things happened here.'

Eden wasn't sure if Lizzy's mother was in command of her faculties. She didn't want to say anything to alarm her, or cause her to become agitated. She felt as if she needed to summon some help from the police, or a psych hospital, or both.

'What things?' she asked carefully.

'You don't remember? It was your mother. Your brother. They died here.' Phyllis looked almost wounded, at Eden's apparent forgetfulness.

'Yes, of course, I remember,' said Eden, as gently as possible. 'Look, we don't want to join them. Why don't we go outside now, Phyllis? It smells awful in here.'

Phyllis frowned and looked helplessly at Eden. 'I'm not done,' she said.

Eden thought about Lizzy, telling her that her mother had had a breakdown when her brother was so ill with Katz-Ellison. Maybe she was having another breakdown now. 'That's probably enough for right now,' she said. 'Why don't we just step out into the yard?'

She reached out and offered Phyllis her hand. She wished she had slipped her phone into her pocket when she left the bedroom. She didn't want to handle this situation alone. But, for the moment, she had to do the best she could.

Phyllis shook her head, still holding the gas can defensively, like a weapon, in her hand. 'NO. It's too cold out. I need to sit down,' she said.

'Okay. Let's put that gas can down now,' said Eden. 'We don't need it.'

Phyllis looked at the gas can as if she had no idea what it was, and set it down on the table. Eden reached out her hand and Phyllis took it. Then she clung to Eden's hand as Eden picked her way through the boxes to the living room sofa.

She gestured for Phyllis to sit down, and Phyllis sat. The overflowing ashtray was on the table in front of her. Phyllis picked up the pack of cigarettes and screwed her face up in dismay. 'Such a foul habit. Your mother hated that. When he would smoke.'

Eden sat down carefully beside her. 'He told me he never smoked in front of her and Jeremy.'

Phyllis set the packet down on the table and shrugged. 'She knew about it, though.'

'I'm sure she did,' said Eden. 'Listen, Phyllis, why don't I call Lizzy for you? Maybe she can come and get you.'

'Oh no,' said Phyllis, shaking her head. 'She'd be upset. She doesn't have any idea.'

Eden peered at the woman narrowly. 'Any idea about what?'

Phyllis sighed. 'About anything. About your mother and Jeremy.' She shook her head. 'When I think about that it just makes me sick.'

'What makes you sick?'

'What I did for him!' she exclaimed.

Eden stared at her.

'I'm sorry,' she said. Phyllis reached out and tried to touch her face. Eden recoiled from her touch. 'What are you talking about?'

'You probably don't know,' said Phyllis. 'I guess it's all right to tell you now. Your mother was very ill. She had a terrible disease. She was going to lose her memory altogether.'

So Phyllis knew about Tara's Alzheimer's diagnosis. She knew, when no one else did. 'How did you know about that?'

'Oh, Flynn told me. I was the only one he could tell.'

'Really,' said Eden flatly.

'And of course, Jeremy . . . All that lay ahead for him was an agonizing death. Just like my Anthony.'

'What did you do for Flynn?' Eden whispered.

'When he went to Toledo that night, I came over to help your mother. I often did that. She needed help by then. She was already beginning to fail. I came over, and I gave her a warm drink

285

with her pills. I told her to sleep and not to worry. I told her I would stay the night.'

Eden stared at the other woman. She suddenly understood that she was hearing a confession. It was coming at her like a runaway train. She couldn't derail it if she wanted to.

Phyllis had taken Eden's hand and was gripping it tightly. Her grip was warm and strong. Eden felt repulsed by Phyllis's grasp, but she did not dare to pull her hand away. Phyllis looked at her earnestly. 'I wanted the end to be as peaceful as could be. And it was. After she was asleep, I injected Jeremy's feeding tube with some of the same drug, crushed up in his liquid protein. I had the note with me. Once they were both asleep, I turned on the car and opened the door between the house and the garage. I stuffed the windows, and left. I locked the door behind me. It was as if they just floated up to heaven.'

Eden snatched her hand away from Phyllis's grasp. 'Oh God,' she cried, shaking her head as her eyes welled with tears. 'You killed them.'

Phyllis looked somewhat affronted, as if she felt unappreciated. 'I released them. I set them free. I know what it's like. I didn't want Flynn to have to suffer like that. Flynn had no one else to help him. Your mother couldn't help him. She was already starting to disappear. The illness, you know.'

'Flynn asked you to do that?' Eden said, her voice shaking.

'Oh no,' said Phyllis. 'No, he never knew. That's why I left the note. So he would think that

286

Tara had done it. She had reason enough, poor thing. He never suspected.'

Eden's heart was hammering as she listened to this confession. So Flynn was not to blame. And she had been right in her surmise about Tara. She would never have left Jeremy to die alone. Tara had never realized what was happening to her. It took every ounce of self-control Eden had not to slap Phyllis Cooper across the face.

'I did it out of kindness,' said Phyllis.

Eden was trying to think. She needed the phone. She needed to get away from this . . . angel of death. She needed to get out of this house.

'And for Flynn, of course,' said Phyllis.

Eden shook her head, as if she had not understood.

'For my son,' Phyllis said.

Twenty-Nine

Eden stared at her, trying to absorb what she had just heard. 'Your son? Are you saying that you are Flynn's mother?'

Phyllis nodded. 'I am.'

Eden shook her head in disbelief. 'But . . . no. Flynn's mother is dead.'

'My parents told everyone I was dead. They wished I was dead.'

Eden shook her head, rocked by this revelation. And then, suddenly, her own confusion cleared. She understood why those photos on Flynn's computer had seemed so unsettling. It was not Flynn's grandmother in those photos with Tara and Jeremy. Of course it wasn't. How could it be? Those photos had been taken in the last year. Flynn's grandmother had never been able to travel to Ohio. It was Phyllis Cooper in the photograph with Jeremy and Tara. It was Flynn's grandmother she had seen in older, earlier Polaroid pictures, when Flynn was a boy and was pictured with his grandparents. The photo images of Phyllis and Flynn's grandmother suddenly superimposed themselves on one another in her brain. Phyllis and Flynn's grandmother looked just alike as they aged. They looked just alike because they were. They were mother and daughter.

'Your parents knew you were alive?'

Phyllis looked down sheepishly. 'Yes. They knew. But they washed their hands of me.'

Eden was dumbfounded by this admission. 'Why?'

Phyllis's cheeks reddened. 'I had a very bad drug problem. I lived in Miami and I sold myself to any man who would pay. I got pregnant and had a baby, whom I neglected. Terribly . . .'

Eden remembered the story of the toddler, left on his own in an apartment by his addict mother. Eating cat food from the bowl on the floor. Filthy and frightened and alone. It was hard to picture this gray-haired, middle-aged woman as that low-life girl who abandoned her child for drugs. Of course, Eden reminded herself, this same neatly dressed lady had just confessed to murdering Tara and Jeremy. And now she was spreading accelerant all over Flynn's house so she could burn it down. 'I heard about that,' Eden said, and couldn't keep the chill out of her voice. 'Poor Flynn.'

Phyllis nodded. 'The couple who lived next door to me found him there. They were my friends, so they didn't call the cops. They called my parents.' She shook her head. 'That was worse.'

'Why?'

Phyllis looked at Eden with a pained expression on her face. 'No one knows about this,' she said. 'Not Lizzy. Not even Charlie. Just Flynn. I had to explain it to him. I owed that to him.'

'What happened?' Eden asked.

Phyllis sighed. 'My father came to Miami and took Flynn home with him. He didn't want a child to raise, but he was so disgusted with me that he took him. He told me that I was dead to Flynn and dead to them. And then he left.

'I'm ashamed to admit that for a while, that was all right with me. I needed my fix and that was all I could think about. I lived that way for several years. Then, somewhere along the way, I decided to kick it. That's a long story . . .'

'I'm sure it is,' said Eden, urging her to skip the details. The smell of gasoline was giving her a headache and her stomach was churning. She knew she needed to get them out of the house, but there was a part of her that felt paralyzed, unable to move until she knew the rest. 'What happened with Flynn?'

'They raised him. They told everyone that I was dead of an overdose. No one was surprised. My drug history was well known. To my father's

289

everlasting shame. He was a cop, after all. When I finally got my life together, I went to see them. Flynn was about . . . nine by then. I wanted to get him back. I had met Charlie, and my life was decent. I was sure that Charlie would welcome Flynn once I explained about him. So I went to my parents. But my father said that I was dead to Flynn, and I was going to stay dead. He kicked me out.'

'And your mother agreed to that?'

Phyllis shrugged. 'My mother never stood up to him. Maybe she didn't want to. I don't know. I'll never know.'

'But you had legal rights,' said Eden.

Phyllis laughed, but the laugh was half a sob. 'There is no fighting my father,' she said. 'You can't win with him.'

Eden had grown up with a father who was kind and loving. All Phyllis knew was a father who was a tyrant. It made Eden feel a little bit of pity for the older woman. But more for Flynn.

'But you both ended up here . . .' Eden said.

'Lizzy was talking about a new family that had entered Dr Tanaka's program. The Darbys. Flynn Darby. Of course the minute I heard the name, I understood. Katz-Ellison is a genetic disease. We moved to be near the clinic because of Anthony. My son and his wife moved here because of Jeremy. Flynn and I were both carriers, you see.'

Eden winced. 'Of course.'

Phyllis nodded. 'I began to go around there, offering to babysit. Your mother was a lovely woman. She was glad for the help. I was just like a mother to her.'

You killed her, Eden thought. She forced herself not to say it.

'After a while, I decided that I had to tell Flynn. I couldn't keep it a secret from him. But when he found out, he didn't want anyone to know.'

What a pitiful story, Eden thought. She shook herself, as if trying to awaken from a trance. She had to think. Pitiful or not, this woman had killed two people. And if Eden didn't move quickly, Phyllis might end up killing her as well. There was no time for pity. No time for anything. Eden was going to need every ounce of sympathy she could feign in order to get Phyllis to cooperate. To get them out of this house. 'Look, your parents were very cruel to you. Your father did something terrible to you. But now, you have a lot to live for. Your family loves you. They want you home. Why don't we get out of here before something sets off an explosion in this house? Let me go get my phone, and we'll get out of here and call for help, okay?'

Phyllis looked torn, but then she nodded docilely.

Eden stood up and reached out her hand. 'Okay?'

Phyllis hesitated, and then nodded. She took Eden's hand.

'Let's go this way,' said Eden, indicating the hallway which led to the bedroom. She wanted to call for help and then escape from this potential inferno. Once they were safely out of here, Phyllis would have to face the consequences of her actions, Eden thought grimly. Eden had every intention of telling the police what Phyllis did to

Tara and Jeremy. But she doesn't have to know that now, Eden thought. The important thing was to get help and get out of there. Before some errant spark started a fatal blaze. The two began to shuffle down the hallway toward the bedroom.

When they reached the door to the bedroom, Eden saw her phone sitting on the nightstand. I should have carried it with me, she thought.

'You know, when I left my parents' house, without Flynn,' Phyllis murmured, her hand still gripping Eden's, 'I was so angry. I wanted to make my father suffer. So I took the only thing he really cared about. Just to pay him back.'

'What was that?' Eden murmured absently, thinking she would grab her phone, take it outside and call from there.

Phyllis smiled with satisfaction at the memory. 'I took his service revolver. His gun.'

The hair stood up on the back of Eden's neck. She froze in the spot where she stood. 'You took it?' she whispered.

Phyllis nodded. 'I knew he would never report that I had taken it. How could he? After all, he had convinced everyone that I was dead.'

Eden's heart was hammering. She licked her lips. 'That was clever of you,' she said.

'Well, it wasn't enough, but it was something,' said Phyllis.

'Let me just get that phone now,' said Eden. She tried to extricate her fingers from Phyllis's grip, but the older woman tightened her hold.

'Who are you going to call?'

Eden tried to edge into the bedroom, pulling Phyllis along with her. 'Um. Probably the fire department. That makes the most sense. I mean, we've got a dangerous situation here. With the gas everywhere . . .'

'I guess you're right.' Phyllis frowned at her. 'What's the matter with you?'

'What?' Eden asked, trying to appear impassive.

'You became awfully nervous all of a sudden.'

'No, I'm fine,' said Eden, though her head was spinning.

'You don't seem fine,' said Phyllis.

'Phyllis, I'm just anxious to get out of here. And that smell of the gas. It's making me nauseous.'

Phyllis peered at Eden's face suspiciously.

'I really don't feel well,' said Eden. 'I feel like I'm going to be sick.'

'I can see that,' said Phyllis, suddenly turning solicitous. 'I've nursed a lot of sick people in my time. Come in here. Come on.'

She began to tug Eden in the direction of the bathroom. Eden marveled at the older woman's strength. 'I think I just need fresh air,' she insisted.

'The way you look? You're ready to throw up all over the carpet.'

At that moment, Eden realized that this was exactly what she was going to do. She bolted past Phyllis into the bathroom and barely made it to the toilet, where she gagged up the contents of her stomach.

Phyllis stood in the bathroom doorway, effectively blocking the exit. Eden scuttled away from the toilet and leaned her head back against the cool tile wall. Phyllis walked in and took a washrag from a holder on the door. She flushed the toilet, then went to the sink and ran cool water on the washrag and bent down, pressing it to Eden's sweaty forehead. 'There now,' she said, as if Eden were her own little girl.

'I feel better now,' said Eden. 'Let's just get outside.'

'I'll open a window,' said Phyllis. She stepped over Eden and reached for the crank on the casement window, turning it till the window opened. 'There,' she said. 'That's better. I'll go get you a can of soda. You need something to settle your stomach. I'll be back in a jiff . . .'

'Phyllis, I don't want . . .'

But Phyllis had rushed off on her mission.

Eden rested her forehead against her knees. She thought about Phyllis, taking it upon herself to end Tara and Jeremy's lives. All for Flynn's sake. And then, today, for some reason, she had used that gun that she had kept for years to shoot Flynn. Her own son.

'Here, have this,' said Phyllis, returning to the room.

Eden lifted her head and saw Phyllis holding out a can of ginger ale, beaded with moisture. Eden hesitated, and then reached for it gratefully. She took several swigs, and handed it back to Phyllis, who set it down on the vanity.

'Why?' Eden murmured.

'Why what?' Phyllis demanded, frowning at her.

'I thought you loved Flynn. He was your son. You wanted him back. And then, today . . .'

'Today what?' Phyllis demanded.

'Why did you try to kill him?' Eden asked.

'Who says I did?' Phyllis cried, taken aback.

'The police found the gun you used, Phyllis,' Eden said wearily. 'They know it belonged to your father.'

'No. I threw it away,' Phyllis insisted.

'The police found it. But why did you do it? Why did you . . . go after Flynn? I thought you were glad to be reunited with him. You went to such great lengths to . . . help him.'

Phyllis's eyes flashed. 'Last night, DeShaun came over and told us what happened. That Lizzy had left him to be with Flynn. That she and Flynn were lovers. She told DeShaun that she could not resist Flynn. It was some kind of compulsion. They had to be together.'

'But that's not . . .' Eden began to say. And then she stopped, suddenly struck by the devastating reality that Phyllis had been forced to confront. Her son. Her daughter. Flynn and Lizzy were siblings. But now they were also lovers. 'Oh my God,' said Eden. 'I see. So . . .'

'So, they're brother and sister,' Phyllis cried. 'Why, of all the people in the world? Lizzy told DeShaun they couldn't help themselves.'

Eden was tempted to scoff at Lizzy's melodramatic version of events, but at the same time, it rang a bell. She had read some news story about siblings who met as adults and became madly infatuated with one another. 'I've heard of that,' she told Phyllis. 'I think it's some kind of psychological syndrome. Siblings who did not grow up together, who meet later in life.'

Phyllis turned on her furiously. 'Are you agreeing that he couldn't help himself? He knew she was his sister. She didn't know it, but he did. He knew exactly, and he went ahead and he did it anyway.' Phyllis wrung her hands, trembling from head to toe. 'My Lizzy was the most perfect thing that ever happened to me. She did everything the way a mother can only dream. Her whole life was like the positive version of my life. No mistakes. No terrible regrets. Just success and goodness. Love and kindness. She was an angel.'

'She is a lovely girl,' Eden said soothingly.

'And Flynn knew how I loved her. He knew exactly what he was doing. Dragging her down to the gutter. Committing incest. After all I did for him, Flynn went ahead anyway and just took her. Took her, like an animal carrying his prey off to his lair.' Phyllis covered her face with her hands and moaned.

Eden hesitated, almost commiserating with the woman's pain. But Phyllis had shot her own son. Eden recalled her earlier conversation with Flynn this evening. And suddenly she realized what he wasn't saying to her. He knew it. He knew he'd been shot by his own mother. That's what he wouldn't say. Eden pushed herself up against the wall and rose unsteadily to her feet.

Phyllis wiped her eyes and looked at Eden accusingly. 'What are you doing?'

'Phyllis, I'm going to call for help. And then I'm getting out of this house. If you have any sense, you'll come with me.' She edged past the weeping woman and hurried to the bedroom. She picked up her phone, and dialed 911.

'I need help,' she cried. 'I'm in a house that's been doused with gasoline.'

'Give me the address,' said the dispatcher.

Eden reeled off the address.

'Okay, we're on our way. Now you need to get out of there. Don't take anything with you. Just leave.'

'I will,' said Eden. She knew the dispatcher was talking about belongings. Not human beings. Still, she hesitated for a moment. And then she went back down the hallway to the bathroom.

Phyllis was seated on the closed toilet seat, her face ravaged by grief.

'Phyllis,' said Eden. 'The fire department is on the way. We have to get out of here. Come on.'

Phyllis slowly stood up and stared at her face in the bathroom mirror. 'I look horrible,' she said.

'It doesn't matter how you look,' said Eden. 'We just have to get out of here now.'

Phyllis stared at the face in the mirror. 'Will I be arrested?'

Eden didn't know what to say. How convincing a liar could she be? 'No. I'm sure not. You'll get an attorney. Everything will work out. You'll see. But you have to get out of here. Now.'

'I smell like vomit,' said Phyllis. She turned and glared at Eden. 'That's your fault.'

Eden rolled her eyes. All she could smell was gas. 'I'm sorry about that. You can have a shower later. Right now, you have to come with me.'

'You probably smell like vomit too,' said Phyllis.

'I don't care,' said Eden. 'I'm leaving this house. Are you coming?'

'After I wash up,' said Phyllis.

Eden thought of grabbing her, and dragging her

out. She reached out for Phyllis's sleeve. Phyllis jerked away from her grasp and hissed, 'Don't touch me. I'm warning you . . .'

'The firemen are going to be here any minute,' said Eden. 'They're going to drag you out of here. You can come with me, or wait till they do it. They won't give you any choice.'

'Leave me,' said Phyllis. 'Please. Leave me alone.' She picked up the bottle of liquid soap on the sink and squeezed it into her hand.

'Fine, have it your way,' said Eden. 'I'm going. I won't stay in this house another minute.' She turned and left the bathroom. Still wearing socks on her feet, she padded down the hallway, clutching her phone with both hands like a good luck charm.

She dodged the boxes lining the hallway, and headed for the front door.

She thought she heard the sound of water running in the bathroom.

And then, just as she reached the front door, she heard a pop, and then crackling. She turned her head to look toward the living room, in the direction of the sound. She saw the leaping flames.

Jesus, she thought. What set it off? Whatever it was, it had begun. She hesitated to throw open the door, for fear the rush of air would cause the fire to intensify. But then, she could stumble outside. Be safe. Out of harm's way.

And Phyllis would still be in the bathroom.

Leave her, she thought. It's her own fault. You tried to convince her. Just go.

But it was no use. She couldn't just leave a

fellow human being to die in the flames. Not without at least trying to save her. Reluctantly, she let go of the door knob and ran back down the hall toward the bathroom.

'Phyllis,' she screamed. 'The fire has started. You have to get out. Now.'

Phyllis emerged from the bathroom, wiping her face with a towel. The crackling at the other end of the house was becoming louder, turning into a faraway roar. She looked blankly at Eden. 'I hear it,' she said.

Smoke was beginning to filter into the hallway. 'Come on,' said Eden, starting to cough. 'We'll go out one of the bedroom windows.'

'All right,' said Phyllis. 'I'm coming.'

Still coughing, Eden grabbed her wrist, and dragged her down the hall, away from the fire, to the last bedroom on the left. She could hear the sound of sirens in the distance. 'Come on now,' she said, pulling Phyllis into the bedroom which had once belonged to her mother and Flynn. She closed the door behind them and went over to the window. She tried to raise the sash on first one, and then another. She was able to raise each one a few inches, and then they stuck. She jiggled them impatiently, but it was no use.

'I'll have to break it,' she said.

'With what?' Phyllis cried.

Smoke was coming under the door. Eden opened the closet and looked inside. Shoes. Clothes. Hangers. Nothing that would break a window. She emerged from the closet, coughing, and looked frantically around the room. On the bureau she saw a lamp. Phyllis was huddled against the wall between the bureau and the corner of the room.

'Phyllis, that lamp. Is it heavy?'

Phyllis turned to where Eden was pointing and lifted the base of the lamp up.

She turned to Eden and nodded. 'It's metal. Cast iron, I think.'

'Great,' Eden said. She crossed over to the bureau and picked up the lamp. It was weighty in her hand. Definitely heavy enough to break the window. 'Here,' she said to Phyllis. 'Hold this.' She handed the lamp to Phyllis and crouched down beside the bureau to unplug it from the wall. The plug was old and felt stiff in the outlet. She worked it loose and tugged it free. 'There,' she cried triumphantly, and then started coughing.

The cord suddenly grew taut in her hand. She looked up and saw Phyllis lifting the lamp base aloft with both hands. Phyllis was looking down at Eden. Her gaze was steely.

'No,' Eden cried. 'Stop!' She reached up to try to cover her head as Phyllis swung the lamp base down on her with all her might.

Thirty

Eden lay on the floor, her head pounding, her cheek pressed to the carpet. She tried to open her eyes. The room was filled with smoke now, and there were flames licking at the door. Her eyes were tearing uncontrollably. Eden tried to think, to remember what had happened, how she had ended up here, but her brain was too muddled to deliver answers. She tried to move, but it was no use. Her muscles felt so weak that she could not even lift herself up. Through the window above her, flashing lights threw patterns on the wall. She could hear the commotion outside as people shouted inchoate orders to one another, and sirens continued to sound. Move, she told herself. Help is here. Get up. Get to your feet. But her body refused to obey her commands. 'Help me,' she whispered. 'Someone help me.'

Outside the window, firefighters rushed to the aid of an older woman whom they had watched climb out of the burning house through one of the bedroom windows. The woman was bleeding in several places from where she had hauled herself across shards of glass still fixed in the window that she had broken. She was coughing uncontrollably from the smoke.

'Hurry up,' cried one of the firefighters, crouching down beside Phyllis and looking at her worriedly. 'Bring her one of those insulated blankets. I think she's in shock.' He put an arm around Phyllis's shoulders. 'We'll take care of you, don't worry. My name is Jimmy, by the way. What's yours?'

'Phyllis,' she managed to say between coughs.

'Okay, well you hang in there, Phyllis. We'll get you all fixed up.'

Another young man in firefighting gear materialized through the smoke clutching a silver blanket, and handed it to Jimmy. Jimmy wrapped

301

it around the woman's narrow, shaking shoulders. 'There you go,' he said kindly. 'Now, Phyllis, how are you otherwise? Anything broken? You took quite a tumble from that window.'

Phyllis coughed, and shook her head. 'It's all right. I'm okay.'

'Well, we'll get you over to the hospital and have them take a look at you when the ambulance gets here. Kheon, where is that damn thing anyway?'

The second firefighter, a broad-shouldered young black man, peered past the phalanx of firetrucks, their red lights blinking, and men in gear training hoses on the house. He looked into the darkness of the street beyond the front lawn. 'Somebody said they got diverted to a three-car wreck on the highway.'

Jimmy shook his head angrily. 'That's typical of this city. They haven't got enough equipment or manpower to cover all they have to cover.'

'Amen,' said Kheon.

Jimmy turned his attention back to Phyllis. 'Don't you worry now, Phyllis. They'll see to you as soon as they get here. Is there somebody we can call for you?'

'Yes, please,' Phyllis began to sob. 'My daughter, Lizzy. My phone is in my pocket,' she said, rummaging in her pocket and pulling out a phone. 'Her number is there. I have it listed under "L". For Lizzy,' she explained, and then collapsed into a coughing fit.

'Okay,' said Jimmy, shifting his weight from one leg to the other, still crouching beside the injured Phyllis. He punched some buttons on the phone and waited. 'Yes,' he said, 'is this Lizzy? Yeah, this is Firefighter James Carmichael from the Seventy-second Precinct. Your mother has just escaped from a burning house. She's asking for you.'

Jimmy listened a second and then put his hand over the mouthpiece and looked up at Kheon. 'What's the address here?'

The fireman told him, and relayed the information to Lizzy. 'Yeah, we'll be taking her to the hospital but the ambulance isn't here yet. No, she's conscious. I think she's more shaken up than anything. Yeah, you're not that far away. You have time to get here. Okay. She's all right. Don't speed.'

Jimmy ended the call and handed the phone back to Phyllis, who put it into her pocket. 'You feel a little better now that you got that blanket over you?'

Phyllis nodded.

'Now,' he said. 'This is very important. Were you the only one home tonight? Is there anyone else still remaining in that house?'

Phyllis looked up at him, blinking back tears. 'No, sir,' she said earnestly. 'I was the only one in there.'

The temptation to just fall back to sleep was almost overwhelming. Eden's eyes were half-closed, and her head was pounding. The idea of giving in to sleep seemed utterly peaceful and appealing. But she knew she should not. Could not. She probably had a concussion from the lamp base. If she fell asleep, she might never

303

wake up. What is wrong with me? she wondered. And then she remembered. She recalled feeling the lamp cord tighten in her fingers. She remembered looking up and seeing Phyllis, hoisting the metal lamp base above her head with both hands.

The memory of it was sickening. She had let herself believe that this woman, who had killed her mother and brother, and tried to kill Flynn, was not a danger to her. How foolish could she have been?

Stop it, she thought. Stop blaming yourself. You were only trying to save her life. Now think! Eden became aware, again, of the commotion outside, but it seemed to having nothing to do with her. And then she forced herself to focus. Get a grip. You're in a burning building, she told herself. You have to get out of here.

Have to get out of here now. She tried to raise herself up again, but it was no use. She was too weak. Her chest felt constricted by the effort to breathe in the room which was filling up with smoke. She looked around her. There was a chair lying on its side not far from her on the floor. She gazed at it, wondering why it was lying on the floor. And then it came to her. Phyllis must have used it to climb out the broken window, kicking it over as she went. Now Eden had to do the same . . . She forced herself to summon up the strength and began to drag herself along the floor. Every inch was painful. The thought of it made Eden want to weep. She knew, vaguely, that she should be angry, but all she could think about was all the despair, all the sorrow that had led her here to this moment. To this house where her mother had lived. To this bedroom which had been her mother's. Suddenly, Tara was all Eden could think about. She felt a longing, suppressed for years, to be sheltered once more in her mother's embrace. To be held in her arms.

And then, as if Tara were whispering in her ear, Eden heard an inner voice that urged her to move. Pick up the chair. Climb on it. Get out the window. She reached the chair and began to try to right it. Her arms felt weak, but the chair was an antique, and somewhat spindly. She knew she could lift it if she just marshaled her forces. She pulled herself up to her knees and reached out for the back of the chair. It took her several tries to turn it over and get it upright. Once she did, she used the chair to help herself rise to her feet. Once she was standing, she wobbled. She was afraid to let go of the chair, for fear she would collapse. Outside the room, in the hallway, she could hear the fire roar, and she could feel the heat emanating through the door, the flames starting to eat through it.

Summoning all her strength, and using the chair to balance, she kept herself upright. Making snail-like progress, she dragged the chair underneath the broken window. Now, she thought, if I can just get under it, climb up on the chair, and somehow lift myself up over the jagged glass remaining in the window frame, I can escape to the world outside.

Every breath was a struggle now, her chest aching from the effort. She finally managed to get the chair positioned beneath the window. Now, she told herself, climb up on it. Her arms shook as she lifted up one knee and placed it on the needlepoint-covered seat of the chair. Now the other, she thought. Almost there. She was kneeling on the seat of the chair. It felt like a moment of triumph. But there was no time to celebrate. Gripping the back of the chair with her trembling hand, she leaned to one side, and pulled one knee up so that she was in the classic marriage proposal position. Next effort, she thought, was to stand up. Then she would be able to easily lean out of the broken window, and fall over the window frame to the ground below.

She shifted her weight off of the other knee, and lifted her leg. She was in mid-effort when she heard a thunderous roar behind her. She turned quickly, startled. The fire had burst through the door like a rampaging beast. Eden cried out at the sight, and teetered. She tried to regain her balance, but it was no use. Her stockinged foot slipped from the frame and broke through the needlepoint chair seat. She fell, tumbling to the floor, the chair landing on top of her, her leg trapped in the space where the seat had been.

'Did you hear that?' Jimmy Carmichael asked to no one in particular.

'There she is,' Phyllis cried. She scrambled to her feet at the sight of Lizzy, dodging fire hoses as she ran across the lawn to her mother. Phyllis opened her arms and Lizzy fell into them.

'Mom, are you all right?' Lizzy cried.

'I am now,' said Phyllis.

'I was so worried when the fireman called. I came straight here.'

Phyllis shushed her and ran a soothing hand over her daughter's hair. 'It's all right now. Everything's okay.'

Lizzy pulled back from the embrace and looked her mother over. 'Are you sure? Is she okay?' she demanded of the passing fireman.

'Well, we're going to send her to the hospital when the ambulance gets here. Just so they can look her over. But I think she's okay.'

'Thank God,' said Lizzy, looking up toward the inky, star-studded sky. Then, she wrapped an arm around Phyllis, who was cloaked by the insulated blanket. 'I was afraid you were mad at me. I was afraid you wouldn't want to see me.'

'Not want to see you?' Phyllis exclaimed. 'That could never be.'

Lizzy gave her mother a tremulous smile. 'I know.'

Mother and daughter embraced, and then Lizzy pulled away and waylaid a passing firefighter. 'Excuse me.'

'This is Jimmy,' said Phyllis. 'He's been very kind.'

'Thank you,' said Lizzy sincerely.

'Just doing my job,' Jimmy said modestly.

'Listen, would it be all right if I took my mother home? If we didn't wait for the ambulance?'

Jimmy Carmichael looked grave. 'I cannot recommend that, ma'am. She should be checked out. That's protocol.'

'Oh. Okay,' said Lizzy.

'I just got word that it's almost here. Won't be long now.'

Lizzy sighed, and beamed again at her mother.

'As long as you're safe.' Then she frowned. 'What were you doing out here anyway?'

Phyllis's eyes went blank for a moment, and then she recovered. 'I was looking for you. I thought you might be staying here. When I got here the door was open, so I went in. I was calling for you. Then I smelled the gas.'

'Oh my God,' Lizzy exclaimed.

'What?' asked Phyllis.

Lizzy turned back to the firefighter. 'Eden!' she cried.

'Come again?' he asked.

'Eden Radley was staying here. I saw her here earlier this evening. She told me she was sleeping here. You have to go in and look for her. She might still be inside.'

'Oh don't be ridiculous. She's not in there. You're asking them to go back in that house and it's dangerous in there,' Phyllis protested.

'Your mother told us that she was the only one in the house,' said Jimmy. 'Do you think there might be someone else in there?'

Lizzy bit her lip. 'Are you sure, Mom?'

'Of course I'm sure,' said Phyllis.

'What if she fell asleep, Mom, and you didn't see her? It's possible that she's tucked away somewhere in the house. I'm sure you didn't go into every room.'

'If she'd been in there, I would have known it,' Phyllis insisted.

'Still, your daughter has a point. If she saw this young woman here earlier, there's a chance she's still inside. We need to go in and check. Hey, Kheon,' Jimmy called out to his fellow firefighter.

'There may be someone still in there. We have to go in.'

The other firefighter nodded, as if this was the most natural thing in the world. Jimmy jammed his carbon-blotched helmet back on his head, and headed back toward the house.

'No,' Phyllis insisted. 'There's no one in there. You're risking your lives for nothing. There's no one there!'

Lizzy spoke soothingly to her agitated mother. 'Calm down, Mom. They're trained to do this. They know what they're doing. And if it was me . . . If there was the slightest chance, you'd want them to go back in, wouldn't you?'

Phyllis was trembling, and didn't speak. Her face had assumed a sickly yellow cast, the reflection from the blaze.

'You know you would. So think of Tara. That's what Tara would want, if she were here,' Lizzy crooned, squeezing her mother's thin shoulders. 'She would want them to make every effort. Of course she would. That's her daughter.'

Thirty-One

Someone was holding her hand. Someone was squeezing it gently, and murmuring her name. Eden felt herself swimming to consciousness, although her eyes were not open. She could feel her mouth now, dry and sticky, and she was aware that she was lying on a bed, in a cool, dark room.

There was a light burning over her head. She knew all this without opening her eyes. She had been forced to stay awake for what seemed like a long time when she first got to this room. Once she was allowed to sleep, the idea of opening her eyes again seemed like too much effort. All she wanted was to sink back into oblivion.

'Oh, Eden. Please come back to us. Please, baby.'

The familiar voice jolted her, roused her. Eden blinked and looked up into her father's worried face. 'Dad?' she whispered.

'Oh, sweetheart. Oh, thank God.' Hugh Radley enveloped her in a brief hug. Then he drew back and looked into her eyes. His own eyes looked weary and bloodshot, as if he had not slept for a long time.

'Where?' she murmured.

'You're in the hospital, sweetie. In Cleveland. You were in a burning house. You've had a concussion, smoke inhalation and a broken ankle. The firemen went into the house and found you there. Luckily, they got you out of there in time.'

'What happened?' Eden asked. But then, she started to remember. The gas spread throughout Flynn's house. Phyllis, hitting her with the lamp base. The smoke. And then voices near her. Around her. She remembered being lifted up, and thanking God, knowing that she was going to live.

'You were in a fire. At your mother's old house. Do you remember that?'

Eden nodded slightly, and closed her eyes for a moment. She licked her dry lips. 'I remember.'

Hugh reached for a small, wedge-shaped sponge on a stick. He dipped it in water and applied it to her parched lips. Eden sucked on it gratefully. 'There was a lot of confusion at first,' he said. 'But they got it sorted out. They checked your phone. I guess you called the fire department and told them that someone had spread accelerant all over the house. It was that woman, Phyllis. Who turned out to be Flynn's mother. Did you know that?'

Eden nodded. 'She wanted to burn it down.'

'Well, she succeeded. They're still sorting through the rubble, but they found the source. There was gasoline spread through the house. Apparently, she put a lit cigarette between the pages of a newspaper, and when the cigarette burned down to the newspaper, it caught on fire and ignited the gasoline around it.'

'No! She couldn't have. I was with her the whole time,' Eden said. And then she remembered. Phyllis had gone to get her a can of ginger ale because she had vomited. Phyllis must have done it quickly, lighting one of Flynn's cigarettes in the living room on her way back from the kitchen, stuffing it in the newspaper. Carrying back a can of soda.

'You could have been killed,' Hugh said, and his voice was torn by a sob.

'I'm okay,' said Eden. 'I'll be okay.'

Hugh nodded and composed himself. 'Anyway, this Phyllis, who, apparently, is Flynn's biological mother, was arrested. She kept insisting that the house was empty. Luckily, her daughter knew that you were in there, and asked the firemen to go back in and look for you.'

'Lizzy?'

'Yes. I think that's her name. Lizzy.'

'She killed Mom. And Jeremy,' said Eden.

'Who did? This Lizzy person?' he cried.

Eden shook her head. 'Flynn's mother.'

'But why? What the hell . . .' Hugh looked at his daughter and then raised a hand as if to signal a halt. 'Never mind. I don't want you to get upset. We can talk about this later. There'll be time for that. You need to rest. We'll talk about this, and everything else later.'

Eden wanted to protest, but the truth was that she felt herself slipping. 'What will you do?' she whispered.

'Oh, I'm okay. Gerri came out to Cleveland with me when I got the news. I was a basket case. Anyway, she's been with me the whole time. We're staying just across the street. Don't you worry about us. You just get well.'

'Dad . . . Thank you. Thank you for being here.'

'Where else would I be?' he said. 'You rest.'

Eden drifted back into sleep and then woke again, numerous times. Nurses woke her with medication, and doctors woke her to ask her questions and examine her injuries. Twice her father was there when she opened her eyes. She didn't know if it was day or night when she awoke. She didn't care. She went immediately back to sleep, drinking in the slumber like it was the elixir of life. When finally she opened her eyes and knew that she was truly awake, it was daylight outside. There was faint, milky sunshine coming through the windows of her room.

Eden blinked and looked around. There were bouquets of flowers along the windowsill. An iPad was sitting on the bedside table. It was not her iPad, but then again, how could it have survived the fire? Her father must have bought this one for her to replace it. She picked it up and checked the date. Three days had gone by since she had last been out in the world. Three days, she thought. Where did they go? She tapped on a few keys. The new notebook seemed to be programmed and ready to go.

Eden moved her feet under the sheet and blanket and felt a shooting pain up her leg. She threw off the sheet and looked. Her ankle was in a cast. She picked up a mirror from the bedside table and looked at her face. There was a long bruise on the side of her pale face, and there were circles under her eyes. She looked about as bad as she could ever remember looking. But she felt better. That was a comfort.

'Oh good. You're awake. I was hoping I wouldn't disturb you.'

Eden looked up and saw Gerri coming into her room, her eyes alight with pleasure. Eden smiled. 'I am awake.'

Gerri enveloped her in a hug and then pulled back to look her in the eyes.

'You've had a quite a time,' she said.

Eden nodded, smiling faintly. 'Thanks for coming out here with Dad. That was so kind of you.'

'It was my pleasure,' said Gerri. 'I'm just so glad you're okay. He has been sick with worry.'

'I know. Where is he anyway?'

'He just went out to stretch his legs and get some decent coffee. The coffee here is terrible.'

'I've heard that,' said Eden.

'Look Eden, while we have a minute, before he gets back, I wanted to tell you something. I probably should wait with this but . . .'

Eden frowned, and her head began to hurt all over again. 'What?'

'Well, your dad told me why you came out here. That you were here to work on Flynn's book.'

'Yes. I did. How is Flynn anyway?'

'I heard he's going to be released tomorrow.'

'That's good. He's been through a lot. Even though I don't like the guy. He made me lose my job!'

'Are you sure about that?' said Gerri, glancing at the array of flowers on the windowsill. 'There's a bouquet here from Maurice DeLaurier, and one from your boss, Rob.'

'Really?' said Eden. 'Wow! That's . . . nice. Who else sent flowers?'

Gerri reeled off a few names. 'Somebody called Vince?' she said, a cheerful question in her voice.

Just then the door to Eden's room swung open, and Hugh Radley entered, carrying two paper coffee cups. His worried face broke into a smile at the sight of his daughter, sitting up and talking to Gerri. 'Eden,' he cried. 'Look at you!'

'Hi, Dad. I'm much better.'

'I'm so glad,' he said, handing one cup to Gerri. 'I would have gotten you one, but I'm not sure it's allowed.'

314

'It's not allowed,' said a nurse who had come in behind Hugh, and was bustling about the room. 'I'm gonna have to ask you folks to leave. I have to get Eden ready for X-ray.'

Goodbyes and promises of later were exchanged all around as Hugh and Gerri took their leave, looking back at her wistfully. Eden smiled until they were out of sight. The nurse unfolded a wheelchair beside the bed and was explaining that they were going down to the first floor, when suddenly Gerri reappeared in the room.

'Did you forget something?' Eden asked.

'That's what I told your dad,' Gerri said. 'But I just wanted to finish telling you . . . When you feel up to looking at it, I have forwarded you an email and an attachment that I received several months ago. From your mother. You will definitely want to read it.' She waggled her fingers. 'Feel better. Talk to you later.'

Eden watched Gerri go, frowning. She was undeniably curious and looked longingly at the iPad.

'All right, missy, let's get you downstairs,' said the nurse.

Eden nodded agreement, and did her best to facilitate her transfer from the bed to the chair. It will have to wait, she thought.

By the time she had been poked, prodded, photographed and tested by every doctor's team involved in her care, Eden was almost as exhausted as she had been in the preceding days. She saw her father and Gerri again, when they stopped in for a last visit that night. She was quick to thank her father for the new iPad.

'Well, the old one didn't make it through the fire. Luckily, most of your stuff was packed and on the plane. But I knew you couldn't manage without one of those.'

'You're so right,' said Eden. 'Really. Thanks.'

'I talked to the doc,' said Hugh. 'We're gonna be taking you home very soon. Just a day or two, they tell me.'

'Can't wait,' Eden admitted. She was too tired for much conversation, and they took their leave early. Finally, the room was quiet, and Eden was left alone.

The thought of sleep was enticing, but ever since her conversation with Gerri earlier in the day, she had been wondering what it was that her mother had said. She felt as if she wouldn't be able to sleep unless she knew.

She lifted the iPad from beside her bed and opened it. She reached for the arm of the moveable tray which she had pushed aside after dinner, and set the iPad on it. Then she went to her email and scanned the emails which had accumulated, unanswered. There were get well wishes galore, including one from an address she didn't immediately recognize. But the name 'Vince' was in the address, which gave her a hopeful feeling. She opened it and blushed with pleasure. The email was, as she hoped, from Vince Silver, the proprietor of the Brisbane.

Eden looked up at the windowsill. That was so . . . kind of him, she thought. They hadn't even been on a date together. Obviously she was not the only one who had felt that attraction between them. His note was short, saying that he was concerned about her, and wanted her to let him know as soon as she got back to Brooklyn. She started to compose a reply. She began by thanking him for the flowers, and then began to torture herself with the wording of the rest. She didn't want to seem needy or pathetic. She didn't want to seem too eager or hopeful. She didn't want to make too much of his gesture, as if it implied that there was something between them when, in fact, they scarcely knew one another. She kept writing and then deleting what she had written.

And then she looked over again at the bouquet of flowers. He had not been afraid to show that he was worried about her. Something wonderful might happen between them, or it might not. But he was saying clearly that he had hopes for them. And in her heart, despite every misgiving about love that she had felt in abundance lately, she found that she was hopeful too. Why not just go for the truth? she thought. And be hopeful. *Hearing from you has made me so happy. I will be home soon. I can't wait to see you again.*

She took a deep breath and pressed send. Then she ran down the list of addresses until she came to the one which was forwarded to her from Gerri. She opened it up, and felt the impact of seeing her mother's email like a blow to her chest.

Gerri had written her a note along with the forwarded documents.

Dear Eden,

I received this from your mother about six months ago. I never mentioned it to your father, because I was afraid it might grieve him to know about it. She wanted my help, but I was not inclined to be generous toward her, and I only answered Tara's request in the most perfunctory manner. It seemed as if anything else would only cause more pain. But when I heard about Flynn's book, I decided it was important to share this with you. Maybe I'm off base. If so, you will tell me.
Much love, Gerri

Eden scrolled down, and began to read.

Thirty-Two

The next morning, despite the fact that she was completely exhausted, Eden was awake and prepared for company. Sitting up in bed, her hair pulled severely back into a ponytail, she glanced repeatedly at the door to her room. She was wearing make-up to try to give color to her face and conceal the dark circles under her eyes. She was wearing fresh pajamas which Gerri and her father had brought for her. Her back was propped up with several pillows. She had her iPad set up on her rolling tray, and her hands were folded calmly in her lap when the door to her hospital room finally opened.

Her visitor sauntered in, wearing an oversized tweed coat and carrying a backpack over his shoulder. His hair was long, wavy and freshly washed. He moved carefully across the room and stood leaning on the visitor's chair at the end of her bed.

'The nurse said that you asked to see me before I left,' said Flynn.

'I did. Have a seat,' said Eden.

Flynn lowered himself carefully into the visitor's chair. 'Still a little creaky,' he said with a crooked grin.

'I'm sure you are,' said Eden. His own mother had shot him. Tried to kill him. How was he able to seem cheerful after that? 'I want you to know that I'm sorry about . . . everything with your mother.'

Flynn sighed, and his eyes became cloudy. Then he faked a jaunty smile. 'My mother. What a gal, huh?'

'She told me a lot while we were in the house. How her parents pretended she was dead. How . . . unkind they were to you.'

Flynn shook his head. 'When she first told me who she was, I actually thought, Hey . . . it's my mother. Second chance. I kept her secret. Hell, I confided in her. About Tara's illness. Everything. So then, I guess she decided that she would do me a favor and kill my wife and son.'

Eden bit her lip. 'I know she did. I'm sorry, Flynn.'

319

'Sorry to you, too. She made the decision for all of us.'

'It's not your fault. What will happen to her?'

'Don't know,' he said. 'I'm washing my hands of her.'

Eden could not help recalling that Phyllis had said that same thing about her own parents. It was like a horrible legacy which continued on. 'And yet, when I talked to you in the hospital that first night, and you knew it was Phyllis, you didn't say a word against her.'

'That was for Lizzy's sake,' said Flynn. 'But now everyone knows.'

'It won't be so easy for Lizzy to turn her back on Phyllis,' said Eden.

Flynn looked uncomfortable. He shifted in the chair. 'If she wants to be with me, she'll have to adjust to it,' he said bluntly.

'Does she want to be with you? Now that she knows that you're her brother?'

'She's having some problems with it,' he admitted.

'I'm sure she is,' said Eden.

'She has to get over worrying about what people will think. Who cares what people think? The hell with them.'

'That's easier said than done,' said Eden. 'Lizzy's life has been turned upside down.'

Flynn took a deep breath. 'Look, is there a purpose to this command performance?' he asked irritably. ''Cause if not . . .'

'There's a purpose,' said Eden.

Flynn glanced at his watch and sighed. 'Okay, shoot.' He shifted in the chair, seeking a comfortable position.

'Okay,' said Eden. She shifted the iPad so she was looking directly at it. 'There's something I want to read to you. It's an email that was sent to Gerri Zerbo, by my mother.'

'That name rings a bell,' said Flynn.

'Gerri and her husband owned the bookstore where my mother used to work. The bookstore where you met . . .'

'Oh right. On that fateful day . . .' he said with a hint of sarcasm.

'I'll read it to you,' said Eden.

Flynn glanced at his watch again. 'I don't have a lot of time . . .'

'It's short,' said Eden coldly. She cleared her throat and began to read.

Dear Gerri,

I'm sure you never expected to hear from me again. I feel a little strange writing this, but I have my reasons, as you'll see. My life has taken some difficult twists and turns, and I'm not sure how long I will be able to communicate clearly, so I am sending this to you now.

I know how much you disapproved of the effect my actions had on Hugh and, especially, Eden. I don't blame you for being angry with me. Whether you believe it or not, hurting them is the greatest regret of my life. But this letter is not about our personal lives. This is about work. I am writing to you because I need your very educated opinion. I want you to know that I always had the utmost

321

respect for you as a book person. You understand books and what makes a good read better than anyone I've ever known. Your choices for the store were always unerring, and if you recommended a book, then I would find, almost inevitably, that it was excellent and that I would enjoy it as well. I value your opinion about books more than anyone I know.

In the last year, when I was not caring for my son, I decided to write a book about all that happened to me. If nothing else, I hope that someday Eden will be able to read it, and maybe understand. Her life was so unfairly ripped apart. I want her to know why I did what I did. I decided to write it as a novel, so that I would have a little distance on it.

I finished it several weeks ago, and have been trying to decide what to do with it. I didn't tell anyone else about it, except for my husband, Flynn. He has read it at several points along the way. Frankly, he does not think very much of it, and that's probably well deserved. He was kind enough to say that it was an interesting effort, which wasn't very encouraging. I thought, before I put it in the drawer, and got on with my life, wherever it may be leading me, that I would send it to you, the best reader I know. If you like it or hate it, I'd still like to hear your opinion. I know that you do not hold a high opinion of me as a person, but if you could judge

*the book on its own merits, and overlook
the author's shortcomings as you read it,
I would be truly grateful.*
  Sincerely yours,
  Tara Darby

Eden folded the iPad closed and looked at Flynn. He stared back at her defiantly. 'Anything you'd like to say?'

'About what?' he demanded.

'I read the attachment my mother sent to Gerri as well. The book you passed off to DeLaurier and your agent as your own. That was my mother's book.'

Flynn avoided her gaze, pursing his lips and gazing out the window. His cheeks were stained a reddish-bronze. 'It's hardly the same book,' he muttered.

'Oh, I can see the work you did on it. Added a few things. Tweaked this and that. Took out anything unflattering to yourself.'

'Tweaked?' he demanded, turning his narrow-eyed gaze on her. 'I did a lot more than tweak it.'

Eden looked at him in apparent astonishment, her eyebrows raised. 'Really? Is that going to be your defense?'

'I don't need a defense,' he said.

'You tried to pass this off as your own work.'

'Oh, get off your high horse,' he said. 'It's not that big a deal. Your mother was dead. It seemed stupid not to go ahead and sell the book.'

Eden shook her head and stared at him. Was that really how he saw it? He seemed to think

323

that none of the rules applied to him. Reading her mother's book last night, as it was written, Eden realized that Tara had come, over time, to understand Flynn, and his limitations. Had she continued to love him? Yes, but her original manuscript made it clear that her rapturous love had been tempered with disappointment as she began to recognize the flaws in his character. Of course he had removed all of that from the manuscript he sold to DeLaurier. 'Whatever possessed you to ask for me as an editor?' she asked. 'Did it amuse you to think that I was working on my mother's book, and I didn't even know it?'

'She wanted you to read it. That was one of her reasons for writing it.'

'I'm sure she did,' said Eden. 'But don't pretend that you did this to fulfill my mother's wishes. After she died you stole her work and claimed it as your own, when she could no longer speak for herself.'

'You don't get it. It wasn't about glory for her. That wasn't her nature. She wanted it to be published,' said Flynn. 'I made that happen.'

Eden shook her head. Did he really believe the words he was saying? 'You discouraged her when she was alive, even though you realized that her work was good. You had to make sure she would not succeed. Between the two of you, there could only be one writer.'

'I am the writer,' he said. 'She only tried her hand at it because she was jealous of me.'

'Do you really believe that?' Eden asked.

Flynn ran a hand through his shaggy mane and

leaned forward, looking at her earnestly. 'Look, let's forget this ever happened. I don't care if the book ever gets published, frankly.'

'Gideon Lendl is not going to forget. Maurice DeLaurier is not going to forget. This is a disgrace.'

Flynn waved a hand airily. 'Obviously, you're going to tell them. Fine. Enjoy your revenge. I'll repay them the advance. They'll be content with that. And the book can go in the garbage for all I care. I wanted to do this for your mother's memory, but I can see that you have to have it your way—'

'My way?' she cried. 'What about the truth?'

'Here's the truth, Eden,' he said. 'I have plenty of money. Hell, I'm a rich man now. The insurance, remember? Thanks to you, the insurance company now knows exactly who killed my wife and son. So they have to pay me. Thanks for that. I don't need this book. It's been nothing but a mistake the whole way.'

'This was no mistake. This was deliberate,' said Eden.

Flynn stood up and slung his backpack over his shoulder. 'Do your worst,' he said. 'I'm getting on with my life.' He turned his back on her and started for the door.

This will follow you everywhere, she wanted to shout after him. When word of this gets out, you'll never publish another word. But she didn't.

Flynn banged the door back on his way out.

Eden watched him go, her anger simmering. She had wanted to shock him. To shake him. But he was not sorry. He would not even apologize

325

for what he had done. He was moving on, and to Flynn, this was just another unfortunate incident in the past. What did you expect? she asked herself. Did you expect him to beg for your forgiveness? Flynn?

In a way, it made her furious. But as she considered it, she realized that it no longer mattered. She had prevented him from stealing her mother's work. That was the important thing. In the end, Tara's book would be published. Eden vowed to accomplish that. She could imagine herself writing a Foreword or an Epilogue to try and put the story into perspective. Judging from that lavish bouquet on the windowsill, she thought that DeLaurier Publishing might just be interested in going forward with this project. Vince Silver would say that it made good business sense. She looked forward to telling him all that had happened over a glass of wine or two. She had a feeling, a hope, one might say, that he would find it all very interesting.

Despite what Flynn had done, it was impossible for her to wish him more harm. It was painful to think of all the loss he had endured. He had grown up abandoned and unwanted by everyone who was supposed to care for him. He had been betrayed at every turn, and cobbled his character together in any way that he could. Tara had seen the need in him, and felt pity and tenderness. She had assumed that her love would be enough to fill that void. But Flynn's was an emptiness that no amount of love could ever fill. Lizzy was the latest to try. Now her life was wrecked on the shoals of that desperate effort. Eden felt sure that there would be many others, most likely with the same result.

Eden leaned back against the pillow and heaved a sigh. Let it go, she thought. You are the lucky one. In the end, Flynn was doomed to be a stranger in the world, forever adrift. Was there anything more difficult to overcome than a void in the heart? It was an invisible burden, crushing, and always with you. There was no escaping it.

Count your blessings, she thought. Get well, and go on home.

CPSIA information can be obtained
at www.ICGtesting.com
Printed in the USA
BVOW08*1934090317
477673BV00003B/6/P